DOUBLE DEALINGS

STEPHANIE HARTE

Boldwood

First published in Great Britain in 2024 by Boldwood Books Ltd.

Copyright © Stephanie Harte, 2024

Cover Design by Colin Thomas

Cover Images: Colin Thomas

A CIP catalogue record for this book is available from the British Library.

Paperback ISBN 978-1-83533-187-3

Large Print ISBN 978-1-83533-186-6

Hardback ISBN 978-1-83533-188-0

Ebook ISBN 978-1-83533-185-9

Kindle ISBN 978-1-83533-184-2

Audio CD ISBN 978-1-83533-193-4

MP3 CD ISBN 978-1-83533-192-7

Digital audio download ISBN 978-1-83533-189-7

This book is printed on certified sustainable paper. Boldwood Books is dedicated to putting sustainability at the heart of our business. For more information please visit https://www.boldwoodbooks.com/about-us/sustainability/

Boldwood Books Ltd, 23 Bowerdean Street, London, SW6 3TN

www.boldwoodbooks.com

To the survivors.
Cancer touches so many lives.
Facing a diagnosis is a terrifying prospect.
This book is dedicated to all those who've bravely fought the battle.

1

DAISY

Wednesday, New Year's Eve

A sea of empty glasses stretched out in front of me. Judging by the hordes of people packed into The Castle pub and the overpowering smell of alcohol, the party was in full swing. As an uninvited guest, my presence hadn't gone down well. I wasn't thrilled about being here, either. Seeing in the new year in a spit and sawdust pub in Dover wasn't on my bucket list the last time I checked.

As we stood face to face behind the bar, MacKenzie's eyes were wide and full of fear as though he was looking down the barrel of a gun, making a satisfied smile play on my lips. Unspoken words hung between us.

I hadn't wanted to entertain the idea that MacKenzie was involved in my sister, Lily's disappearance, but now that I knew he owed money to the Albanian mafia, it changed everything. They ran a prostitution ring, and my twin was a twenty-three-year-old blue-eyed blonde. I couldn't bear to think about the trouble she was in. It turned my stomach, so I forced myself to focus on the job in hand. MacKenzie had upset the boss, and I'd been sent to flush him out.

Regret was swirling around me. I wouldn't be in this position if I hadn't accused my old boss, Samson Fox of kidnapping Lily. It had been a stupid move that had cost me dearly. But she'd vanished into thin air, so desperation had brought me to his door. Big mistake. To get myself out of the shit, I'd agreed to do his dirty work.

Midnight was fast approaching, so a racket from the playlist and partygoers filled the room, but I tuned them out to give MacKenzie my undivided attention. I'd had such high hopes for him. I'd fallen head-over-heels for him the first time I'd met him when Lily and I auditioned for the gig at Eden's. It was a shame it had come to this. But he'd turned out to be a total prick. Slept with me and then blanked me. Our fledgling relationship was dead in the water. Saving my own skin was far more important. Samson's ultimatum was looming over me. 'I'll exchange your life for MacKenzie's,' he'd said, and I had no intention of going to an early grave.

With the warning still ringing in my ears, Gary gave me the nod. Samson's hired muscle was about to make his move. Gary pulled a gun from the waistband of his black suit trousers, pressed the muzzle of it against MacKenzie's back, then leaned forward and whispered into his ear. 'Right, it's time to get going. Don't try anything dodgy.'

Gary forced MacKenzie away from the timber-beamed bar strung with lobster pots and fishing nets and frogmarched him along the corridor leading to the back door, keeping the weapon's barrel pushed against his spine to help him focus.

'Open it,' Gary said.

When MacKenzie pressed down the bar of the emergency exit, a blast of ice-cold air hit me straight in the face. The wind had picked up since we'd gone into the dingy pub. Stepping outside, I shivered. It was well below freezing. Despite the cold, it felt good to be away from the chaos. My head was pounding from the tanked-up revellers. The sound of the waves crashing on the shingle as we walked towards the car was a welcome relief. Soothing for the senses.

The noise inside the pub had been deafening. The countdown to the new year had begun, so I'd decided to wait until we'd got outside to phone Samson and give him the good news. I couldn't wait to tell him that we were on our way back to London with MacKenzie. But I never got the chance. We only made it halfway down the narrow passageway at the side of the building when a man's booming voice cut through the darkness and stopped us in our tracks.

'I wouldn't go any further if I were you. And unless you want me to blow your brains out, get your grubby mitts off MacKenzie,' he bellowed in a cockney accent.

I flattened myself against the wall as Gary looked over his shoulder to see who had made the threat while keeping the gun in contact with MacKenzie's back. The pub was heaving, so I hadn't noticed the man with dark, crew-cut hair and large side-burns following us.

'Well, well, well, Roscoe Allen. Fancy seeing you here. So you've finally decided to show yourself and crawl out from the rock you've been cowering under since the boss sent you packing,' Gary replied.

My ears pricked up. I knew MacKenzie's old boss was called Roscoe. It was good to finally put a face to a name.

'I don't think so, mate. I haven't been hiding from Samson. I just fancied a change of scenery, that's all.' Roscoe laughed.

'Is that so? I thought you'd know better than to try throwing your weight around again. It didn't get you very far last time, did it?'

My pulse went into overdrive as Roscoe and Gary stood eyeballing each other. Tension hung in the air. It was plain to see there was no love lost between them and as they were both armed, the situation was volatile. Explosive. I was seriously worried I was going to get caught in the crossfire if it all kicked off.

'I'm not going to ask you again. Take your hands off my boy, before I put a bullet in that thick skull of yours,' Roscoe said.

His voice shattered the silence with the subtlety of a sledge-hammer and made me jump. I was on edge. My nerves were jangling. Roscoe was about to ruin everything. I'd already fucked up once by not delivering MacKenzie to Samson's door so that he could settle the score. He'd reluctantly given me a second chance. I wasn't going to get a third. My life was on the line.

I stayed where I was, glued to the brickwork as Gary turned away. He prodded MacKenzie in the small of the back to prompt him to move. The moment he took a step forward, a shot rang out, making my ears ring.

'Fuck!' Gary's voice sounded pained.

He pulled his right hand away from MacKenzie and covered the back of his left arm with it, dropping his weapon in the process. MacKenzie scrambled to pick it up, then he pointed it at Gary. My heart was pounding as I stood metres away, shaking like a junkie badly in need of a fix.

'You bastard,' Gary yelled at Roscoe, his eyes filled with hate as blood seeped between his splayed fingers.

'You're lucky I left you alive to tell the tale. Now, I want you to run back to Samson with your tail between your legs, you big wuss, before I change my mind. Tell him to stay away from my patch, or there's going to be an all-out war,' Roscoe warned.

'Get in the car, Daisy,' Gary snarled while glaring at Roscoe.

'You stay right where you are,' Roscoe said when I peeled myself away from the wall. I felt the weight of his stare.

My eyes darted between the two men as panic inched its way up inside me. I was torn between the Devil and the deep blue sea. I didn't know what to do for the best. Both options were equally grim. I'd sold MacKenzie out to save my own skin, so who knew what would happen if I hung around. Payback was never pleasant. But it couldn't be worse than what Samson had in store for me if I turned up without MacKenzie again. We'd made a deal. It was him or me. If I didn't stick to it, there'd be consequences. Deadly ones. He'd made that perfectly clear.

My head was all over the place. Fear had scrambled my thoughts. As I waited to see how things would unfold, something terrifying suddenly occurred to me. There was a good chance Roscoe might shoot me too, if I tried to go with Gary. I wasn't prepared to take a bullet, so I stayed rooted to the spot.

'You fucking bastard,' Gary cried out moments after the sound of another gunshot snapped me from my thoughts.

His fingers had dropped to the crook of his arm as a wave of fresh blood began seeping through the fabric of his jacket.

'I've already told you to fuck off back to London. I'm not going to tell you again. Unless you want to end up completely full of holes, I suggest you start moving your feet.'

Roscoe's finger hovered in front of the trigger as a gentle reminder of what would happen if Gary decided not to follow his orders this time.

'Didn't you hear what the man said, shit for brains?' MacKenzie pressed Gary's gun into the base of his skull.

Gary was outnumbered, so he had to swallow his pride and back down. Then he paced down the alleyway, muttering obscenities under his breath. MacKenzie trained the gun on him until Gary's black Range Rover disappeared into the distance.

When MacKenzie turned around to face me, my heart started galloping in my chest. I froze, and my breathing became laboured. It felt like my lungs were being crushed by a vice.

'And all this time, I thought we had something special going on.' MacKenzie tilted his head to one side and fixed his large greeny-hazel eyes on me.

I knew I should beg for forgiveness, but my voice had deserted me.

'For what it's worth, I'm gutted, Daisy.'

A sob escaped from my lips as I fought to hold back my tears. What the hell had I done? MacKenzie looked genuinely hurt by my betrayal.

'I never expected you to turn on me like this. Why did you sell me out to Samson? I thought you hated his guts.'

MacKenzie's unanswered question hung between us. My legs started to tremble even though both of my feet were planted firmly on the ground. I was struggling to control my fight-or-flight response. The temptation to run was overwhelming. But it would be a suicidal move on my part. The tables had well and truly turned. Our bond of trust was in tatters, and now my fate lay in MacKenzie's hands.

2

MACKENZIE

Thursday, New Year's Day

'Come on, sweetheart, let's get you inside,' Roscoe said.

Daisy was so busy looking at me that she hadn't noticed Roscoe approach her. She jumped out of her skin when she realised he was right beside her. It pricked my conscience when she shied away from him. I could see she was terrified, so I put Gary's gun into the back pocket of my jeans.

Every time I saw a woman cower from a man, it brought back memories of my own mum being beaten by my dad. It caused me so much pain. The scars ran deep. There was no valid reason why a man should ever hit a woman. It didn't matter how fucked off she'd made you feel or what she'd done to hurt you. Lashing out wasn't the answer. That was the coward's way.

Roscoe placed his gigantic hand on Daisy's back and steered her towards the pub. His fingers were splayed so they spanned the width of her shoulders. She was pretty tall for a woman, but she was slender, so she looked childlike next to my boss's broad six-foot-one frame.

'Jesus, that was close! It's a bit of luck you appeared when you did,' I said as I followed them. My nine lives were rapidly running out.

'Luck had nothing to do with it, son,' Roscoe replied, glancing at me over his shoulder. 'I knew that bastard would come for you when you turned up out of the blue, so I wanted to be ready for him.'

Roscoe had saved my bacon, so I didn't want to tell him that I'd purposely never mentioned The Castle or Dover to Samson for that very reason. Biting the hand that fed you was never a good idea. Nobody liked a smart arse, did they? But I definitely recalled having a conversation about what I'd do if I lost my job with that beautiful angel-faced woman Roscoe was wrapping in cotton wool. I'd told her that if Samson ever fired me, Roscoe would welcome me back with open arms, which must have led her to my door. There was no point in wasting brainpower on the technicalities. It didn't change anything. The minute I took the money out of Samson's safe, my card was marked. But he didn't want me to clear the debt. He wanted my head on a plate.

Roscoe's wife, Bernice, was standing in the doorway of the emergency exit, looking like an Amazonian ready for battle. Dressed head to toe in black, she looked every inch the warrior queen I knew she was. She was the real deal. She took no prisoners. As soon as Daisy was within reach, she pulled her towards her, then wound a long arm around her shoulder.

'Come on in, darling. You're safe now,' she said, ushering Daisy into the closest room. Her waist-length, dark brown ponytail swished behind her as she walked.

I'd never been in this room before, but when I stepped inside Bernice's private lounge, I felt like I'd been transported to the set of *Moulin Rouge*. It had an air of brothel madam about it. Black damask wallpaper lined every wall. A huge black velvet sofa draped with ruby-coloured throws and cushions sat in the middle of the red carpet. Antique lighting gave the space a soft glow. A gilt-framed mirror hung on the wall opposite the door, to the side of which stood an ostrich-feathered floor lamp with a gold base. Ooh la la! I couldn't imagine Roscoe had played any hand in the room's design, but it summed Bernice up to a T. It was a million miles away from the rustic, piratey-looking bar, which had smugglers' retreat stamped on it. The Castle was a proper seaside boozer.

Gary had been pointing the gun into the small of my back, but anyone would have thought Daisy had been the one in the firing line the way Roscoe and Bernice were clucking around her. It was a fucking joke. Talk about misplaced concern. Admittedly, she looked shocked by what she'd witnessed, but she'd brought the trouble to my door. If Roscoe hadn't stepped in to save my skin, Samson wouldn't have shown me any mercy.

'Take a seat, and I'll get you a drink,' Bernice said, leading Daisy over to the sofa.

'I think we could all do with one, doll,' Roscoe replied.

The light bounced off Bernice's black wet-look jumpsuit as she slinked over to the drinks trolley parked next to the ostrich feather lamp. I watched her pour generous measures of a dark spirit from a cut-glass decanter into crystal tumblers. The zip on Bernice's suit was so low it struggled to contain the contents. When she leaned forward, her huge boobs nearly spilt out. I couldn't imagine my mum wearing a figure-hugging outfit like hers, but she had the confidence to carry it off, so good luck to her. All she needed was a set of ears and a tail, and she could easily pass as Catwoman. Although, given the setting, a whip might have been more appropriate.

Bernice handed Daisy and Roscoe their drinks before bringing one for us on her return journey. She then sat next to

Daisy, who was clutching the glass with both hands as if her life depended on it.

'We've got a couple of hours at the most to get you both out of here and into a safe house before The Fox comes prowling,' Roscoe said.

I saw the colour drain from Daisy's face.

'Don't be scared, we're going to look after you,' Bernice said.

'We'll put you in two different locations to spread the risk of him sniffing you out,' Roscoe said.

When a sob escaped from Daisy's lips, Bernice pulled her into her arms. I'd never seen this side of Daisy. She was terrified. She looked so vulnerable. She was more like her sister Lily than she realised.

'Shush, shush. There's nothing to worry about,' Bernice said, holding Daisy at arm's length.

'That's easy for you to say.' Daisy's voice cracked.

'Don't upset yourself over this, sweetheart.' Roscoe locked eyes with Daisy.

'I don't want to go into hiding on my own. Can't I stay here?' Daisy asked and her big blue eyes filled with tears.

Roscoe glanced over in my direction. I knew what he was thinking, so I shrugged my shoulders. Daisy had done the dirty on me, but I'd walked away unscathed. Luckily for her, I didn't hold grudges. Life was too short.

'This is the first place Samson will look. Would you prefer to stay with MacKenzie?'

I smiled over at her to show her there were no hard feelings, but it didn't have the desired effect as I watched her expression darken. Little did I know it was a precursor to the surge of anger that was about to come barrelling towards me.

Daisy shook her head. 'No way. Not after what he did to my sister.'

What the hell was that supposed to mean? She threw me a toxic glare. The hatred in her eyes was so intense that I could feel her subconsciously injecting me with poison.

'Come again?' I asked, hoping she'd elaborate.

'Don't act all innocent. You know damn well you sold Lily into a prostitution ring.'

'I did what?' If Daisy thought that, she'd lost the plot.

'There's no point in trying to deny it.'

'I'm sorry to disappoint you, but I don't know what you're talking about.' I threw the palms of my hands up.

'You're a fucking liar, MacKenzie. How much did you get for her?' Daisy screeched. Her blue eyes were blazing. 'I trusted you. And you let me down in the worst way possible.' She was so mad, it was hard to get a word in, but I had to try.

'Don't talk to me about being let down. After what you've just done to me, you're not on solid ground.' I spat the words out as though they were burning the inside of my mouth.

'That's enough! Samson's after both of you, so you need to put your differences behind you and start working together. I haven't got time to get to the bottom of what's gone on, but I can vouch for the fact that MacKenzie wouldn't have seen your sister come to any harm no matter what you think,' Roscoe said, turning to face Daisy.

She looked at me out of the corner of her eye. The movement was so subtle I almost missed it. 'I want to believe what you've just said. But I'm afraid I don't.'

Roscoe gave her a weary grin. He didn't want to listen to this bullshit. None of us did. The clock was ticking. Samson might already be on his way.

'Daisy, love, the way I see it, you've got two choices. You either stay under the radar on your own or with MacKenzie. What's it to be?' he asked, taking the no-nonsense approach.

'In that case, I suppose I'll have to stay with MacKenzie,' Daisy huffed.

I was surprised to see her do a U-turn. I'd expected her to dig her heels in to the bitter end.

'Is that OK with you, son?' Roscoe tilted his head to one side while he waited for me to reply.

'No problem,' I said, but I wasn't sure I meant it.

3

DAISY

Roscoe had a terrifying stare – his left eye sat slightly off-centre and didn't seem to move when the right one did. When I'd first noticed it, I'd wondered if it was a birth defect, but the presence of a large scar that ran from his temple to his jaw made me think otherwise. Every face told a story. It seemed like his had seen more action than most.

Roscoe was scary looking. A stereotypical bad guy with a facial disfigurement. But looks could be deceiving; he clearly had a heart of gold. That's why I'd backed down without putting up too much of a fight and agreed to stay with MacKenzie. He was going out of his way to help me. A total stranger. So I didn't want to be difficult in case he thought better of it.

Maybe MacKenzie was telling the truth. He'd sworn blind he had nothing to do with Lily's kidnapping and Roscoe had vouched for him. From what I'd seen, he was a really decent guy. Whereas Samson, the man who'd put that idea in my head in the first place, was an untrustworthy dickhead. Why had I been so quick to believe him? He hadn't shown me a shred of evidence. I could kick myself for falling for the crap he'd fed me. My brain ached just thinking about it. It was all so confusing, and that was before I added the video Lily sent me into the mix. If she was alive and well, why hadn't she contacted me again?

'You'd better go and pack your stuff. No offence, but I want you out of here sooner rather than later,' Roscoe said, breaking my train of thought. MacKenzie didn't need to be asked twice. He took off like a prize-winning greyhound let out of the trap.

I felt jealousy stab me in the gut. MacKenzie had belongings to take with him. I only had the clothes on my back. And they weren't even mine. I was wearing Lily's trackies, sweatshirt, coat and Ugg boots. I'd left the house this morning disguised as my twin and had expected to be back at home now tucked up in bed, not disappearing into the night with a guy I'd betrayed. Nothing ever went to plan. Why did life constantly throw hand grenades in my path?

'Where are you going to take them?' The sound of Bernice's voice caught my attention.

Roscoe sank his teeth into the side of his lip as he mulled over her question.

'I'm not sure. One of the apartments at the Old Mill House is empty. They could stay there for the time being,' Roscoe replied after a brief pause.

The conversation was going on around me as though I wasn't in the room.

'Wouldn't somewhere more private be better? If they're going to be holed up together for a while, they'll need a bit of space, or they'll get on each other's nerves. What about the farmhouse?'

Roscoe pulled a face as he considered his wife's suggestion. I could feel my features mirror his as dread rose up within me. I couldn't stand the thought of being holed up somewhere remote for the foreseeable future, especially with MacKenzie. We'll probably end up killing each other and save Samson the trouble.

'It's too isolated, and it's a long way from here if there's an emergency...'

An emergency. What emergency? My heart started galloping in my chest. Roscoe's words were bouncing around in my brain, scattering my thoughts as I tried to concentrate on what they were saying. But there was so much to take in. I was muddled. Confused. Fear was slowly squeezing the life out of me. Its grip was suffocating.

'I'm ready.' MacKenzie bounded into the room shortly afterwards which brought me back to reality.

I looked over at him. He was standing in the doorway with a small black holdall gripped in his right hand. So, I wasn't the only one travelling light.

'Come on, sweetheart, let's get moving,' Roscoe said.

I hadn't touched the drink since Bernice had handed it to me, but I needed some Dutch courage so I knocked it back in one. I closed my eyes as the brandy burnt a trail down my throat before it landed in my empty stomach. I hadn't eaten since I'd had breakfast, and it was the early hours of the morning now. But skipping meals was the least of my worries.

Bernice got to her feet. 'Don't worry about a thing. You're going to be fine. Roscoe will look after you,' she said, sensing my hesitation. 'It really is a beautiful apartment. It's fully equipped, so everything you need is there. And as soon as the shops open, I'll go and get some clothes for you. What size are you, darling?'

'I'm a ten.' I felt so choked up by her kindness the words almost got stuck in my throat. 'Thanks for everything.'

'My pleasure,' Bernice replied before she threw her arms around me and gave me a tight squeeze.

When she released her grip, I felt like I'd been cut adrift. I had to force myself to put one foot in front of the other so that I could catch up with Roscoe and MacKenzie. I followed two steps behind as though I was on automatic pilot. Moments later, I was sitting on the back seat of Roscoe's midnight blue Jaguar F-PACE.

'I'm going to take you to the Old Flour Mill. I refurbed the building a few years ago now. One of the top floor apartments is empty. It'll be perfect for the two of you. It's only five minutes from here, and it's got a balcony with patio furniture at the back so you can get a bit of air without going outside,' Roscoe said.

'Sounds great!' MacKenzie replied.

It sounded like hell on earth if you asked me. Being cooped up with a man I'd done the dirty on was going to be awkward at the very least. Uncomfortable. Unpleasant. The list went on. MacKenzie might have been acting as if my betrayal meant nothing, but I was pretty sure it was just a front he was putting on while the boss was here. Once we were on our own, I had a horrible feeling it would be a different story. Nobody could be that forgiving.

'I'm sure I don't need to tell you that leaving the apartment is out of the question. If you need anything, call me. Don't be tempted to venture out...' Roscoe tore his eyes away from the road and looked at MacKenzie.

My stomach flipped over as his words registered.

Other people's New Year celebrations were either still in full swing or were done and dusted. We barely passed another car on the short journey. When we pulled up outside the brick-built building, which, as the name implied, had been converted from a Victorian mill, the street was deserted, too. Roscoe leaned in front of MacKenzie and opened the glove compartment. He rummaged around inside it and then pulled out a large bunch of keys. The heavy-duty key ring with swivel attachments and split rings made him look like a jailer. How ironic, I thought. Although MacKenzie and I weren't being held prisoner, we weren't free to leave the confines of the apartment either, not if we knew what was good for us. Having a death threat hanging over me was terrifying. Overwhelming. Nothing could stop the inevitable wave of darkness heading my way.

In an attempt to stop myself from losing the plot, I fixed my gaze on Roscoe. He scrutinised the entire bunch of keys one by one before unclipping a set from the metal ring and handing them to MacKenzie.

'Those are for the front door,' he said, holding up a set of brass keys. 'Once you're inside, lock the door behind you and put the alarm on. The code's the same as The Castle's. It's linked straight to my gaff, so if anyone tries to break in, I'll be the first to know about it.'

If Roscoe was trying to put my mind at rest, he was failing miserably. I was becoming more and more anxious by the minute. I needed to get a grip of myself before I had a meltdown in front of everyone.

'Any questions?' Roscoe locked eyes with MacKenzie.

'Nope. That all sounds straightforward enough, boss.'

'Great. The apartment's on the second floor. It's number six. You've got your own private entrance, so you'll be able to slip in unnoticed. See those stairs on the right?' Roscoe pointed through the windscreen, and MacKenzie nodded in response. 'They'll lead you to the front door.'

The black metal staircase bolted onto the side of the building looked like a fire escape.

'You better get going. You don't want to be taken out like a sitting duck. I'll call you later, but remember, if anything doesn't feel right, phone me.'

I'd known Roscoe for less than an hour, but I was putting all of my trust in him. I hoped I wasn't going to end up regretting that decision. But I didn't have another choice. I couldn't go home, and I didn't fancy my chances if I tried to go it alone.

By the time I'd unfastened my seat belt, MacKenzie was standing on the pavement waiting for me. As soon as my foot made contact with the ground, he began walking with purpose towards the stairs. I practically had to run to keep up with him while turning up the collar on Lily's pale pink teddy borg coat to try and keep the Arctic gusts of wind out. They were swirling around me, lifting my hair off my shoulders and making it splay out behind me. I tucked my chin down as I pushed against the force of the gale, willing myself to dig deep.

By the time I looked up again, MacKenzie had already made it to the platform at the halfway point, where the stairs changed direction. My heart started galloping in my chest. Being out in the open made me feel vulnerable. Alone. When I finally managed to catch up with him, MacKenzie was placing a key in the Yale lock, having already undone the Chubb.

'Ladies first,' he said when I reached the top of the stairs.

Warm air flowed out of the open doorway, so I quickly stepped inside. I couldn't wait to get out of the cold. Out of danger. MacKenzie closed the door behind him and put the deadlock on as instructed before arming the alarm. My teeth chattered as I stood in the hallway. It was a response to the sub-zero tempera-ture outside and the adrenaline dump I was experiencing.

'You OK?' he asked, ever the gentleman.

I gave him a half-hearted nod. My lips were numb with cold, so I didn't trust myself to speak.

MacKenzie walked down the hall and poked his head around every door he came to. 'So, the kitchen and living area's on this side. And over here there's a double bedroom, a bathroom and another double bedroom,' he said.

He'd given me a guided tour without me having to move a muscle, which was just as well really as I was glued to the spot. Paralysed by fear.

4

MACKENZIE

Life was full of choices and paths not taken, so I'd made the decision years ago to never let myself get bogged down with regrets. They only complicated things, and I liked an uncomplicated existence. What was done was done, nothing good came from dwelling on the past. If you did, you missed out on the here and now. Much as I hated to admit it, staying in London and working for Samson had been a huge mistake. Things could have been so different if I'd been brave enough to take the leap of faith and follow Roscoe to the coast.

Roscoe had done well for himself since he'd moved to Kent. He'd been ploughing a lot of the profits he made from selling gear into property development and if this apartment was anything to go by, he'd found his calling. Every inch of the place was immaculately presented with high-end fixtures and fittings. The best that money could buy. Not that there was anything wrong with the room above the bar in The Castle that Roscoe threw in with the job offer, but it wasn't in the same league as this place. The apartment was incredibly tasteful which made me wonder how much input Bernice had had in its design. There wasn't a trace of her madam whiplash anywhere.

Roscoe Allen was a top bloke. I hadn't seen him for years until I'd walked back into his life at lunchtime yesterday. But he'd bent over backwards to help me, greeting me like I was the prodigal son, and now he was doing the same for Daisy. He'd brought her into the fold as though she were one of his own. I wasn't sure how this arrangement was going to work out. I didn't have a problem being holed up with a gorgeous, leggy blonde. I could think of worse ways to spend my time, but Daisy was strong-willed and she was convinced I'd sold Lily into prostitution, so I knew I hadn't heard the last of it, even though Roscoe had done his best to smooth things over. She was a lousy judge of character if she thought I was capable of doing something that evil. It cut me to the quick that she held such a low opinion of me. How she'd come to that conclusion was a mystery, but I had a feeling all would be revealed soon. Bring it on; I wanted to get to the bottom of it.

Now that I came to think about it, Daisy hadn't said a word since I'd opened the front door and she hadn't bothered to join me when I'd checked the gaff out. Where was the mini-skirted Judas hiding? Surely she wasn't still standing by the front door shaking in her boots. I poked my head out of the living room door. Lo and behold, there she was. I'd never seen Daisy like this before. I was worried about her. Admittedly, we were still up to our necks in crap, but we were out of immediate danger. The way she was carrying on, you'd think somebody was holding a gun to her head.

'Hey, Daisy,' I called. She jumped out of her skin at the sound of my voice, so I went over to where she was standing. Her big blue eyes looked twice the size they normally did.

'Jesus, you frightened the life out of me,' Daisy said, covering her heart with her hand.

'You can't stay out here all night. Come in, and I'll get you a drink. You look like you could do with one.' Daisy made no attempt to move, so I caught hold of her hand and towed her along behind me. 'Have a seat,' I said when I stopped in front of a pale grey sofa with large squishy-looking cushions. 'What's your poison?' I asked and then immediately regretted my choice of words when the tiny amount of colour left in Daisy's face made a hasty exit.

She looked like she was about to burst into tears, and even though I was desperate to confront her over what she'd done, I wasn't that much of a bellend. That particular conversation could wait. We were going to have more time on our hands than we'd know what to do with, so an opportunity would present itself in the near future. I was sure of that. The last thing I wanted was to be shacked up in a hostile environment. Being on bad terms with Daisy would make things ten times worse than they already were.

Daisy hadn't bothered to answer me, but I didn't think she was intentionally trying to be frosty. I'd witnessed her ice maiden routine first-hand. This seemed different. She looked shell-shocked. It seemed strange to see her like this, as though all the fight had been sucked out of her. I couldn't help feeling her present state was nothing a good measure of Courvoisier couldn't fix. Alcohol never failed to loosen somebody's tongue. A more sensible person than myself would steer away from the sauce so that they could keep a clear head, but after the shit I'd been through in the last twenty-four hours, I desperately needed a drink and a few lines of rocket fuel. A drinks trolley similar to the one in Bernice's lounge was calling to me. I'd put money on the fact that the dark spirit in the decanter was Roscoe's favourite tipple.

'Get that down you. It'll make you feel better,' I said, handing Daisy the glass. She took it from me with trembling hands.

'Thanks,' Daisy said before taking a large gulp.

Her face contorted as she swallowed the liquid. Fair play to her. Not many women would be able to down a neat spirit. Brandy was a lot harder to knock back than Baileys.

'I owe you an apology,' Daisy said, putting her glass on the side table next to where she was sitting.

You could have knocked me down with a feather, but if that was the route she wanted to go down, I owed it to her to listen to what she wanted to say without interrupting.

'I really am sorry I brought trouble to your door, but Samson forced me into it...' Daisy let her sentence trail off.

She sat on the sofa stony-faced, staring into the middle distance so that she didn't have to make eye contact with me. I could see she felt awkward, so I didn't want to push it, even though I wanted to hear the whole story from start to finish. I had to gain her trust so that I could find out what I was dealing with. If I could get her to open up, hopefully, she'd tell me what Samson had in store for me. I'd have to adopt the softly-softly approach and take baby steps. But it was going to take a monumental effort. I was still reeling from the fact she'd sold me out. And to Samson of all people. She was meant to hate him with a passion.

'Don't worry about it. Shit happens. As far as I'm concerned, it's water under the bridge. Let it go.'

Daisy turned her head towards me and looked me right in the eye.

'Really? Do you mean that?'

'Absolutely. Don't beat yourself up over it. I forgive you,' I smiled. 'Another drink?'

'No thanks. I'm shattered. I think I'll go to bed,' Daisy replied.

'Fair enough. Pick whichever room you prefer and I'll have the other one.'

'Thanks,' she said as she got to her feet.

Her eyes bore into mine for several seconds before she turned away and walked out of the room. She'd looked as though she was about to say something else, but then she thought better of it. Daisy was being cautious, but I could feel her walls were already starting to crumble.

5

SAMSON

'You don't get many of those to the pound!' Travis said as one of the strippers jiggled her enormous tits in his face.

The tiny bikini she was wearing barely covered her nipples, but none of my guys were complaining. We were all enjoying the view. I thought Travis was going to bend her over and shag her on the spot when she gyrated her pert little arse above his lap. And why not? He was on a boys' night out. So he was entitled to let his hair down and have some fun while the trouble and strife wasn't looking. He'd left her at home, chained to the sink where she belonged.

Unluckily for Travis, the prick-tease took herself off before he had the chance to get his end away. I tore my eyes away from her and fixed them on a different bird wearing a white sparkly thong. She'd wrapped her never-ending legs around the pole before performing a one-armed spin. When she flipped herself upside down and let her legs drop into a scissor split, she ramped things up a notch. The woman was a contortionist. She was every man's fantasy. Watching her was mesmerising. I found myself in a trance-like state, dreaming about screwing her long and hard at the end of the night, so I was preoccupied with my dick hardening and hadn't noticed Gary walk in. I only realised he was standing next to me when I heard him speak.

'I need to talk to you urgently,' he boomed in my ear.

I begrudgingly tore my attention away from the tart on the pole and locked eyes with Gary. He was looming over me like an avenging angel. He didn't look happy so something must have gone catastrophically wrong. But I wasn't impressed that he'd come barging in and interrupted me just when things were heating up.

I'd been having such a good night with my close friends that I hadn't given Daisy or MacKenzie a second thought until now. But seeing Gary standing alone in my function room suddenly made my anger spike. Even the sight of Crystal Tits shaking her stuff on the dance floor couldn't snap me out of it. With steam practically coming out of my ears, I knocked back the single malt in my glass and got to my feet.

'Hey, Samson. Where are you going?' Travis called after me as I stormed out of my private entertaining space.

I didn't bother to reply. The sooner I found out what the issue was, the sooner I could get back to my party. Not that I was in the mood for celebrating now.

'What the fuck's going on?' I bellowed at Gary as soon as he closed my office door behind him. I didn't want every Tom, Dick or Harry listening in to our conversation, so I'd held my tongue until we were on our own. 'Where's the scrawny little scrote you were meant to be delivering? Let me guess, he gave you the slip again...' Silence settled in the room, so I fixed Gary with a death stare. If he knew what was good for him, he'd better start talking. A few seconds later, he broke eye contact with me. 'And what's happened to the blonde bimbo I sent you out with? What the fuck is going on?' I shouted. I'd never been a patient man, so my blood was already starting to boil.

'They're with Roscoe Allen,' Gary blurted out.

I felt my mouth drop open. Now, there was a ghost from the past. I hadn't expected to cross paths with the guy again, so hearing his name was a big shock.

'What do you mean, they're with Roscoe Allen?'

'I was leading MacKenzie to the car when the fucker appeared from nowhere and told me to sling my hook,' Gary replied without making eye contact with me.

'And you were only too happy to oblige? Why didn't you stand up to the spineless git?'

I let rip at Gary, who was very sensibly keeping his distance from me. He'd been on the receiving end of one of my right hooks more times than he cared to remember. The speed at which he answered told me he'd registered the weight behind my questions.

'I tried to, but he was tooled up. The bastard shot me twice in the arm.'

Gary's voice had a defensive edge to it. He turned to the left and the right to show me his war wounds. I'd like to say my heart bled for him, but taking a slug came with the territory. It was part of the job description, so he wasn't going to get any sympathy from me.

'You're about as useful as a set of tits on a bull. When are you going to grow a pair?' Gary's lips moved into a straight line as he accepted the verbal assault he knew was heading his way. But instead of the white noise pacifying me, it made my blood boil. 'Roscoe shot you in the arm, and you ran away like a fucking pussy to lick your wounds. I've got a good mind to plant a bullet between your eyes for coming in here and ruining my night. You're a wanker, Gary!'

'I'm sorry, boss. If it's any consolation...'

'Shut the fuck up.' I cut Gary off mid-flow.

His apology seemed genuine enough, but his words were lost on me. I was stuck in the red mist, so I couldn't tolerate listening to him bleating on with excuse after pathetic excuse. He'd had one job to do, and he'd fucked it up. I couldn't hold my fury any longer. I swung my arm back and swiped the phone and paperwork off my desk, then paced over to the bar, took out a bottle of Dalmore single malt, poured myself half a tumbler and knocked it back in a couple of swallows. While I waited for the alcohol to take effect, I faced the wall, clenching and unclenching my fists.

'Roscoe asked me to give you a message.'

Did the stupid fucker have a death wish? I spun around and glared at Gary. He was standing in front of the office door with his shoulders hunched and a sheepish look on his big, ugly mug. His timing was lousy. I'd had as much as I was prepared to take. I stomped over to Gary and grabbed hold of the front of his jacket, pulling him towards me. Then I looked up into his face. I didn't care how big the bastard was, he wasn't going to get away with ruining my favourite night of the year.

'So come on then, don't keep me in suspense, tell me what the boss-eyed git had to say for himself.'

I knew my spit had landed on his face, but he had the good sense not to wipe it away in front of me.

Gary cleared his throat. It was obvious he wasn't looking forward to being the messenger. I didn't really blame him. I had a habit of lashing out at the bearer of bad news. 'Roscoe said to tell you to stay away from his patch, or there's going to be an all-out war.'

'What a fucking liberty!' I shouted in Gary's face before head-butting the bridge of his nose.

Blood started pouring out of both of his nostrils a moment

after my concrete head made contact. I dusted off the front of my grey silk suit and walked out of my office. I had a different type of business to attend to. Crystal Tits was about to get the ride of her life. I needed to take my fury out on something or someone, and I couldn't think of a more satisfying way to relieve my aggression than fucking her brains out.

6

DAISY

The two bedrooms were almost identical, so I chose the one furthest away from the front door just in case we were broken into in the middle of the night. Closing the door behind me, I walked across the room and perched on the edge of the bed. I opened my phone to check for messages. I hadn't heard from Lily since she'd sent me the video. Something was wrong. I was sure of it.

I only had the clothes on my back so I briefly considered stripping down to my underwear before I hit the sack, but I decided against it. If we needed to make a hasty exit, I didn't want to waste precious time putting my clothes back on. And it was far too cold to go streaking outside in my bra and pants, so I slid fully clothed under the duvet to be on the safe side.

When I lay down, the first thing that hit me was the linen. It smelled divine and was luxurious to the touch. Five-star hotel quality. The bed was also incredibly comfortable. Not too soft. Not too hard. But sleep wasn't going to come easy, which was a shame as I was exhausted.

I hadn't been lying when I'd told MacKenzie I was shattered but that wasn't the reason I hadn't joined him for another drink.

Even though he was making light of the situation. I felt awkward. Embarrassed. He was being a complete gentleman about the whole thing which made me feel even worse about what I'd done. If he'd screamed and shouted and called me every name under the sun, I'd have known what I was dealing with. His water off a duck's back response was alien to me. I didn't know how to handle it, so I decided to put some space between us.

I was used to arguing nonstop with my dad. We were often locked in battle for days, but I hadn't expected MacKenzie to be so forgiving. His attitude was like a breath of fresh air. I could feel myself falling for him all over again. He had a power over me that I couldn't explain. It was magnetic and I couldn't resist the pull.

MacKenzie had told me to let it go, but I wasn't going to be able to. I was my own worst enemy. I wouldn't be happy until I'd explained myself. He deserved to know why I'd sold him out. I'd been trying to kid myself into believing that I'd lost interest in him but if I was totally honest, I liked him more than ever. He was a decent guy. Now I had to do the decent thing and come clean.

I was just starting to drift off when I heard a thud from somewhere in the apartment. I blinked. Dazed momentarily. My eyes scanned the unfamiliar room. For a brief moment, I'd forgotten where I was. But as soon as I remembered, my stomach lurched and my heart began galloping in my chest. I pulled back the covers and got out of bed, tiptoeing over to the door and pressing my ear up against it so that I could hear what was going on. There was no sound of an intruder and I wondered if I'd imagined the whole thing. I'd been half asleep. Perhaps I'd been dreaming. But I'd never be able to go back to sleep if I didn't investigate. I pushed down on the handle and eased open the door. My eyes travelled towards the front door. There was no sign of anyone in the hallway. When I turned the other way, I could see the reflection of a shadowy figure in the kitchen window. I gasped. My heart was in my mouth. As the person turned around to face me, I realised it was MacKenzie.

'Jesus, you frightened the life out of me!' I said putting my hand up to my chest while breathing a sigh of relief.

'Sorry, babe. I didn't mean to wake you. I've been on the puff and now I've got the munchies, so I was rooting through the cupboards to see what I could rustle up and I accidentally knocked over some tins of beans,' MacKenzie explained.

I used to hate it when he called me babe. But I had to admit I liked how it sounded. It made me feel a bit giddy. Gave me palpitations. Butterflies. I needed to snap myself out of this. I took a deep breath to calm myself down before I replied. 'I heard the bang and thought we were being broken into.'

'No, nothing like that. It was just me being clumsy. I'm sorry I scared you. I'm just about to make something to eat. Are you hungry?'

I shook my head and glanced down at my watch. It was quarter to four in the morning.

'I'm going to try and get some sleep.'

'No worries. I promise I'll keep the noise down,' MacKenzie smiled as I retreated back to the bedroom.

I couldn't trust myself to stay. The temptation was so strong. I was struggling to resist throwing myself at him, but I didn't want to be a notch on his bedpost for a second time so he could get his dick wet.

7

SAMSON

I prided myself on my generosity. I liked to spread my wealth around. People were impressed by money and if you had a lot of it, you naturally found yourself high up on the social ladder without even having to try. I could hear my guys laughing and joking, enjoying the entertainment I'd put on, but my mood had taken a nosedive. When I walked in and saw my friends having so much fun at my expense, it thoroughly pissed me off. It was time to call an end to the evening. I stormed over to the booth, my nostrils flaring. The DJ turned to look at me and grinned. No doubt he was expecting me to request a song, but that wasn't on my agenda.

'Turn the fucking music off,' I said.

'Don't you like this one?' the dopey arsehole asked.

'The party's over,' I bellowed.

He looked shocked that I was pulling the plug so abruptly, but he didn't question my decision. He just did as he was told. When the track stopped halfway through, I received a barrage of complaints from my beered-up buddies. As I turned to face them, every pair of eyes in the room was on me. Even Crystal Tits was managing to stare at me while she hung upside down on her pole as though she was frozen in time.

'Hey, Samson, what's going on?' Travis threw his hands up in the air.

'Haven't you bunch of scroungers got homes to go to?' Tonight had cost me a small fortune and I wasn't as flush as I used to be. Not that anyone would have noticed. I was still flashing the cash while keeping that little nugget of information to myself. What I had in my bank account was my business. Nobody else's. I glanced down at my Rolex and slowly shook my head from side to side. 'Didn't you know outstaying your welcome is very bad manners, Travis?'

I decided to single out the group's mouthpiece. Name and shame him to try and embarrass him into taking the unsubtle hint. The majority of the guys had finished their drinks, put their coats on and were headed for the door without making a fuss. A few stragglers were still skulking in the shadows waiting to see how things panned out. I should have known Travis wouldn't bail without getting a blow job at the very least. The man had an insatiable appetite for sex. He was like a horny old goat and would mount anything with a pulse. I wouldn't have minded if he was single, but he had a young wife at home that he could ride anytime he chose to.

'You can't send me home when things are just getting interesting,' Travis protested.

His tone was challenging, but I wasn't about to get into an argument with him about it. 'I can do whatever I want. My club. My party. My rules.'

'You're being a dickhead, and it doesn't suit you.' Travis eyeballed me.

'That pink flowery shirt doesn't suit you either. You look like a prize twat in it. I'm surprised your missus let you go out dressed like that!'

'Meow.' Travis bent his fingers and pretended to claw me as he roared with laughter. 'Proper little bitch you're being. Are you on your period?'

'Trust me, mate. I speak the truth,' I replied.

The colour did nothing for Travis. It made his bright pink face look worse than usual. If I hadn't known better, I'd have thought he'd been on holiday in the Sahara Desert and forgotten his suncream.

'What's up with you all of a sudden? You were fine until Gary turned up.'

Travis and I were great friends, and I didn't usually keep secrets from him, but I was fucking furious that Roscoe Allen was trying to mug me off, and wasn't in the mood to talk about it.

'Come on then, spit it out. I can see something's bothering you,' Travis continued, refusing to back off.

He was standing in front of me with his liver-spotted chest puffed out like a peacock.

'Just drop it will you.' I felt my lip snarl as I clenched my fists down by my sides.

'OK, you win. Don't get your knickers in a twist!' Travis said, holding his hands out in front of him in an attempt to pacify me. He'd read my body language correctly and had taken note of the angry vibes radiating off me. 'Get your coat, darling, I'll give you a lift home.'

Crystal Tits didn't reply but she slinked over to where her cheap-looking faux fur jacket was slung across the back of one of the chairs.

I didn't mind sharing birds with Travis as long as I got to go first, but there was no way I was going to let him take her away before I'd finished with her.

'Not so fast, mate, she's coming home with me,' I said.

The stripper picked up her nylon Arctic Fox and turned to face me. Then she batted her false eyelashes while flashing her unnaturally white teeth. 'You're making me blush. It's not every day a girl like me has two handsome men fighting over her,' she giggled as though she was a twelve-year-old schoolgirl.

'We're not fighting over you, darling. There's no contest. I paid the bill, so I get to take the goods home.'

My choice of words wiped the smile off her face. But I didn't feel bad if they offended her. If she didn't want to be considered a commodity, she shouldn't make her living as a stripper and an escort. A high-class one admittedly, but a hooker all the same. I could see Travis watching our exchange, but he didn't get involved.

'Thanks for your hospitality, Samson. It's been a pleasure as always. I'll give you a bell later after you've had time to catch up on some beauty sleep.'

Travis knocked back the drink in his glass and headed for the door. Even though he'd initially tried to put up some resistance, he'd finally taken the hint. I didn't need to spell it out in any more detail. He knew his company was no longer required. I wasn't about to defend my behaviour. I was a spoilt brat. Always had been. Always would be. I had my mother to thank for that.

8

DAISY

When I woke from a few hours of fitful sleep, it was still dark in my room. I glanced at my watch and was surprised to see it was just after nine. The blackout curtains were doing a good job of keeping out the daylight. I scrambled out of bed and headed for the door, pausing with my ear up against it as I listened for sounds of life. I could hear the kettle boiling in the distance, so I decided to brave leaving the room.

MacKenzie was standing by the sink with his hands shoved into the front pockets of his jeans. He looked over in my direction when I appeared in the doorway.

'Hi, Daisy,' he said, greeting me with a smile.

'Morning,' I replied.

'You look tired. Didn't you sleep well?' MacKenzie asked while his greeny-hazel eyes drank in the details of my face.

Sleep well? He had to be joking, right? How could he expect me to get a wink of sleep? Had he forgotten our lives were on the line? If Samson found us, he'd kill us. I was shitting myself. Stressed out of my mind. We were up to our necks in crap, but I couldn't even begin to imagine the horror Lily was facing. I was worried sick about her.

'It's pretty hard to switch off when you're sleeping with one eye open.'

'I know it's easier said than done, but try not to stress yourself out. Roscoe's got our backs. And believe me, having his protection counts for a lot.'

MacKenzie was attempting to reassure me. It wasn't working.

'No offence, but Samson seems like he's in a completely different league.'

From the first moment I'd met Samson Fox, the owner of the nightclub Eden's, I'd felt uncomfortable in his presence. That awkwardness had been replaced by fear. True heart-pounding terror. The man scared the shit out of me.

'Never underestimate the underdog.' MacKenzie flashed me one of his winning smiles.

I was more at ease in his company now, so I decided it was time to set the record straight. I felt really bad that I'd let Samson fill my head with rubbish. I was annoyed with myself for being so gullible. I thought I was a better judge of character. MacKenzie seemed genuinely gutted that I'd betrayed him. The least I could do was explain why.

'I know you told me to let it go, but I can't. I want you to know what drove me to throw you under the bus.' I paused long enough to take several deep breaths as I tried to compose myself. 'It's a long story, but don't worry, I won't bore you with unnecessary details.'

'I don't understand why you feel the need to confess all. You're not on death row, you know,' MacKenzie laughed.

Wasn't I? It certainly felt like my fate was in somebody else's hands. But that conversation would have to wait. Right now, I was psyched up and ready to spill the beans.

'Maybe not, but just humour me, will you?'

'Suit yourself, but what's done is done...'

'I don't know what possessed me to do it, but I turned up at Samson's house yesterday morning and accused him of kidnapping Lily,' I began.

'Oh, shit!' MacKenzie stretched out the two words as his large hazel eyes doubled in size.

'As you can imagine, he wasn't impressed by the unexpected intrusion, so he threatened to let Gary carve up my face unless I agreed to find out where you were hiding. He was fuming that you'd shot through without giving notice.'

'Fuck!' MacKenzie's voice was barely a whisper.

'The reason I thought you were behind Lily's kidnapping was because Samson told me I should look closer to home before I started throwing wild accusations around. I didn't want to believe you were behind her disappearance, but...' I let my sentence trail off.

'Jesus, Daisy. I still can't believe you thought I'd have anything to do with it—'

MacKenzie shook his head. He looked pained and I could see he was offended. But I pushed the guilt away.

'Please let me finish,' I cut in so that I could continue with my defence. 'I knew you were hiding something from me, but I didn't know what it was. Samson told me that you were involved with the Albanian mafia and that they ran a prostitution ring.' The words caught in my throat and my voice cracked. He'd also said that the pimp who bought her would want to get his money's worth, and Lily could expect to service ten to fifteen clients a day. My eyes filled with tears, so I shook that thought from my head and pressed on. 'Samson said you owed them a lot of money and that you were going to use Lily as a bargaining tool.' Once I started talking, the words spilt out of my mouth. There was no holding them back. The floodgates had opened and MacKenzie was almost swept away by the deluge.

'I swear on my mum's life, I honestly had nothing to do with Lily being snatched. I hope you believe that. Shit rolls off Samson's tongue. You shouldn't believe anything he says,' MacKenzie replied – his tone was flat.

I'd learned that lesson the hard way. A wave of embarrassment forced me to change the course of our conversation. 'I'm sorry I flushed you out, but Samson was threatening me.'

'I was gobsmacked when you turned up at The Castle yesterday, but when you walked back in with Gary, I did a double take. I thought you'd gone back to London,' MacKenzie said.

'I'd intended to, but Samson told me to stay put. By the time Gary drove down, you were nowhere to be seen.'

'What time was that?' MacKenzie asked.

'I'm not sure, I suppose about 7 p.m.'

'I'd gone on my break.'

'I'm surprised you left the pub unlocked and unmanned.' That seemed like a weird thing to do.

MacKenzie stared at me with a puzzled look on his face. 'Carly was meant to be covering for me. She was behind the bar when I went up to my room.'

'Well, the place was deserted when we walked in, so Gary started rampaging around looking for you. There wasn't a soul about. I can't believe you didn't hear the commotion.'

'I didn't hear a thing, but Roscoe's not going to be happy when he finds out that Carly made herself scarce while the pub was open. Anyone could have walked in off the street and robbed the place. Talk about getting off to a bad start. That was only her second day on the job. He'll show her the door before the punters have a chance to learn her name at this rate,' MacKenzie said, steering the conversation in a different direction.

'Gary was absolutely livid that you'd done a disappearing act, so he bundled me into the car and took me back to Samson's house,' I replied, getting back to the point. 'I was shitting myself. I thought Samson was going to kill me. I'm sorry I threw you under the bus, but I didn't have a choice.'

Tears started rolling down my cheeks. I couldn't hold them in any longer, they'd been threatening to spill since the beginning of our conversation.

'Hey, don't cry,' MacKenzie said.

He walked across to where I was standing in the doorway of the open-plan room. He hesitated for a moment, but then he threw his arms around my shoulders and pulled me towards him. I buried my face into the side of his neck. It felt good to be held by MacKenzie. There was nothing quite like a hug. It never failed to make a person feel better. I wasn't usually an emotional kind of girl, but before I knew what was happening, I was sobbing on his shoulder. The guilt behind my confession had weighed heavily on my conscience and I was gutted that things hadn't worked out between us. Knowing this was probably the last time he'd hold me was more than I could bear. I wanted to tell him how I felt, but I could deal with his rejection. Why did I always fall for the love 'em and leave 'em type?

MacKenzie loosened his grip and held me at arm's length. 'Like I said, don't beat yourself up over it. I'd have done the same thing. When Samson orders you to do something, the terms are non-negotiable. He expects you to jump to it and not ask questions.'

'Thanks for being so understanding.'

I knew I didn't deserve his compassion, but I was trying to

build bridges. I knew I wouldn't have been so generous if things were the other way around, though.

'Think nothing of it, and anyway, I owe you an apology, too. I'm pretty sure you thought I was blanking you because I hadn't replied to your texts. I promise you, it wasn't intentional. I was up to my neck in shit and I had to focus on staying alive,' MacKenzie laughed.

He'd been acting weird around me since we slept together, so I didn't believe a word of the crap he'd just spouted. He'd said it himself. Texts. Plural. Not just one message. I could kick myself for being such an idiot. I should never have let him get inside my pants. But I'd naively thought I had a future with him. It was too late to turn the clock back, so I'd just have to brazen out the fact that he'd used me. Slept with me and jogged on. Now that we were face to face, he obviously felt awkward about it, so he was trying to pretend it was all a big misunderstanding. As if!

'What kind of shit?' I asked to take the focus away from myself.

'Samson was right, I am involved with the Albanians. But it has nothing to do with prostitution. I owe them money. I owe him money, too.'

I looked down at my feet when I felt my cheeks flush. I'd behaved like a total bitch and torn into him without thinking things through. 'I feel bad that I thought you were involved but I didn't know what to believe. I still don't know who's taken Lily. She sent me a video yesterday evening when I was at Samson's place telling me she was alive and well.'

MacKenzie let out a sigh of relief. 'That's great news, but I'm surprised you didn't mention it earlier.'

'I think it's a hoax, though. If Lily was OK, why haven't I heard from her since? I didn't think too much about it at the time because Samson was looming over my shoulder, and then all hell broke loose. But now that I've digested it properly, it doesn't make sense. I think Lily was forced to send it. She looked too upbeat. Too unaffected. I know my twin better than anyone, and that's not how she'd react. She's still in danger. I know she is.'

I'd thought once I'd delivered MacKenzie to Samson, I'd go home, be reunited with my twin and put all of this behind me. But instead of it being the end, the journey was just beginning.

9

MACKENZIE

The words had barely left Daisy's mouth when my phone pinged. I took it out of the back pocket of my jeans and unlocked the handset. I almost jumped out of my skin when I saw an image of Lily staring back at me. It was another video. Fuck! Now what was I going to do? I didn't want to open the message in front of Daisy, so I wandered over to the kettle. 'Fancy a cuppa?' I asked, doing my best to sound casual while my heart pounded against my ribcage.

'Yes, please,' Daisy replied.

Even before I played the clip, I was pretty sure it was different to the last one I'd received. The background didn't look the same. With my back to Daisy, I turned down the volume of my phone and hit play while I waited for the water to boil. The video was short but I could see Lily's wrists were restrained by zip-tie hand-cuffs which were attached to a metal chain bolted to the wall. She was sitting on a sofa with her knees pulled up to her chest. She looked absolutely terrified.

'Is everything OK?' Daisy must have read the look of horror on my face as I put two mugs of tea down on the breakfast bar.

I didn't know what to do for the best. How could I tell her about the footage? I'd done my best to convince her I'd nothing to do with Lily's abduction. If I showed her the clip, she'd probably think I was involved after all. What I didn't understand was why the kidnappers kept sending them to me.

'You've been quiet since that text arrived. Did you get bad news?' Daisy asked, still hovering in the doorway.

'No, everything's fine. It was just my mum wishing me a Happy New Year,' I lied.

I could tell from her expression that she wasn't buying the lame excuse I'd just given her. Daisy was smart; she wasn't a dumb blonde by any means. She'd run rings around me if I wasn't careful. She'd already proved she paid attention to detail. I'd dropped in about The Castle and Dover as a passing comment in a far heavier conversation about me dealing drugs. But she'd stored it away in the deep recesses of her mind, pulled it out when required and used it against me.

I'd trusted her completely back then. I'd never thought I'd have a reason not to, but when a person was facing their own mortality, self-preservation would always be their main priority. Loyalty counted for nothing in a situation like that where your life was on the line. I'd probably have done the same thing. But I was only human and now I was wary of telling her too much in case she used it against me again. Once bitten, twice shy.

'Are you sure you're OK, MacKenzie?'

The sound of Daisy's voice brought me back to reality.

'I'm fine,' I replied. I tried to hide my concern behind a smile as I gripped the sparkly counter with tense fingertips.

'You don't look fine. All the colour's drained from your face.'

That didn't surprise me. Whoever was holding Lily was playing games telling Daisy she was alive and well and then sending me a clip showing her bound and chained to a wall.

'Can you stop lying to me and tell me what's up? I've been talking to you and you've just been staring into space,' Daisy said.

A million thoughts were rushing around in my head and I was trying to process them while trying to act normal. I was obviously failing miserably and Daisy wasn't easily fooled.

'Sorry, what were you saying?'

'It was nothing important. But you've been acting really weird since you got that text. I think we both know it wasn't from your mum. If I had to put money on it, I'd say it was from Samson. Why don't you tell me what's going on?'

Silence hung heavy between us. I couldn't think straight. My mind was whirring.

'Look, I know I let you down and I'm really sorry about that, but if we're going to move forward and put this behind us, we need to be able to trust each other. Please tell me what's bothering you.'

The sound of Daisy's voice interrupted my thoughts. She wasn't going to let this go any time soon. She was going to keep chipping away at me until I caved in. I wanted to confide in her, but I was worried about the repercussions. Trust had to be earned, but holding onto a grudge wasn't the way I rolled. It was time to take my own advice and let it go.

'You're right; my mum didn't text me, but I honestly don't know who the message is from.'

Daisy locked eyes with me. She looked confused.

'The text was sent from a withheld number, so it could have been from Samson, but it could just as easily have come from Arben Hasani.'

Daisy pulled a face. 'Who's that?'

'He's the Albanian I owe money to. A proper nasty piece of work. He's charming on the outside but he's rotten to the core when you scratch beneath the surface.'

Now it was Daisy's turn to go pale.

'What did the text say?'

I took a deep breath and exhaled slowly. 'I think you'd better sit down.'

Daisy's big blue eyes grew wide. She looked terrified.

'Why? What's going on?'

I pulled two high-backed stools away from the black sparkly breakfast bar and sat on one of them. A moment later, Daisy came and perched next to me. Beads of sweat broke out on my upper lip and my heart started pounding in my chest. I was all fingers and thumbs as I tried to open my phone and locate the message. I tilted the screen towards Daisy. She gasped and covered her mouth with her long, slender fingers when she saw an image of her sister frozen behind the play arrow. I hesitated before starting the video.

'Oh my God. I knew the video Lily sent was a hoax.'

Daisy's voice broke with emotion, so I pressed the arrow. There was no point prolonging the agony any further.

Lily looked terrified as she stared into the camera's lens. She didn't say a word. She didn't need to. Her eyes were pleading for help. Seeing her like that was unsettling. At the end of the ten-second clip a man, whose voice had been distorted said, 'Tick tock, MacKenzie.'

Daisy turned to face me. She wasn't tearful any more. Her eyes were blazing. Even before the words left her mouth, I knew she was furious with me.

'You're a selfish bastard. The only person you give a shit about is yourself,' she shouted.

'What the fuck's got into you?'

Daisy's mood had done a one-hundred-and-eighty-degree flip. She'd gone from being apologetic to wanting to rip my bollocks off in the blink of an eye. I would never understand the way women's minds worked.

Daisy pushed her stool back and got up in my face. 'You don't get it, do you, even though it's staring you in the face. Lily's life is in danger because of you. I can't believe you tried to fob me off by saying she'd got herself mixed up in trouble. Talk about trying to take the heat off yourself by fabricating a load of crap.' She jabbed her finger at me as she spoke.

Fuck me. Why did shit always land on my doorstep? I wished I hadn't shown her the video now. I could have saved myself from the ear-bashing from hell. There was no point trying to explain myself, she wasn't going to listen.

'This is all your fault! She's clearly being held by one of the people you've upset. It's down to you to get my sister back in one piece before anything happens to her. Tick tock, MacKenzie. You caused this situation. What are you going to do about it?' Daisy put her hands on her hips and fixed me with a death stare.

I would have replied if I could have come up with a decent answer, but I was so shocked by the change in her behaviour I didn't know how to respond. I wasn't usually slow at coming forward, but I was lost for words. Daisy stormed off, and as she left the room she slammed the door behind her. I felt guilty enough without her making me feel ten times worse. She was right, though; whoever had taken Lily had done it to punish me. But I honestly didn't know whether it was Arben or Samson. Both possibilities deserved equal consideration. It could have just as easily been either one of them. There was a fifty-fifty chance.

10

SAMSON

Who the fuck did Roscoe Allen think he was, warning me off? What a joke. The man was a comedian with a seriously short memory. Had he forgotten the last time we'd crossed paths? He'd tried to stand up to me, and it had ended in tears. His tears. I'd pounded the fucker so hard I'd felt his eye pop out of its socket. But that didn't stop me. I kept hitting him until he surrendered and begged for mercy.

I'm glad to say the fucker was scarred for life, so every time he looked in the mirror, he'd be reminded of that night. The disfigurement was plain to see. Not that he'd been at the front of the queue when looks were handed out. He had the kind of face only a mother could love. The ugly gene ran in the family. There was a reason everyone called Roscoe's older brother Fester. He looked exactly like the guy from *The Addams Family*.

Roscoe was acting the big man, but his card was marked again. If it was a war he wanted, a war he was going to get, make no mistake. Not only was he harbouring MacKenzie, who'd turned out to be a snake with legs, but he'd also taken Daisy in. You'd have to go a long way to find a bigger tramp than that little whore but Roscoe clearly had no taste in women. You only had to look at the ageing plastic dolly bird he was shacked up with to know that. There was nothing natural about her. I didn't usually go for the girl next door type either, but she was too long in the tooth by about forty years to be obsessing about her appearance.

Tempting as it was to jump in the car, drive down to Dover and beat the crap out of him again, I was going to resist the urge. That would be the predictable thing to do. And I didn't like to be predictable. Roscoe was on high alert at the moment, so I'd leave him to sweat for the time being. Watching and waiting was stressful. It took its toll on a person. Letting him wear himself out would work to my advantage. I'd make my move when he was least expecting it.

In the meantime, if he knew what was good for him, he'd pipe down and slink back into the shadows he should never have come out of. When the time was right, I'd muscle in on his new patch. Nothing would give me greater pleasure.

11

DAISY

I'd been lying on the bed with my knees hugged into my chest, feeling sorry for myself when the smell of sausages wafted under my door. My stomach grumbled in response. I rolled onto my back and picked my phone up from the bedside cabinet. I glanced down at it. It was ten past twelve. I hadn't eaten for well over twenty-four hours, and I was starving. But my pig-headedness wouldn't let me go in search of food. Not while MacKenzie was in the kitchen, anyway. I couldn't help myself. I wore my stubborn streak like a badge of honour.

The high-pitched tone of the burglar alarm suddenly rang out in the silence, making me jump out of bed. The air felt charged. Electric. I couldn't shake the feeling of danger as I kept my eyes glued on the door. Watching. Waiting. My heart was in my mouth. I was trapped in here. There was no escape route.

'It's only us.'

I let out a sigh of relief when I heard Roscoe's voice call out before he entered the code that stopped the alarm from counting down.

'I'm in the kitchen,' MacKenzie replied.

Much as I didn't want to see him, I didn't want to appear rude by staying out of the way. I blew out several deep breaths to try and compose myself before I opened the bedroom door.

'Good morning, Daisy,' MacKenzie said as I finally stopped sulking in my room and came into view.

'Morning,' I grunted before pursing my lips together. I didn't need to glance in the mirror to know a sour look had settled on my face. Just when he was starting to come up in my expectations, he'd gone crashing back down again.

MacKenzie flashed me a sheepish smile, and I threw him a filthy look in response. When I broke eye contact with him, I realised that Bernice had witnessed the frosty exchange, but thankfully, she didn't say anything to draw attention to it.

'How are you feeling?' she asked instead.

'I'm OK, thanks.'

That statement couldn't have been further from the truth, but this wasn't the time or the place to tell her what had happened.

'You'll be pleased to hear I've got nothing to report. All's quiet on the Western Front. There's been no sign of Samson or any of his goons,' Roscoe laughed. 'But I've put the word out just in case the sly fox starts prowling around. If he crosses the county line, somebody will tip me off.'

'That's good to hear. What time do you want me to start work?' MacKenzie asked.

I became aware of the sound of my heartbeat pounding away inside my chest. Even though I couldn't stand the sight of MacKenzie right now, I didn't want him to go out and leave me on my own.

'I think it would be better if you stay away from The Castle for the time being. Carly's going to cover your shifts,' Roscoe replied.

'Fair enough,' MacKenzie replied.

Roscoe had just given MacKenzie a golden opportunity to tell him how unreliable Carly was. But he hadn't taken it. Why was he protecting her? Maybe something was going on between them. I felt a stab of jealousy, which was ridiculous. I had no right. MacKenzie was a free agent. What he chose to get up to in his spare time was none of my business. Yeah, right! My feelings for him were complicated. Extreme. I kept swinging between love and hate. But there was a fine line between the two.

'I've got a shipment coming into Dover in the next few days, so you can help out with that instead,' Roscoe said.

My face slackened as his words registered. He hadn't gone into details but I'd be amazed if the shipment he was talking about didn't contain drugs of some description. I'd seen MacKenzie dealing cocaine from behind the bar at Eden's, and he used to work for Roscoe, before he became the manager of the club. I didn't like the idea of him being mixed up with this. But there was nothing I could do about it.

'Take a pew; the food's almost ready. Who wants an egg?' MacKenzie cast his eyes around the kitchen and looked at us in turn.

'Go on then,' Roscoe replied.

'Not for me, thanks, darling. I'll just have a black coffee. I have to watch my figure.' Bernice smiled as she ran her hands over the generous curve of her hips.

She was wearing skin tight leather trousers and a slinky black polo neck top. She was in great shape for a woman her age and she obviously intended to keep it that way. I briefly considered saying no to his offer, but I would have been spiting myself. It would be absolute torture watching them tucking into mounds of food while I had nothing just to prove a point. MacKenzie knew I was pissed off with him. It was going to take more than cooking a fry-up to smooth things over between us.

'Yes, please,' I replied before my stubbornness got the better of me and I talked myself out of it.

'Coming right up.' MacKenzie beamed.

He scooped rashers of streaky bacon and sausages out of a frying pan with a fish slice and put them on white plates he'd just taken out of the oven. Then he added half a large tomato, mushrooms and baked beans before placing a perfectly cooked egg on the side. A moment later, MacKenzie put the peace offering down in front of me.

'Thanks,' I said.

My mouth was watering. The food looked incredible. You couldn't beat a full English.

'Here you go, boss. Enjoy!' MacKenzie said, beaming with pride.

Roscoe picked up his knife and fork, but before he started eating, his eyes scanned the plate.

'Is something wrong?' The smile slid from MacKenzie's face.

'Where's the black pudding and hash browns?' Roscoe asked.

'Roscoe,' Bernice said in a reprimanding tone.

'What? Everyone knows they're the best bits!' Roscoe looked gutted.

'Aww, I'm sorry, boss, I just cooked up what I found in the fridge,' MacKenzie replied.

'And you did a great job,' Bernice said to try and soften the blow of her husband's disappointment. 'Now you get stuck in while I make the tea.'

I didn't need to be asked twice. As I chewed my first mouthful, I watched Bernice delve into a Waitrose shopping bag sitting on the counter. She pulled out a white bloomer loaf, cut it into thick slices and then brought it over to the table along with a tub of Lurpak she'd taken out of the fridge. Then she went back to the bag and took out two boxes of jam and cream-filled doughnuts.

'These are Roscoe's favourites,' she said with a big smile on her face.

Roscoe's eyes lit up as they fixed on the cakes. 'You're spoiling me, doll,' he smiled.

I barely came up for air until I'd devoured the food. When I did, I noticed all eyes were on me.

'You look like you enjoyed that,' MacKenzie smiled.

'I did. Thank you.'

'Would you like a doughnut?' Bernice asked.

'No thanks, I'm stuffed.'

'Right then, let's leave the men to it; they can do the washing up while we go and see what I've bought you.'

When Bernice held up the shopping bags that were down by the side of her chair, a lump formed in my throat. I was humbled by her kindness and felt the stab of tears at the back of my eyes.

Bernice tipped the bags out onto the bed. There were enough clothes to fill half of the wardrobe. I dreaded to think how much she'd spent.

'Thank you so much. I don't know what to say. You've been so generous,' I said.

'Honestly, you don't need to thank me. It's my pleasure,' Bernice flashed me her bright, white smile. 'How are you getting on with MacKenzie? I couldn't help noticing there was a bit of friction between the two of you.'

I'd only met Bernice yesterday, but I felt so comfortable in her presence that it made me want to confide in her.

'I have a twin sister called Lily,' I began.

'Wow, how lovely,' Bernice replied.

'Somebody kidnapped her...' I let my sentence trail off as the words caught in my throat.

'Oh my God! When did that happen?' Bernice's manicured fingers covered her mouth.

'In the early hours of Wednesday morning. She told me she was safe, but then MacKenzie was sent a video of her bound and chained to a wall. I don't know what to do. I haven't even told my parents yet,' I blurted out and felt my eyes fill up with tears.

Bernice wrapped her arms around me. Held me close. Swaddled me in a warm blanket of compassion. I wasn't accustomed to displays of affection like this, so I didn't know how to react. This was unfamiliar territory for me. I was like a cardboard cut-out inside her embrace.

'You poor thing,' Bernice soothed. 'Do you know who's taken her?'

Bernice loosened her grip and held me at arm's length. She looked at me with a grave expression on her face.

'No.'

I broke eye contact and looked down at my feet, hoping my tears wouldn't start to fall. Then, I entwined my fingers to stop my hands from shaking.

'Don't worry, darling. Roscoe will sort this out.'

My efforts were in vain. Bernice's kindness broke through my defence barrier and freed my emotions. I began sobbing my heart out. Weeping. Wailing. An endless river of tears.

'Don't cry, Daisy,' Bernice said as she pulled me into a hug.

I'd spent all that time hoping something nasty would happen to Lily, and now that it had, I felt responsible. I wished we'd never walked through Eden's doors. We had Dad to thank for pushing us in that direction.

But it was too late for regrets. Much as I'd love to turn back the clock, the damage was done. Lily and I had been sucked into the underworld and I had a horrible feeling we were in too deep to ever get out.

12

MACKENZIE

'Roscoe, can you come in here, please?' Bernice asked.

As Roscoe and I stared at each other, I froze mid-motion, with a soapy scourer in one hand and a frying pan in the other.

'On my way,' Roscoe called out.

Bernice's voice had an urgency about it, and Roscoe jumped to attention. I was hot on his heels, still wiping bubbles onto a towel, when I made it to Daisy's room.

'Daisy's twin sister, Lily, was kidnapped in the early hours of Wednesday morning. She doesn't know who's holding her, but MacKenzie was sent a video of her,' Bernice blurted out.

My balls started to tingle when Roscoe turned towards me with a look of horror on his face. 'Why didn't you mention this to me?'

How the hell was I meant to answer that question and not look like a bellend. The tone of Roscoe's voice indicated he was going to judge me whatever I said. I'd start with an apology. If I adopted a submissive role, it might help to calm the undercurrent.

'I'm sorry. I should have, but so much has happened since I arrived in Dover...'

I let my sentence trail off before I dug myself into a hole I couldn't get out of. It wasn't as though Lily being taken had slipped my mind. I couldn't get the image of her terrified face out of my head. But I was ashamed to say I'd put my own needs before hers.

'Is that it? That's all you've got to say on the matter?'

Roscoe didn't look impressed, but there was no point in going into a long-winded explanation. There was no excuse. I should have told Roscoe everything and not just part of the story, but I was worried he'd be reluctant to help me if he knew how much trouble I'd got myself into.

'I know it's pathetic.'

I glanced over at Daisy. She looked distraught which made me feel like the biggest arsehole on the planet. Seeing a woman cry always tugged at my heartstrings.

'Roscoe, look at the state she's in. She's in turmoil,' Bernice said. She had her arm wrapped around Daisy's shoulder in a bid to comfort her.

'Dry your tears, sweetheart. I'm going to sort this shit out.'

Roscoe offered her a sympathetic smile while I breathed a silent sigh of relief. Bernice had refocused the conversation, and in doing so, she'd taken the heat off me, albeit momentarily.

'Has Samson taken Lily?' Roscoe asked. His eyes drilled into mine.

'I honestly don't know.' Roscoe looked confused, so I was forced to elaborate. 'He might have, but Arben Hasani could also be holding her. He's an...'

'You don't need to tell me. I know who he is,' Roscoe cut in before I had a chance to finish. 'He's a nasty piece of work.'

You could say that again, but I hoped for Daisy's sake Roscoe didn't go into any more detail. She was worried enough already without hearing the danger her sister might be facing in technicolour.

'I think you'd better show me the footage,' Roscoe said.

'I've got two clips,' I replied.

'You've got two?' Daisy questioned.

Fuck! Me and my big mouth. I hadn't told her about the first one I'd received, but it was too late to backpedal now. I'd have to come clean, or I was going to make myself look like a right scumbag.

'When did you get the first clip?' Daisy's tears evaporated into thin air as she perched on the end of the bed glaring at me.

'It literally came through just before you walked into The Castle yesterday afternoon.'

'And you chose to keep that to yourself? My God, MacKenzie, you're a selfish bastard.' Daisy's words hit me like weapons of mass destruction. Friction was building between us like tectonic plates before an earthquake. I could sense an eruption wasn't far away.

'It's your fault Lily was kidnapped in the first place.'

Daisy leapt to her feet and started jabbing her finger at me. Her features froze for a brief moment, and I'd thought she was going to pipe down, but then she got a second wind.

'But instead of trying to do something to help her, you just buried your head in the sand.'

'Believe it or not, I don't know who's holding her. There aren't any clues. The videos just show anonymous-looking, soulless rooms. They're indistinguishable. Don't you think I'd sort this mess out if I could?'

Bernice caught Roscoe's eye, then gestured with a flick of her head towards the door.

'Right, son, come with me. We've got business to attend to,' Roscoe said, leading the way out of the bedroom.

I flashed Daisy an apologetic glance but she looked straight through me.

'Daisy's upset, so I think it's best we give her some space and formulate a plan out of earshot,' Roscoe said once we were behind the closed door of the open plan living space. 'I can see you feel bad about what's happened, but I have to say you've behaved like a bloody idiot. Delays can cost lives in a situation like this. I'm sure I don't need to tell you we've got to find Lily before she comes to any harm.'

We both knew there was a real possibility she had already come to harm. But second guessing never got you anywhere, so it was better to focus on the facts.

'Before we go any further, let me see the footage.'

I angled my phone towards my boss and played both of the clips, but instead of watching the distressing images of Lily, I focused on Roscoe's reaction instead. He was a hardened criminal but he was visibly moved by what he'd seen.

'She looks absolutely terrified. We've got to do something to help her. I think you'd better tell me what's been going on,' Roscoe said.

He walked over to the fridge, took out two cans of Kronenbourg and handed one to me. I released the ring pull and took a huge gulp before I started to speak.

'You know I owe Samson money.'

Roscoe nodded. 'You said he's holding you accountable for the cash he lost in the break-in.'

My blood ran cold. I should never have tried to keep him in the dark. The truth always came out in the end.

'Yeah, but I haven't been completely honest with you about that.'

Roscoe's features hardened. 'For fuck's sake, MacKenzie!'

He shook his head slowly from side to side. I was gutted to see the disappointment written all over his face. I wasn't sure I could handle another guilt trip right now, but I'd have to suck it up and take the ear-bashing like a man. It was the least I could do.

'I've always treated you as though you were my own flesh and blood, haven't I? I've looked out for you. Given you a roof over your head and money in your pocket. And what do I get in return? A whole load of bullshit. Show me some respect, son.'

'I know you have, and for what it's worth, I'm really, really sorry.'

Offering him another grovelling apology was a small step in the right direction, but he deserved to hear the truth, ugly as it was.

'I told Samson the club was broken into over Christmas, and most of the takings were stolen from the safe because I'd used the cash to pay Arben off. He'd lent me a kilo of cocaine to tide me over until our shipment cleared customs, but then he changed his mind and insisted I pay for it before I had time to shift any of it,' I began.

'Why didn't you ask me to lend you the money?' Roscoe looked hurt that I hadn't come to him in my hour of need.

'Believe me, I wish I had. But it all happened so quickly, and the money was just sitting there. I didn't think Samson would realise. I'd intended to pay it back before he found out...'

Roscoe shook his head again while he processed what I'd just said. It was as though he couldn't believe I'd been that stupid. But I'd been desperate. And desperate people did stupid things. Guilty as charged.

'So what happened?' Roscoe asked.

'After I gave Arben the money, Samson discovered the cash was missing. I panicked and told him that Eden's had been burgled, thinking he'd claim for the loss on his insurance, but he didn't buy the story I'd spun him and said it was my responsibility to pay back the dosh.' I closed my eyes and let out a big sigh.

'Sounds like you were getting it from every angle.' Roscoe's tone had softened.

'I was. As soon as I dealt with one threat, another one was there to replace it. I was meant to pay Samson back by New Year's Eve, or he said there'd be a price to pay. And he wasn't talking about cash.'

'So you missed the deadline, and now Samson wants your head on a plate. But why's Arben still threatening you if you've cleared your debt?'

'He sent a message early yesterday morning saying I'd given him some counterfeit notes, which I'm sure isn't right, but I've got no way of proving it. He said there'd be consequences.'

'Fuck me!' Roscoe said before finishing off his can.

He walked over to the fridge, took out another two Kronenbourgs and passed one to me. Roscoe stared into space as he sipped his drink.

'So this all came to a head yesterday?' Roscoe quizzed after a lengthy pause.

'Yeah.'

Time was dragging by so slowly it felt like years had passed.

'But didn't Daisy say Lily was kidnapped in the early hours of the morning?'

'Yeah. They'd just finished their set at Eden's. Daisy had gone outside for a smoke, and Lily was alone in the dressing room when she was snatched,' I explained.

'So she was taken before you missed your deadline with Samson and before the text from Arben came through?' Roscoe was trying to work out how the pieces of the puzzle fitted together.

I nodded.

'That doesn't make any sense,' Roscoe concluded.

'I know. I'm wondering if Lily was taken as a case of mistaken identity. Daisy and I had a bit of a fling before, and Arben threatened to sell my girlfriend into prostitution if I didn't stick to our deal,' I said to explain why Lily had found herself in the middle of the equation. 'And we all know Samson likes making his vendettas personal.'

'You don't need to tell me that.' A flash of anger spread across Roscoe's face. I'd unintentionally hit a nerve.

'Let's face it, either of those bastards spell bad news for Lily. We need to work out which one of them it is. But we'll have to act quickly. Time is of the essence,' Roscoe said and then he downed the rest of his can.

I just hoped Lily hadn't been given a one-way ticket to the sex trade. If she had, we might as well give up the fight. We'd never be able to trace her. She could be anywhere in the world by now. I shuddered at the thought and then pushed it from my head. I had to get out of this mindset.

'I've replayed the night she was snatched over and over, looking for clues, but I keep coming up with blanks. I didn't see the men, and Daisy didn't give me a description, so it's hard to say who they were working for,' I replied.

'Daisy saw them?' Roscoe snapped his head around to look at me.

'Yeah. She was in the alleyway when Lily was snatched.'

Roscoe walked over to Daisy's room, knocked on the door, but opened it before anyone replied. 'I'm sorry to disturb you, sweetheart, but I need you to tell me what Lily's kidnappers looked like.'

'I only saw them from a distance. All I know is they were huge, they towered over her.' Daisy was doing her best to disguise it, but I could hear the tremor in her voice.

'Did you notice what they were wearing?' Roscoe asked.

'Black suits, white shirts and black ties,' Daisy replied without hesitation.

'That's a great help. Thank you, sweetheart.'

Why hadn't I thought to ask Daisy what they looked like? It was a simple enough question. Maybe I would have done if the circumstances had been different, but right now, I had so much pressure weighing down on me that I didn't know my arse from my elbow.

A moment later, Roscoe walked back into the room.

'I don't know a lot about how Arben's operation runs, but the fact that the goons were suited and booted makes me think Samson's actually the one behind this.'

I agreed with Roscoe's suspicion. 'I think you're right. I'm definitely leaning towards Mr Fox orchestrating this. Arben's always smartly turned out, but his heavies dress head to toe in Adidas.'

I felt a small glimmer of hope for Lily. Samson holding her was the lesser of two evils. At least we had a chance of finding her now.

13

DAISY

I was struggling to process the fact that MacKenzie had two clips of Lily. I literally had to force it out of him to tell me about the one he'd received while we were in the kitchen. He'd tried to fob me off by saying the message was from his mum. I knew he was lying, but nothing could have prepared me for what he showed me. My muscles tensed and I held my breath as my heartbeat went into overdrive.

'MacKenzie still hasn't shown me the first video. I don't get it. Why all the secrecy? Is he deliberately trying to torment me?'

'No, that's not his style. MacKenzie hasn't got a cruel bone in his body,' Bernice replied.

'Hasn't he?'

I wasn't convinced. I didn't know what to make of him. He was a multi-faceted, complex character. Both intriguing and infuriating at the same time.

'Just ask yourself why he'd want to make you suffer more than you already are? What would he possibly gain from that?' Bernice's tone was soothing. Sympathetic.

'Revenge.'

How could one word hold so much power? It felt like it was coated in ice as it left my lips.

'I'm not buying that, but you're entitled to your own opinion, it's a free country.' Bernice flicked her head, and her waist-length dark brown ponytail swished in response.

'It makes perfect sense to me. I sold MacKenzie out to Samson, so this is my payback.'

'Look, love, I get where you're coming from, but you're wrong. It's my fault he didn't play you the clip. I thought it might be too much for you, so I gave Roscoe a nudge to take MacKenzie outside. You've been through enough without having distressing images of your twin replayed over and over again.'

Bernice reached for my hand and squeezed my fingers, but I pulled away.

'That wasn't your decision to make.'

I replied too quickly. My tone was unnecessarily harsh. Snappy. Once again, my temper had derailed my manners. Bernice looked hurt. Wounded by what I'd said. I hadn't meant to lash out at her. But I was feeling stressed. Irritable. Agitated. I hated myself sometimes. Why was I being such a bitch to the person who was going out of their way to help me? I'd never understand the way my mind worked. I always pushed the self-destruct button.

'I'm sorry, darling. I shouldn't have interfered, but you looked so upset, and there's only so much a person can take.'

Genuine concern poured out of Bernice. Her words were so compassionate they almost reduced me to tears. I had to get a grip of myself before I totally lost the plot.

'You shouldn't be apologising to me. I shouldn't have spoken to you like that. I really appreciate everything you've done for me. I'm feeling a bit overwhelmed. My emotions are all over the place, but that's no excuse for being rude.'

That was an understatement! The stress I was under was fucking with my brain, and I was struggling to think straight. Finding Lily was proving to be an impossible task. But I wouldn't give up on her. I couldn't. I was determined to help her before it was too late.

Bernice had every right to turf me out onto the street. It would serve me right for behaving like a stroppy little madam. I should have tried harder to keep this ugly side of my nature hidden.

'You've had a lot to deal with. But Roscoe and I will do our best to take some of the pressure off you. We'd be only too pleased to help you sort things out.'

'Your kids are lucky to have parents like you,' I said.

A lump formed in my chest. Nobody ever really looked out for me. I felt like an outsider in my family. An outcast. Bernice had become my biggest ally. More than that, she was acting like a surrogate mum. Showing me the love and kindness I didn't get at home. My mum wasn't affectionate and caring like this. She never gave me much attention. Even though this was all new to me, it was good to have somebody to lean on. I needed Bernice's support more now than ever.

'Roscoe and I don't have a family.'

'Seriously?'

'What are you going to do about your mum and dad?' Bernice asked.

'I'm not sure. I've got loads of missed calls and texts on mine and Lily's phones from my dad. I've been ignoring them, but I'm going to have to make contact with my parents soon. I can't keep putting it off,' I blurted out.

'Are you going to tell them the truth?'

I considered how to answer the question. But before I had a chance to reply, Bernice continued to speak.

'The way I see it, you've got two choices. You either come

clean, or maybe you could pretend to be Lily to buy yourself some time.'

Bernice made it sound so simple. The best plans always were. But I wouldn't be able to pull off the deception, not to the people who knew us best. We might look the same, but we had different mannerisms. Lily didn't smoke or drink, and I had no intention of giving up the fags or going teetotal any time soon.

'I'll never get away with pretending to be Lily. My mum and dad have no trouble telling us apart.'

'I'm sorry, love, that wasn't what I meant. I was just thinking you could send some texts from her phone.'

It was a good idea, but I couldn't shake off the sense of impending doom. I didn't want to tempt fate in case I jinxed things.

'I think I'll have to come clean.'

'In that case, you're going to have to tell them in person. You can't deliver news like that in the text.'

I felt my eyes widen as I shook my head. 'I don't want to go to the house, though. Samson might be waiting for me.'

'Don't be scared. Roscoe and I will go with you for moral support.'

Dread started welling up inside me. I appreciated Bernice's offer, but she was underestimating the situation. She had no idea how unreasonable my parents could be. Samson threatening me was one thing, but facing my mum and dad was an equally terrifying prospect. The news wasn't going to go down well.

A missing child was every parent's worst nightmare. Lily might be a grown woman, but she would always be their baby. Their firstborn. Their golden child.

14

MACKENZIE

I should have told Roscoe about Lily yesterday. Who knew what that decision had cost? Her life? Her sanity? Her dignity? I couldn't bear thinking about it.

'Let's go back over what we know and see if that sheds some light on anything,' Roscoe suggested snapping me back to reality. 'Lily was snatched in the early hours of yesterday morning. When did the first video come through?'

'Not long after I got here. I'd been familiarising myself with the stock's layout when a message came through from a withheld number.'

I shuddered at the memory of Lily hugging her knees with her wrists bound. Her eyes were huge as she stared into the camera's lens. She was terrified. Her fear was palpable.

'The culprit would have used a burner phone. So you watched the clip and...' Roscoe let his sentence trail off and waited for me to fill in the blanks.

'I got distracted because then Daisy walked in. I felt like I'd seen a ghost. I almost shit myself.'

'I can imagine. Why didn't you tell her about the footage?'

'Because she came in all guns blazing and accused me of taking her sister! Samson told her that I owed money to the Albanian mafia and that I was going to sell Lily to them to clear the debt. Daisy's convinced they've got her, but that's exactly what Samson wants her to think to keep the heat off himself.'

'Exactly. I'm sure that slippery bastard's holding Lily. But where the hell is she? The room in the video was featureless, and there weren't any background sounds. So there's no clues to go on...' Roscoe broke off.

'I won't be a minute. I'm just going for a slash,' I said.

I needed some rocket fuel to help me think straight, but I didn't want to take it in front of Roscoe, so I slipped away to the privacy of the bathroom to snort a couple of lines. Feeling more alert, I walked back into the open-plan living space. Roscoe was still lost in thought.

'I take it Samson still controls all the pubs in the area,' Roscoe said.

'Yeah, apart from The Railway Tavern and The Bell,' I replied.

'Do you think he's keeping her in one of the cellars?' Roscoe asked.

I was desperately scouring the deep recesses of my memory in the hopes I'd unearth something that would lead us to Lily. It was a decent suggestion, but I wasn't sure he was right.

'I doubt it. The room didn't look like a boozer's underground lock-up to me. Everything was bright and white. It was almost clinical.'

But I'd never had the pleasure of visiting the basements of the other establishments he controlled, so I couldn't say for certain. My observation was just a hunch. Although, I wouldn't put it past Samson to have an immaculate storage facility for his wines and beers. He was incredibly particular when it came to personal grooming and his house was like a show home, so it would be reasonable to assume that fussiness followed through to other areas of his life.

'Do you reckon he'd be stupid enough to hold her at his house?' Roscoe's eyes widened as though he'd just had a light bulb moment.

'I honestly couldn't see him taking that risk. He usually likes to put as much distance as possible between himself and his dodgy deals.'

My response seemed to drain my boss's energy. I wasn't intentionally stamping on any possible leads. We had to go through a process of elimination and dampening the beacon of hope was the last thing I wanted to do, but going on a wild goose chase was just going to waste everyone's time. And thanks to me, we'd already done enough of that.

'Roscoe, darling, I'm sorry to interrupt, but Daisy needs to tell her mum and dad about Lily. I told her we could take her. Is that all right with you?'

Bernice pulled her ponytail over her shoulder and began running her long nails through the length of it while fluttering her false eyelashes at Roscoe. She knew exactly how to twist her hubby around her little finger, acting all coy when she'd already volunteered his services without running it past him first. But Roscoe didn't seem to mind. He'd do anything to please the woman in his life.

'Of course it's OK, doll. When do you want to go?'

'Sooner rather than later before she loses her nerve and talks herself out of it. She's teetering right on the edge,' Bernice replied.

'Let's get going then,' Roscoe said, picking up his car keys.

'By the way, Daisy's dad is an arsehole,' I warned. It was only right to give Roscoe the heads up after everything he'd done for me.

'Is he now? Thanks for the tip off.'

'Do you want me to come along?' I asked.

'There's no need. But while I'm gone, do me a favour and have a think about any other properties Samson has access to and see if you can find one that might match the footage. We should be back in a couple of hours,' Roscoe said as he walked out of the room.

15

LILY

I had no idea who had kidnapped me or why. I didn't have any crazy ex-boyfriends lurking in the shadows or stalkers that I knew of, and it was too early in my career to have attracted the attention of an obsessive fan. From the moment I'd been snatched, I'd been trying to work out who was behind this. Warren Jenkins was the only person who came to mind. He was the local villain who'd lent Dad money fifteen years ago after he'd remortgaged our house and couldn't keep up the repayments to the bank. But we were in a far worse position now. The debt to Warren was spiralling out of control; Dad owed him a ton of money. Surely, Warren realised it was a pointless exercise holding me to ransom. I wasn't the heiress to a vast fortune. My parents were skint.

Visions of my family started running on a loop through my head. I could see Mum and Dad so clearly. Then images of Daisy and me, from little girls to teens to grown women, shuttered through my mind. I desperately wanted to go home, but my restraints were too strong. Escape wasn't an option. I had to accept my fate. My destiny. But I was going out of my mind. The anticipation was unbearable. I'd been expecting the boss to make an appearance by now. When we'd arrived at the warehouse, the older of the men guarding me had said he'd be here soon. But daylight had come and gone, and I'd survived my first night in captivity, yet there was still no sign of him. I was a nervous wreck. Scared of my own shadow.

I'd been moved to a room on the mezzanine level, which was sparsely furnished with a single bed and a two-seater sofa. The presence of several sets of clothes and underwear made me realise my kidnapping hadn't been a spur-of-the-moment decision. It had been carefully planned. There was a shower room next door to the bedroom which was fully stocked with toiletries, so I had everything I needed. I couldn't complain about the conditions. This place was better than some budget hotels I'd stayed in before. But it was still a terrifying ordeal. My thoughts kept wandering to dark places.

Who knew what was planned for me? The men hadn't questioned or tortured me. They were just holding me, awaiting further instructions. I was being fed and watered regularly, although their fast food diet was adding to my distress. But it was the fear of the unknown that kept me awake last night.

I'd turned my back on the younger man who was guarding me because I could feel the heat of his eyes boring into me like laser beams, scrutinising my every move. But I couldn't escape from his glare. His shadow projected onto the wall. It was a menacing shape as it loomed over me, instilling me with terror as intended. I'd been relieved when morning finally came and the night watch ended.

The sound of a mobile ringing in the warehouse below broke into my thoughts. Moments later, the older man said, 'Hello.'

I listened to the one-sided conversation with barely contained panic, desperately trying to block out the sound of my pulse pounding in my ears.

'There's nothing to report. She hasn't given us any trouble.'

I was glad I'd done what came naturally and been obedient, reasoning that if I was compliant, they were more likely to keep me alive. Was that a pipedream?

'Are you coming over today?'

Those seemingly unthreatening words sent a shiver down my spine. My nerves started jangling. The thought of coming face-to-face with the man who gave the orders escalated my terror. It was as though his presence might change everything. Upset the balance. My heart began thundering in my chest, so I had to force myself to stay calm.

'No reason. I was just asking,' the man said.

I wondered what the response to his question had been. Was the boss on his way or not? I was trying to stay positive but it felt like time was running out for me. I was on edge. Anxious.

'No worries. We've got it covered. We can handle it between us.'

That sounded like reinforcements weren't coming. Whoever was on the other end of the phone was making themselves scarce, which was good news for me. Three men plus a driver had kidnapped me, and now only two of them remained. Should I wait to be rescued or try and make a run for it while I wasn't heavily outnumbered? I might die trying, but they were probably going to kill me anyway. Daisy would fight tooth and nail to survive. She wouldn't go down without a struggle. But I wasn't Daisy. I didn't have her reckless nature, so I was in two minds about whether to chance it or not. If I was going to brave it, I should sit tight for now and try and slip out under the cover of darkness.

I slumped back on the sofa to mull things over. I couldn't be sure, but I reckoned it was around lunchtime. I could see a watery blue sky streaked with grey and white wispy clouds through the glass roof. It got dark early at this time of year, but the light hadn't started to fade yet.

'I'm starving,' the younger guy said.

The sound of his voice made me jolt upright.

'There's no fear of you fading away any time soon, is there, Tank?' the older man laughed.

'Stop fucking calling me that! You know I hate it,' Tank shouted.

'I'm only pulling your leg. Don't be such a tart.'

'I'm going to get fish and chips.' Tank sounded sulky.

'No, you stay here and watch the girl. I'll go and get the food. Will you be all right on your own?' the older man asked.

'Fuck off. Of course I will,' Tank snapped.

My heart started galloping in my chest. If I was going to do this, I needed to do it now. I wasn't going to get a better opportunity. This was the moment I'd been waiting for. It was time to stop weighing up the pros and cons and take action, but I was terrified of the consequences if my plan failed.

'I won't be long,' the older man said, then I heard the door below me open and close.

I had to stop overthinking the situation, or I was going to miss the opportunity. The natural instinct to survive was hardwired. Fight or flight was an ingrained mentality. And before I even realised what I was doing, it bypassed my emotions and took control.

'Help, help me!' I called, trying to get Tank's attention.

He was down in the warehouse, but he'd turned the radio up so he couldn't hear me above the sound of 'Flowers' blaring out over the airwaves. I didn't have him down as a Miley Cyrus fan, but he seemed to know all the words as he sang along at the top of his voice. My wrists were cuffed with plastic cable tie restraints, which were attached to a metal ring on the wall via a chain so I couldn't go far. But I moved as close to the door as possible and shouted again.

'Please, can you help me? Please, please, I need some help,' I called, remembering to use my manners.

I wasn't 100 per cent certain why the older guy was calling him Tank, but I had a pretty good idea, so I didn't want to rile him up and start off on the wrong foot. When there was still no response, I started banging my feet on the floor over and over as my legs weren't bound. The clock was ticking. The older guy would be back soon. I knew he'd finally heard me when he stopped singing and the music's volume lowered.

Beads of sweat formed on my upper lip when his trainers connected with the metal steps. The sound was eerie as it echoed around the cavernous space. My breath caught in my chest when his outline approached the frosted, half-glazed door. When he opened it, I froze. My composure was evaporating into thin air. But I couldn't allow myself to shut down. Not now.

'What's all the racket about?' Tank asked from the doorway.

'I really need to go to the toilet,' I forced myself to say.

My eyes bored into his, silently pleading. Hoping desperately that he'd release me. He was the youngest of the four kidnappers so I assumed he was also the least experienced.

'You'll have to wait until Smithy gets back.'

'Please let me use the toilet. I've been holding on for ages. I can't wait any longer. I'm absolutely bursting.'

I looked up at him with a pained expression on my face.

'For fuck's sake. If I let you use the bog, you'd better not drop me in it. I'm supposed to keep you restrained.'

'I promise I won't say a word.'

'Go on then, but you'll have to be quick. Smithy will be back soon, and you'd better not be sitting on the throne when he gets here, or there'll be trouble.'

'I swear I'll be quick.'

He reached into the pocket of his jeans, pulled out a bunch of keys and quickly located the one to the padlock. Once he'd opened it, he unthreaded the chain from my wrists. Then he unclipped a Swiss Army knife hanging from his belt loop and cut off the plastic restraints with a serrated blade.

'Now, hurry up.'

My hands felt so much lighter without the weight of the tether.

'And make sure you leave the door open,' Tank said as I rushed out of the room.

I raced straight past the bathroom door and took the stairs two at a time. I could hear him start to run after me before I got to the entrance. My heart was in my mouth when I reached ahead and grabbed hold of the handle, pulling the door towards me. It didn't budge, so I pushed it the other way and it flew open. I tumbled out, breathing a small sigh of relief. But the relief was short lived.

The hesitation had cost me valuable time. To add to that, I didn't know which way to go. I only had a split second to decide, so I looked to the right. The warehouse was at the edge of the industrial estate. The only things beyond the spiky-topped boundary fence were railway lines and waste ground. As my feet were bare, I didn't fancy trying to run in that direction. Out of control, shrubby undergrowth, brambles and all manner of debris littered the floor. Not that I'd have been able to make it over the fence. It was too high. Too sharp. Too impenetrable. So I turned left and raced through the development, hoping to flag down a passing motorist, but the place was deserted. I shouldn't have been surprised nobody was about. It was New Year's Day.

When the soles of my feet slammed against the icy tarmac, pain shot through my body, but I had to push through the agony. I couldn't give up now. The bitter wind was stinging my face, making my teeth chatter. I was cold. So cold. Within minutes, I couldn't feel my feet. They were numb.

Tank was closing in on me, but I wasn't about to give up. I just kept running. If I could make it a bit further, I might stumble upon somebody. Anybody. I let out a scream when I felt the tips of his fingers make contact with the back of my sweatshirt. I hadn't managed to get very far before he'd caught up with me. I thought my bid for freedom was over, but he didn't have a good enough grip, and the fabric of my top slipped through his grasp, which motivated me to keep going. My lungs were screaming from the exertion. I could hear him panting, too, which gave me the strength to carry on as I clung to the hope that I'd be able to outrun him.

The industrial estate was huge. I felt like I'd been running for an eternity, but I'd only passed two units. I still had a long way to go. There was no sign of the road or civilisation. Every muscle in my legs burned. I knew how the runners in the London marathon felt now when they hit the wall. My pace was slowing, but thankfully, his was, too, so I was still managing to stay just out of reach. Then disaster struck. I tripped and lurched forward, helicoptering my arms as I tried desperately to stay on my feet. But I failed miserably and hit the ground like a sack of spuds, skinning the palms of both of my hands as I attempted to break my fall. They hurt like hell. They were throbbing. Stinging. I was in the process of getting up from the floor when I felt his fingers tightening around my upper arm, squeezing my flesh like a blood pressure cuff. I did my best to wriggle out of his grip, but he was holding me too tightly. He yanked me onto my feet and started dragging me back in the direction of the warehouse.

I started screaming blue murder, so he clamped the fingers of his hand over my mouth and pulled me around to face him. I'd never hit anyone in my life. But if I could stop him in his tracks,

I'd still be in with a chance of breaking free. Even the smallest chance had to be worth the risk. The alternative was unthinkable. He began shaking me like a rag doll. Like I weighed nothing. If I really was as light as a feather, maybe a gust of wind would blow me away. Save me from the fate waiting for me.

'Shut the fuck up.' Tank's breath was stale as it hit me full force in the face.

Fear swirled around me, tightening my chest. Making it hard to breathe. As he locked eyes with me, I swung my leg back and tried to knee him in the balls. I made contact with his groin, but there was no power behind the strike. I'd used up all of my energy trying to escape, so I didn't manage to disable him the way I'd hoped. What the hell had I been thinking? He was so much bigger than me. There was no contest.

'So you want to play dirty, do you?' Tank shouted.

His question was met by silence.

'Answer me, you fucking bitch,' Tank barked in my face.

'I shouldn't have done that. I'm sorry,' I snivelled.

I'd tried my best to stay strong, but I couldn't hold back my tears any longer.

'By the time I've finished with you, you'll be bawling your eyes out.'

Tank curled his lip. Then he frogmarched me back to the warehouse. As we got closer to the building, I started screaming again in a last-ditch attempt to raise the alarm.

'Zip it. Nobody can hear you. Nobody's coming to save you,' Tank said as he pulled the door closed behind him. He dragged me up the stairs and pushed me into the mezzanine room. 'Take your clothes off.'

I couldn't. I wouldn't. I considered dropping to my knees and begging for his forgiveness, but it was too late for that. He was going to make me pay good and proper by doing something that was far worse than death. Tank was blocking the doorway. Blocking my escape route. I was trapped. There was no way out.

'I said, take your fucking clothes off. Now!' Tank roared.

His eyes were blazing as he paced over to where I stood shaking like a leaf. He swung his right arm back and punched me in the stomach, winding me, which made me bend forward. I cried out as a flash of searing pain ripped through me. Before I could catch my breath, he pulled down my leggings and pants and pushed me back onto the bed.

'No. No. Noooo. Please don't do this,' I sobbed. I was hysterical. Clawing. Biting. Fighting.

He pinned me down with ease and yanked my clothes over my feet, leaving me naked from the waist down. Then he pulled his tracksuit bottoms and boxers down to his knees. The next thing I knew, he was between my thighs. I tried to close them. Tried to push him off. But he was stronger than me. He was a dead weight pressing down on me.

'Please stop. Please don't hurt me!' I yelled.

He tried to force himself inside me, but he couldn't get it up, so he started tugging away at his cock in a bid to get an erection. I closed my eyes to block out the sight of him. I'd thought if I was ever in this situation, I'd scream blue murder. But now that it was actually happening, I froze. Counted to ten. Then started to count again. Willed it to be over. Willed Smithy to come back. My heart was racing. I couldn't catch my breath. I silently begged for somebody to help me. Anybody. Nobody came.

'If you breathe a word of this to anyone, I'll kill you,' Tank said, finally abandoning attempts to bring his dick to life.

I opened my eyes when I heard him speak. His face was inches from mine. Tears rolled down my cheeks. I felt helpless. I *was* helpless. He glared at me, got to his feet and pulled his clothes up. Then Tank reached under the bed, took a plastic restraint from the pile and secured my wrists with it before reattaching the chain.

'You need to get dressed before Smithy comes back. And remember, don't you dare say a word about this, or I'll kill you.' He ran his finger across his throat to reinforce the threat.

As I watched him leave, I'd never felt more alone or frightened. I should have been relieved that he hadn't managed to rape me, but I was too traumatised by what had just happened to feel grateful. He'd failed this time. What if he tried again? He might succeed. The thought sent a fresh wave of terror crashing through my body, which released a flood of bitter tears.

16

DAISY

On the long drive back to London, I had time on my hands to work out what I was going to say. How could I tell my parents that Lily was missing? I could picture their faces now, contorted with grief. They'd be beside themselves. Utterly devastated. My hesitation grew the closer we got.

I glanced down at my watch as Roscoe's Jag pulled up outside our house. It was just after 5 p.m. So much had happened in the last forty-eight hours. I'd barely had a wink of sleep and felt like I was running on empty, but I had to summon every ounce of strength I had left. I was going to need it.

When Roscoe turned off the engine, I leaned back against the headrest and closed my eyes. I wasn't sure I could go through with this. Why didn't I just send a text? I could have spared myself the ordeal.

'Are you ready, love?' Bernice shifted in her seat and looked at me.

'As ready as I'll ever be,' I replied, hoping I sounded more confident than I felt. My actions didn't match my words. I was glued to my seat.

'I'm going to wait in the car. Bernice will go in with you,' Roscoe said.

I knew he was prompting me to make a move, but my hand had frozen on the seatbelt button. Bernice got out of the car and opened my door from outside. So, I forced myself to push down the release. The belt unclicked instantly, but I had to drag myself away from the cream leather interior. As soon as the doors clunked shut, I saw Dad twitch the curtains. My heart started hammering in my chest, and I had to resist the urge to turn around and get back in the car. I felt like I was about to face the firing squad. My legs were wobbling like jelly, and my breathing had become shallow. Bernice must have sensed I was on the verge of a meltdown as she suddenly threw her arm around my shoulder and steered me towards the front door. Dad had already flung it open by the time we were halfway up the garden path.

'What the bloody hell is going on? Where's Lily? I've left God knows how many messages, and she hasn't responded to any of them,' Dad barked.

I left his question hanging in the air between us as I paced towards the door. He was wearing a look of fury on his face when I stepped over the threshold. But he wasn't the only one who was angry. I was boiling mad, too. He hadn't even waited until I got inside the house to tear into me.

'Hello,' I heard Bernice say from behind me.

'Aren't you going to introduce me to your friend?' Dad asked. His tone was far from friendly.

A scowl rested on his face as he looked her up and down. Talk about making the poor woman feel awkward. We stood facing each other. Our eyes locked with each other. I was determined I wouldn't look away first.

'This is Bernice. Bernice, this is Des,' I said without breaking eye contact with my dad.

'Pleased to meet you,' Bernice replied.

Dad said nothing. His rudeness astounded me. I imagined Bernice's insides were squirming as the tumbleweed moment played out. Why was he trying to make her feel so uncomfortable? She hadn't done anything to him to warrant being given the cold shoulder. He'd never met the woman before.

His ignorance lit a fire in my belly, but I hadn't come here to have an argument, so I'd have to bite my tongue. I just wanted to tell them what had happened and go back to Dover. Roscoe and Bernice had been good enough to bring me here. But it was too dangerous for us to be in London. We were in Samson's prime hunting ground. The sooner we got away from here, the better. Without Lily assuming the role of the referee, the hostility between Dad and me would quickly get out of hand. So I did the only thing I could think of doing. I let him win the stare-down and became the one to fill the silence.

'How's Mum? Is she feeling any better?' I asked in quick succession, letting the sentences roll into one.

It was a tactical move. I'd hoped if I could refocus Dad's mind in the direction of his queen, it might dilute his spikiness. The task ahead was going to be hard enough without him trying to take shots at me. Turning the other cheek didn't come naturally to me. There was a limit to how much of his bitchiness I could take. And I was fast approaching my cut-off point.

'She's still not good. And now she's worried sick about Lily on top of everything,' Dad replied.

They hadn't had any contact with me either, but they didn't seem concerned about that. I shouldn't have been surprised. That was the story of my life.

'I'm in here,' Mum called from the living room. Her voice was barely a whisper.

I stepped past Dad and pushed open the door. My mum was

lying across the sofa which had been set up as a makeshift bed, tucked under a fleece blanket and propped up against a pillow. She looked drained and sleep deprived with dark circles under her eyes.

I faltered in the doorway. I could feel Lily's presence woven into the fabric of this house. It was unsettling but also comforting. Confusing. I didn't approach Mum when I walked into the room but parked myself on one of the armchairs on the far side of the room. Vomiting bugs were highly contagious, and I didn't fancy catching the one that had floored her. I couldn't remember the last time my mum was ill. She never usually caught anything, but she'd been wiped out by this.

'Hello,' Bernice said to Mum. Then she followed me across the room and took a seat on the chair next to me.

'Now that you're sitting comfortably, perhaps you'd like to tell us what's going on?' Dad's words were laced with sarcasm.

Just the sight of him standing next to Mum with his hands on his hips made me see red. It didn't take much to reignite the fire, but I'd have to keep a lid on my temper. I paused for a moment, wondering how to start the conversation, wavering with uncertainty. There was no way to soften what I had to say, so I told it plain and simple.

'I don't want you to freak out, but somebody's taken Lily.'

Mum's gasp silenced the room temporarily. Then she let out a howl from deep within her like an injured animal. By the expression on her face, I could tell she'd sensed something terrible was wrong before I'd even started to speak.

'What the hell are you talking about?' Dad asked.

I glanced over at Mum. She was still trying to wrap her head around the idea. 'This doesn't make any sense. There must be some mistake. Lily can't have been taken. She's such a gentle soul. Who would want to harm her?' Mum shook her head from side to side, refusing to believe what I'd just told her. She gripped Dad's hands with both of hers as she searched his face for answers. 'Tell me it's not true, Des.' The desperation in her voice was plain to hear.

Dad didn't answer. He stared into space as he weighed up how to respond. But when he did reply, he directed his response to me. 'When did this happen? She was here as large as life when we got back from York yesterday morning.' The words came spilling out of Dad's mouth like a deluge. There was no stopping them. He hadn't come up for air long enough to allow me to explain.

'In the early hours of Wednesday morning. She was taking her make-up off after our gig. I'd gone outside for a...' I suddenly stopped mid-sentence, pretending to clear my throat. I'd almost dropped myself in it by saying I'd gone for a smoke. Dad would have hit the roof if I'd let that slip out. I might be twenty-three, but it was a closely guarded secret. 'Bit of fresh air,' I added instead.

'The early hours of Wednesday morning,' Dad repeated. I could almost see the cogs inside his brain turning. 'That can't be right. She was standing in the kitchen talking to us yesterday morning. Wasn't she, Tara?'

Dad turned to face Mum, but she was in a world of her own, rocking backwards and forwards. The intensity of his stare made my pulse speed up. Deep down, I knew I'd never get away with impersonating my twin. But at the time, he'd been too preoccupied with Mum being ill to notice his mistake. I'd been wearing Lily's dressing gown, so he'd presumed I was her. When the penny finally dropped, he began jabbing his finger in my direction, and I felt my cheeks redden. The game was up.

'So it was you we were talking to in the kitchen, not Lily.' He fired me a look of contempt then slowly shook his head. 'If you're going to lie, the very least you should do is remember the backstory. It's not rocket science. Otherwise, this happens. You've tied yourself in knots.'

I was raging by the time he finished speaking.

Mum's expression turned from disbelief to fury in a split second. Her eyes were blazing. 'I can't believe you'd blatantly lie, knowing your sister's in danger. What's wrong with you? Is there no end to your jealousy? This is totally unforgivable.' Her voice was tinny. Robotic, as though it wasn't her speaking. As though she'd become possessed by something demonic.

On the surface, I kept my composure. Inside, I was dying. Mum's words were like daggers to my heart. The best thing I could do was focus on things within my control, or her toxicity would dissolve my self-esteem like poison.

Silence hung between us. The atmosphere had changed and the room started to spin. My vision blurred. I felt faint. Weak. I didn't know what to say to defend myself. I had nothing to feel guilty about. Or did I? Should I have ignored MacKenzie and called the police the moment Lily had been taken?

'Why didn't you do something to help her?' Mum's question was accusatory.

I didn't need her pointing the finger at me. Guilt was smothering me already. My imagination had been running wild since Lily went missing. I kept picturing all sorts of horrors. All sorts of atrocities.

'This is all your fault.' Dad delivered the line I'd been expecting since I'd walked through the front door.

'That's absolute bullshit!' I shouted, as the urge to fight back got the better of me.

I knew they'd hold me accountable. Even from this distance, I could feel the bitterness radiating off them. I tore my eyes away and started staring into space. I couldn't bear to look at them putting on a united front. Whatever happened to innocent until proven guilty? Had they forgotten I wasn't on trial here?

'Why are you blaming me? I didn't kidnap her,' I fired back after a lengthy pause.

'Maybe not, but you should have told us as soon as it happened. I can't believe you tried to fob us off by pretending you were Lily,' Dad roared, flipping over the side table next to the sofa.

His rage exploded without warning, blindsiding me. My heart started pounding. He was riled up and ready to fight. Surely he wouldn't dare hit me in front of Bernice. But I wouldn't put anything past him. Not when he was lost in the red mist.

Mum looked at me for a moment with tears welling up in her eyes before her face crumpled and she began to cry. More than cry. She was wailing. Bawling. Great, heaving, gut-wrenching sobs.

Despite everything, I felt a rush of sympathy for her, until my jealousy spiked. Mum would never have broken down like that over me. I carried the weight of how my parents' favouritism made me feel like my own personal cross to bear, pretending it didn't bother me. When in reality, never being good enough hurt like hell.

'We have to call the police,' Mum eventually said with an unfamiliar tremor in her voice as her eyes darted left and right.

She was panicked. Her body was trembling uncontrollably. She was beside herself with grief.

'Have you completely lost your mind?' Dad looked horrified.

Mum suddenly pulled herself together and challenged Dad. 'Why not?' she asked, fixing him with a steely stare.

'If Warren Jenkins gets wind that the Old Bill are sniffing around, he might jump to the wrong conclusion. And we both know he's looking for any excuse to snuff me out, so let's not make it easy for him.'

How typical of Dad to only think of himself!

Mum gave Dad a withering glare before she dropped her head into her hands. Then she suddenly looked up at the ceiling with the palms of her hands clamped together as though she was in prayer. She'd never been religious, so her behaviour seemed strange. I wasn't sure what she thought was going to happen. Was she expecting some divine intervention? A sign that everything was going to be OK? After a few moments, she gave up waiting and slumped back in the chair. Defeated. Deflated.

Dad crouched down and took hold of Mum's hands. 'Don't worry, Tara. I'll find Lily and bring her home where she belongs.'

Who the fuck did he think he was? Liam Neeson?

I straightened my posture and wiped my tears from my cheeks. Their rejection stung. I wanted them to put their arms around me. Pull me close. Hold me. Comfort me. Tell me everything was going to be OK. Not shun me. Blame me. Treat me like the villain. Then I got to my feet and walked out of my parents' house with my head held high.

17

SAMSON

I had better things to do with my time than overseeing staff, especially on New Year's Day. There was no point being the boss if you had to do all the work. That was why I employed people. Running the club didn't interest me in the slightest. If Eden's hadn't been a fanny magnet, I'd have closed it years ago.

I'd barely parked my arse on the chair behind my desk when somebody started hammering on my door. I needed to find a new manager. I could do without this shit.

'What is it?' I snapped, then reached for my drink.

I was hoping the hair of the dog would sort me out. My head was pounding. I'd overindulged at the party last night, but instead of being tucked up in bed with Crystal Tits, giving her another seeing to, I was holding the fort. So I was in a filthy mood. I couldn't even lick my wounds in peace.

'I'm sorry to disturb you,' Igor said, his huge frame filling my doorway. 'Four of Arben's guys are in the foyer. They're looking for MacKenzie...'

'Aren't we all? They'll have to join the fucking queue,' I interrupted, cutting the Pole off mid-flow.

MacKenzie, the scrawny little runt, had gone behind my back and bought cocaine from the Albanians. I'd have sacked him the minute I found out if he hadn't gone on the run. But now his card was doubly marked for bringing trouble to my door.

'I tried to get rid of them. I told them he doesn't work here any more, so they've asked to see you instead.'

I could see the beads of sweat glistening on Igor's bald head and across his forehead. He had good reason to feel nervous. He was about to bear the brunt of my temper.

'Why did you tell them I was here, you dopey fuck?'

As my fingers gripped the tumbler tighter, Igor eyed the lead crystal in my hand. He must have sensed I was going to hurl the heavy glass at him, so I didn't bother. It wouldn't have the same impact if he was expecting it.

'I never mentioned you were here, but they're refusing to leave until they speak to the boss,' Igor said.

'For fuck's sake,' I said as I pushed my chair back. 'Tell them I'll be with them shortly.'

Igor threw me a sheepish look as he retreated into the corridor.

I could have just put an end to this by going with him now, but I had no intention of making this easy for them. I wasn't in any hurry to face them, and it would send the wrong message if I jumped when they clicked their fingers. My time was more important than theirs, so they could wait until I was good and ready, which wouldn't be anytime soon. I waltzed over to the bar at the back of my office and poured myself half a tumbler of Speyside single malt then I settled myself down on the sofa. My headache seemed to be improving with every sip I took.

I was halfway down the same-sized refill when there was another knock on the door. I'd been expecting it to be fair. I was surprised it hadn't come sooner.

'What now?' I bellowed.

Igor edged open the door and fixed his eyes on me; gauged my reaction from the safety of the hallway. I never had him down for a coward. I knew he wasn't a pussy. He faced violence head-on every day of the week, but he was proceeding with caution. He was good at reading a situation, and he knew his presence wasn't welcome. It was good to see he respected the hierarchy. Respected me, which was more than I could say for the bunch of hooligans that worked for Arben. He had a pained expression on his face. He looked like he'd just trodden in a huge pile of dog shit in his bare feet.

'I'm sorry to disturb you—'

'Again,' I cut in. This was the second time he'd invaded my privacy.

Igor pulled a face and then continued to speak. 'I really am sorry. You know I wouldn't bother you if it wasn't important, but I really need you to come and speak to the guys right away. They're fed up of waiting and they've started to trash the lobby.'

'They've done what?' I felt my temper spike.

'They're smashing up the place,' Igor reiterated.

'Why haven't you thrown the fuckers out?'

It was a simple enough question, but Igor seemed lost for words.

'We tried, but there are only four of us,' Igor eventually replied. His white-blond eyebrows had become animated and taken on a life of their own.

'And there are four of them, so what's the problem?'

'But two of my guys are controlling the queue,' Igor said, throwing the palms of his massive hands skywards.

That was a pathetic excuse if ever I'd heard one. And I'd heard a few in my time. Most of them from MacKenzie.

'So while you're fannying about in here, that bunch of little pricks are destroying my property. Let me tell you something, nobody does that and gets away with it.'

I knocked back the contents of my glass. As the liquid raced towards my stomach, it lit a fire in my belly. I was on my feet in an instant, fists clenched, ready to pound the life out of the first arsehole that crossed my path. I shot out of my office like Usain Bolt on steroids, pushed past the six-foot-plus Pole and then charged along the corridor. I was a man on a mission. Igor was having trouble keeping up with me.

As we neared the foyer, I could see Caleb trying to talk the Albanians down. They weren't taking a blind bit of notice of him. They were squaring up to him and getting into his face. Goading him because their confidence was buoyed up. Jermaine was attempting to watch his back, but there were four on two, so I didn't rate my guys' chances even though under normal circumstances they were great scrappers. If we didn't kick them to the kerb soon, there was going to be a blood bath. And I had no intention of losing a drop.

'What the fuck's going on?' I roared, pacing towards the mouthy twat I presumed was the ringleader. As soon as I got within reach, I pushed him in the chest with the heel of my hand. He staggered backwards several steps before he managed to right himself. The unexpected contact had taken him off guard. 'How dare you force your way into my club and start tearing up the joint.' I was absolutely fuming. I could feel a vein pulsating at the side of my neck.

'And how dare you keep us waiting. Arben will not be impressed when he finds out how badly you've treated us and how little respect you've shown us.'

The Albanian's nostrils flared as we stood facing each other in a death stare contest. He could posture all he liked. He wasn't going to win this battle.

'You're a fine one to talk about respect.' I tore my eyes away from his and cast them around the foyer. Tables and chairs had been tipped over, and the exotic plants I'd spent a small fortune on had been upended, and soil was scattered all over the carpet. The once immaculate place was an absolute mess. I hated mess, so what they'd done really hit a nerve with me. 'You're a bunch of fucking animals.' My fists were clenched, and I was grinding my teeth, seconds away from rearranging the ringleader's features. Alarm bells must have been ringing in his ears loud and clear. Before I had a chance to get my hands on the fucker, he gave his guys the nod, and they scuttled out of the entrance.

'You haven't heard the last from us,' the ringleader said, picking up one of the overturned chairs and hurling it at the glass frontage as he rushed out of the club.

It was just as well Leroy was keeping the people queuing at a safe distance because a second later, the glass shattered into millions of tiny pieces. It somehow managed to stay contained within the frame, but the slightest disturbance could see the whole thing giving way. It left me with no option but to shut up shop for the night. I couldn't risk one of the punters getting injured. Not that I gave a shit about their welfare, but I didn't want to have to pay an expensive medical insurance claim if I was sued.

'Get rid of them before somebody gets hurt,' I said, gesturing with my thumb to the wall of people behind the cordon. 'There's no way the live bands can perform tonight.'

Igor, Caleb and Jermaine stared at me in astonishment, but I wasn't sure why they were so surprised. Health and safety measures had gone through the fucking roof in recent years. The council's risk assessment team would hang me out to dry if they got wind that I'd continued to trade before the damage was repaired. I could have called out an emergency glazier, but that would cost an arm and a leg as it was a bank holiday.

Pulling the plug on the evening was the more cost-effective thing to do in the long run. But it riled me up. Eden's was in enough financial trouble without me having to send a queue full of customers away. Tonight had cost me dearly. So it seemed only right that I should repay the favour. MacKenzie had just earned himself another nail in his coffin.

18

LILY

After Tank left, I didn't move from the bed. My brain whirred as I tried to process what had just happened. I was dazed and confused. Dumbstruck. This was all my fault. If I hadn't tried to run, I wouldn't be in this position now.

I rolled onto my side and curled into a ball. Foetal style. Closing my eyes to block out the horror. I tried to shut off my emotions by focusing on my breathing. Long, slow breaths. In and out. But it didn't help. My body began trembling. I was in shock. The terror wasn't going to ebb away any time soon. What I'd been subjected to had been traumatic. Panic inducing. I was so scared. I thought I was going to die. An involuntary shiver ran down my spine. I swallowed hard. Attempted to erase the memory. But it was too vivid.

The only way I got through the ordeal was to shut down and not allow myself to mentally be there. As his hand had moved harder and faster, trying to magic up an erection, I'd tried to focus on something else so that I wasn't in the room with him. But it was almost impossible to ignore him pumping away at his flaccid cock. I thought it would never end. Eventually, he gave up the battle. But he didn't get up. He lay on top of me, crushing me under his weight for what felt like an eternity until he sauntered off as though nothing had happened.

My breath caught in my throat when I heard the door below open and close. Had Tank gone out, or had Smithy returned? It didn't take long for my question to be answered.

'You were fucking ages. What took you so long?' I shuddered at the sound of Tank's voice.

'I've been driving all over the place trying to find a chippy that was open,' Smithy replied.

'Oh, for fuck's sake! The food better not be cold.'

'Why don't you do us all a favour and stop moaning, you ungrateful little prick.'

It astounded me that Tank was thinking of his stomach at a time like this, but he wasn't traumatised the way I was. It repulsed me to imagine him tucking into his meal as though he didn't have a care in the world. As though his actions didn't have consequences. For him, they didn't. He'd got away with assaulting me, but I'd have to find a way to compartmentalise the trauma. Put it behind me. Bury it deep within me and throw away the key. Otherwise, I'd end up being ruled by fear. And then I'd miss out on life.

Initially, I froze when I heard footsteps echoing off the metal steps. I could see the large outline approaching, but it was impossible to tell which of the two men it was through the frosted glass. They were both a similar height and size. Tall and broad, had short brown hair and were clean-shaven.

I scrambled to sit up so that my legs were out in front of me and my back was against the headboard. My heart was hammering in my chest, and by the time the figure stopped outside the door, I'd almost pushed myself through the other side of the mattress as I'd burrowed deeper into it. Please don't let it be

Tank, I said to myself as I pulled my knees up to my chest and wrapped my arms, still bound at the wrist, around them. Relief flooded through my veins when I saw Smithy standing in the doorway.

'There you go,' he said.

He walked across to where I was huddled and held the white bag with the blue fish emblem towards me, but I didn't move a muscle. I stayed where I was.

'What's up with you?' Smithy asked. 'You look like you've been crying.'

I was tempted to tell him exactly what had happened to me while he was out, but Tank's threat was ringing in my ears, and I was too scared to speak up. So I clamped my lips shut and did what came naturally. Retreated into my shell.

'Eat it before it gets cold,' Smithy said when I didn't reply.

He put the bag down on the side table next to me before he turned his back. I stared at his retreating figure as he walked out of the room and closed the door behind him.

The smell of the fried food made my insides flip over and I started retching. But nothing came up. I hadn't eaten for hours. My stomach was empty.

'Hello. Hello,' I called out in as loud a voice as I could muster.

My throat was dry and croaky from all the screaming earlier. I hoped I hadn't damaged my vocal cords. If I had, my career as a singer would be over before it had barely got off the ground.

'What the fuck do you want?' I heard Tank shout from below.

'Please, can you take the food away? The smell of it is making me feel sick.' I was on the verge of tears.

'What do you think this is? A fucking hotel?' Tank shouted back.

Nobody came. The silence stretched on for an eternity until it was broken by a rumble in the distance, slowly growing closer.

The sound of the train reminded me of Eden's. Gave me the faintest glimmer of hope that I wasn't a million miles away from civilisation. If only there had been a window in the room, I might have been able to attract a passenger's attention. Alert somebody to the fact that I was being held against my will. But the train came and went, and my mood nosedived again.

I glanced over at the bag on the table while pinching my nostrils. I tried to resist the urge to look at it, but the pull was too strong. My eyes kept being drawn to it. Watching the grease seeping through the paper was compelling viewing. The thought of soggy chips and stone-cold fish, shrunk inside its wobbly battered jacket silently tormented me. The unopened bag was adding to my misery. When I heard the sound of footsteps on the metal steps, I tore my attention away from the oily wrapper and focused on the shape coming towards me. Hoping and praying it wouldn't be Tank.

'I thought you might want to have a shower,' Smithy said as he stood filling the doorway.

Relief swept over me. But panic wasn't far away. So far, I'd resisted the urge to wash. I couldn't handle the thought of somebody watching me while I was stripped naked, but I felt so dirty after what Tank had done to me, I wanted to scrape myself from head to toe with a Brillo pad, or remove the top layer of my skin with a potato peeler. I somehow doubted I'd ever feel clean again. My body felt like it was crawling with maggots.

My knees felt like they were going to give way when I swung them over the side of the bed and put weight on them. But the thought of scrubbing myself with shower gel gave me the strength to put one foot in front of the other. I rubbed at the raw skin around my wrists when Smithy cut the restraint off.

'I'll be right outside, so don't get any ideas,' Smithy warned as I walked into the bathroom.

I'd never take something as simple as warm water for granted again. As the shower rained down on me, it felt so good. For a brief second, I almost forgot where I was until the memory of the assault came flooding back. I backed myself against the tiles and slid down in the cubicle while silent sobs escaped from my lips. Smithy was right outside, so I couldn't afford to make a sound. I didn't want him to invade my privacy. I tried to lift my arms up to wash my hair. My limbs were heavy from underuse and I struggled to coordinate my movements. After I rinsed off the lather from my third scrub with shower gel, I switched the water off. I still felt dirty. I supposed I always would.

19

MACKENZIE

'How did it go?' I asked when Roscoe and Bernice walked into the living area.

'As you can imagine, they didn't take the news well,' Bernice replied.

'Where's Daisy?'

'She's gone to her room.' Roscoe's tone was flat.

'Is she OK?' I might not be Daisy's favourite person right now, but I still had a soft spot for her.

'She's trying to hide it, but she's very upset. I offered to stay with her, but she wants to be on her own.' Bernice looked concerned. 'The poor girl has been through enough without her mum and dad blaming it all on her.'

I couldn't say I was surprised to hear that.

Bernice wafted her long, manicured fingers in front of Roscoe and me, beckoning us to come closer. 'Her parents are absolutely vile. Especially her dad. I still can't get over the way he spoke to her. I had trouble holding my tongue.'

'It's just as well I was in the car. I'd have grabbed the guy by the throat if he'd treated her badly in front of me,' Roscoe chipped in.

'I haven't had much contact with Tara, but Des is a complete tool. He manages to remember his manners when he's speaking to me, but he treats Daisy like shit,' I added.

Roscoe's features hardened. 'Don't tell me any more. I can't bear the thought of it. Men like that shouldn't be allowed to have children.'

Wasn't that the truth? My dad was also a scumbag who thought his offspring had been put on this earth to serve him. I'd washed my hands of him years ago. If somebody gave you nothing but aggro and grief, they didn't deserve your respect.

'Poor Daisy. Des should be treating that beautiful girl like a princess, not reducing her to tears.' Roscoe's eyes misted over.

He was as hard as nails on the outside but as soft as butter on the inside. I often wondered why he and Bernice never had a family. Taking in waifs and strays was their favourite pastime. They would have made great parents.

'I know, love, it's heartbreaking,' Bernice rubbed the side of Roscoe's arm with her fingertips.

'It was awful seeing Daisy so distraught, but I didn't want to do anything to draw attention to it because she was doing her best to hide how upset she was,' Roscoe said.

Bernice nodded. 'But every now and again, a little whimper cut through the silence.'

'What did you get up to while we were out?' Roscoe asked, changing the subject.

'I've been wracking my brains trying to think of buildings that Samson has access to,' I replied.

They didn't need to know that I'd also snorted a few lines of cocaine and had a wank.

'So did you manage to come up with anything?' Roscoe asked then he ran his fingers through his dark brown hair.

I shook my head. 'Nothing that resembles the room in the video.'

'Where does he store his drugs?' Roscoe fixed his close set, dark brown eyes on me.

'All over the place. He tends to split the shipments up to spread the risk in case any of it gets seized.'

'That's standard procedure. I do the same thing. Let's have another look at the footage,' Roscoe said as he sat down next to me.

'Do you mind if I take another look?' Bernice asked.

'I think you should. You've got an eye for detail, so you might spot something we've missed,' Roscoe replied.

Bernice slipped in next to her husband, and I started the first clip, then I played the second. They were short, a matter of seconds, but they weren't pleasant viewing. We sat in silence as we absorbed the harrowing scenes, eyes wide with horror.

'What's confusing me is the place looks so clinical,' Roscoe said after a lengthy pause. He was still looming over my shoulder, squinting at the screen.

'That's exactly what I thought. It's almost like one of those private psychiatric units you'd see in a film,' Bernice added.

'I know what you mean, but he can't be holding her in an institution. There's nothing wrong with her,' I said.

'The room does have an industrial look about it even though it's immaculately clean, which is weird because the two things don't sit naturally together,' Bernice replied.

Roscoe's thick, dark eyebrows knitted together. 'I don't know why, but I've got a hunch it's somewhere close to his home.'

Bernice pressed her index finger onto her full lips as she

mulled Roscoe's suggestion over. 'Why don't we pull up a browser and look for rental units near Battersea Park?' she said.

'Good thinking. She's not just a pretty face, is she, MacKenzie?' Roscoe beamed with pride.

I couldn't help feeling it wouldn't be that obvious. I was Samson's right-hand man. Surely I'd know if he had access to an empty warehouse on his doorstep.

'We'd best get back to The Castle and see what Carly's been up to. Can I leave you to do the search?' Roscoe asked.

'No problem,' I replied. I could hardly say no.

'Make it your top priority. We need to get moving on this. We can't afford to sit around doing nothing,' Roscoe threw in for good measure.

'I'll just go and say goodbye to Daisy,' Bernice said, getting to her feet.

'I wouldn't, doll. Leave her be. She needs some time on her own.'

Roscoe offered her a weak smile, and the dimple in his chin widened. A wordless exchange passed between them before the two of them walked out of the apartment. A short while later, my mobile began to ring.

'MacKenzie, it's me. Carly's done a runner, but not before she had her hand in the till. Talk about biting the hand that feeds you. Any idea where she might have gone?' Roscoe asked.

For fuck's sake! I had a feeling something like this was going to happen. I should have told Roscoe when I found out she cleared off on New Year's Eve while I was on my break and left the pub unlocked. But I'd wanted to give her the benefit of the doubt. More fool me. It was too late to come clean now without facing some backlash.

'I'll see what I can find out,' I replied instead.

'Do me a favour, drop everything and get on it straight away before the little tea leaf spends all of my hard-earned dosh,' Roscoe said before he hung up.

I let out a groan. I thought finding Lily was my top priority. I'd barely had time to open the browser, let alone come up with a lead, and now he wanted me to abandon the search until I tracked Carly down. Something told me that was going to be a tall order.

20

SAMSON

Since MacKenzie struck his deal with Arben, the fucker was giving me no end of grief. Lording it around my manor like he didn't have a care in the world. The way he was conducting himself made my anger spike. His sheer arrogance blew my mind. It was as though he thought I owed him something. Anyone would think I worked for him.

I slipped out of my office, intending to do a quick sweep of my premises when I clocked a bunch of shifty-looking guys who appeared to be up to no good. Warning bells started ringing in my ears once I spotted the Adidas logos. Arben's crew wore nothing else and he knew I had issues with supply, so I wouldn't put it past him to try to muscle in. I hung around and kept them in my sights to see if they were carrying drugs. If the wankers had gear, the chances were they'd also have weapons. The two went hand in hand.

MacKenzie used to be my in-house dealer. I hadn't got around to replacing him yet. But that didn't mean I'd given every Tom, Dick or Harry the green light to bring their own gear in. Two of the geezers were doing their best to create a diversion while the third member of the team carried out dancefloor transactions right under my nose. The cheeky fucker wasn't being a bit subtle. I let my glare burn into his flesh. The cocky bastard had the audacity to shoot me a passing glance, then carried on with what he was doing.

Tolerating another operation dealing *close* to my territory would have been bad enough, but this tosser was doing the rounds in my establishment. Selling gear in my club. Who the fuck did he think he was? My jaw started twitching as my temper came to the boil.

I pushed my way through the crowd and tapped him on the shoulder. He slowly turned around to face me and looked at me as though I was a turd on the sole of his brand-new trainer. I felt my eyes widen in response. It was a precursor to me losing my rag. I always did it when I was riled up. I'd been told I appeared mentally unstable when I stared at people with the whites of my peepers visible around the entire perimeter of my irises. Apparently I looked crazy. That suited me just fine. I could almost guarantee it unnerved my opponent, but this bellend wasn't fazed. He gave me a cursory glance and then turned his back on me.

It was about to kick off. My patience had been stretched to its limit. In a situation like this, did you fight, or did you talk? If I followed the official guidelines, I'd open the lines of verbal communication. Fuck that! Fists won, hands down, if you asked me. Words were never enough to quash trouble. I wasn't going to feel satisfied if I dished out a reprimand. I needed to beat the shit out of the dickhead.

I tapped him on the shoulder a second time. When he turned around, I swung my right arm back and let my fist connect with his mouth. I had so much rage contained within me, I knocked three of his front teeth out with one blow.

'Aaagh! Aaagh!' he yelled as blood spurted from his mouth and seeped through the fabric of his white Adidas T-shirt.

His friends looked on in horror. Their eyes darted from side to side, but they didn't move a muscle. I grabbed the pussy by the scruff of the neck and dragged him across the room. The crowd of people parted like the Red Sea as I approached them. His pearly whites were long gone. Hopefully, trampled to dust by the panic-stricken clubbers. I wasn't going to waste precious time trying to reunite him with his gnashers. The gaping hole in his smile would act as a gentle reminder of what happens to people caught dealing on my patch.

I shouldn't have to spell it out to people. We went to enough lengths at the door to confiscate gear. Although, something had clearly gone wrong, as the Three Amigos had slipped through the net. But after tonight's fiasco, maybe I should consider putting up a sign stating only drugs bought from Eden's could be consumed within its walls for any dimwits uncertain of the rules.

'You, my friend, are barred for life,' I roared, getting up in the tosser's face before I slung him out onto the pavement.

He staggered around like a newborn giraffe before he managed to find his feet. Moments later, his accomplices shot out of the door after him, fussing around him like a couple of blue-arsed flies. They swung protective arms around him as they led him away. It amused me to see he wasn't looking down his nose at me now that I'd rammed the message home. I'd won the dick swinging contest as expected, while he limped away with his tail between his legs.

I watched the front steps with beady eyes as I waited for them to disappear out of sight. My dad might have given me a leg-up on the ladder, but I'd built up a tasty reputation for myself. I sailed through life making up the rules as I went along and had zero tolerance for people taking liberties. If Arben knew what was good for him, he'd stop trying to flex his muscles.

21

DAISY

My parents' words were still dominating my thoughts. Despite my best efforts to silence them, they played over and over in my mind. I didn't need them laying the blame at my feet. I already felt guilty. I was tormented by a vision of Lily meticulously removing her make-up, totally oblivious to the fact that moments later she was going to be frogmarched out of Eden's and driven away into the night.

I screwed my eyes closed, forced the image away. I had to push it to the back of my mind. Hiding away in the bedroom wasn't going to bring Lily back. It was time to dust off my big girl pants, push my shoulders back, and face the problem head-on. I didn't know what had got into me. I didn't usually shy away from anything. I was impulsive. Acting first and worrying about the consequences later was how I did things.

I was surprised to see MacKenzie was on his own when I walked into the open-plan living area. He was sitting on one of the high-backed stools, drumming his fingers on the black sparkly work surface, looking defeated. Deflated. His fingers hovered in mid-air as he glanced over at me. His body language stiffened. He seemed tense. Uncomfortable. Awkward in my presence. Much as I was still pissed off with him, there was no point in going over old ground. What was done was done. We couldn't change what had happened, so there was no point in dwelling on it. The best way forward was to draw a line under the incident and move on.

'Have Bernice and Roscoe gone?' I asked to break the fingers of tension stretching out between us.

'Yeah, they left about twenty minutes ago.' MacKenzie looked relieved I'd asked him a civil question and hadn't torn a strip off him again.

'Can you show me the videos of Lily again, please?' I asked, getting straight to the point. There was no point pussyfooting around.

'Agh, Daisy, don't ask me to do that.' MacKenzie closed his greeny-hazel eyes.

I could see he wasn't happy, but I steamrolled on regardless. 'Why not? It's a simple enough request.'

Our eyes locked in a power struggle. I was confident I wouldn't be the first to look away, but he was giving me a run for my money.

'Why do you want to watch them again? You'll only end up upsetting yourself,' MacKenzie said.

'I need to see the room one more time so that I can try and work out where Lily's being held.'

'Roscoe's already asked me to deal with it, so chill your beans, I've got it sorted,' MacKenzie replied.

'What have you come up with?'

'Nothing yet, but as soon as I track Carly down, I'll be able to give it my full attention.'

'Carly?'

'Yeah, she went off with the takings, so now there's a bounty on her head,' MacKenzie smiled.

'Are you serious? I would have thought finding my sister was more important,' I snapped.

MacKenzie threw his eyes to heaven. I could see he was under pressure.

'Give me a break, will you? I'm following Roscoe's orders. I've got so much on my plate I don't know which way to turn. My head's fucked.'

'Sounds like you're up to your neck in it.'

'Tell me about it. Finding somebody who doesn't want to be found is no easy task.' MacKenzie shook his head. 'It's going to take time.'

'I seem to have a bit of a knack for it.' I grinned.

'I'd forgotten about that. I'd barely stepped inside The Castle when you turned up. Eat your heart out, Miss Marple!' MacKenzie smiled back.

'Roscoe can't seriously expect you to do all of this on your own. Why don't you focus on tracking down Carly while I try and find Lily?' I suggested.

'It's a good idea, but I'm not sure he'll be happy if I ignore his instructions. He told me to sort it out,' MacKenzie replied.

'You said yourself, it's going to take time and every second counts. I dread to think what's happened to Lily. It's eating away at me that I didn't do more to help her when I had the chance.' As my eyes welled up with tears, MacKenzie reached for my hand and gave it a squeeze. His touch felt good. I appreciated his support more than words could say. 'I'm determined to make it up to her. I want to be the one who finds her. Who saves her. It's really important, so please don't take the opportunity away from me.'

'I didn't realise you felt like that. You and Lily never seemed like you were that close,' MacKenzie said.

'We weren't. We had a terrible relationship. I'm embarrassed to say I used to hate her guts. Blamed her for everything that went wrong in my life. I feel guilty about the way I treated her, so I want to put things right. Make amends. Hopefully, it's not too late to build bridges.'

'It's never too late. But Roscoe will hang me out to dry if I don't follow his orders.' MacKenzie looked troubled.

'Well, I won't tell him if you don't.'

MacKenzie shook his head. 'In that case, you've got yourself a deal!'

My lips lifted into a smile. He was putty in my hands.

22

SAMSON

Friday 2 January

'Samson, it's Willem.'

The sound of the Dutchman's voice made my blood pressure spike. 'What do you want?' I asked. I had no time for pleasantries even though he was the big cheese who ensured my shipments had safe passage through Rotterdam. The four-eyed git had caused me no end of hassle.

'I've been phoning MacKenzie's mobile, but the number's unavailable,' Willem replied.

'That's because he doesn't work for me any more,' I said in a frosty tone.

'Oh, I see. I wasn't aware he'd left your employment.'

Willem seemed surprised he hadn't been informed, but it was none of his business. He was just another cog in the machine, so he didn't need to know who was currently on my payroll.

'Why did you want to speak to him?' I asked to put an end to the silence that had stretched out between us.

If Willem was hoping for a long-winded explanation as to why

MacKenzie was no longer on the scene, he was going to be bitterly disappointed. My lips were sealed on the subject.

'Your container is due to be released the day after tomorrow.'

That was music to my ears. 'On the fourth?' I asked to clarify.

'Yes. I'll be in touch once the ship sets sail with your cargo safely on board. It's booked on the 7.45 a.m. ferry, which should arrive in Felixstowe at 11.40 a.m.' Willem said before he ended the call.

When I'd heard his voice, I was dreading what he was going to say, but he finally had some good news for me. There'd been nothing but trouble with this shipment from the moment it left Ecuador, so I wasn't going to get too excited until I clapped eyes on the van transporting the cocaine on the final leg of its journey. Having said that, I was quietly confident that things were on the up. Pretty soon, I'd have more surplus cash than I knew what to do with.

23

LILY

I woke with a start and sat bolt upright. The rattle of the chain startled me. I blinked several times so that my eyes could adjust to the darkness. It took a moment for my foggy brain to register where I was. I felt confused. Disorientated. Had I been drugged?

'Are you OK?' Smithy asked. 'You've been screaming and shouting and thrashing about.'

I couldn't remember doing any of that, but my long hair was stuck to the sides of my face and the back of my neck. I was literally dripping with sweat. I must have had a night terror. I hadn't had one of those since I was a kid.

'Would you like some water?' Smithy asked.

He looked at me intently, which made me feel uncomfortable. When I found something intrusive, I retreated into myself. I was desperate to break eye contact, but I forced myself to hold his gaze. 'No, thank you. I'm going to try to go back to sleep,' I replied. But I knew that wasn't likely to happen.

I must have drifted off at some point because when I woke again, I was alone, and it was daylight. I could hear voices below me, so I threw back the quilt, sprang out of bed and tiptoed towards the door. I couldn't go far because the chain tethering me to the wall restricted my movements.

'Did something happen while I was out yesterday?' I heard Smithy ask.

I waited, heart pounding, to hear Tank's response. It seemed to take him an eternity to reply.

'Nope.' His tone was dismissive.

He didn't even have the decency to sound rattled. Let alone remorseful.

'Are you sure about that?'

It sounded as though Smithy didn't believe Tank. Was he about to get caught out?

'Yep.' Another one-word answer.

My frustration was bubbling under the surface. I was the victim, and yet I didn't have a voice. All I could hope was that Smithy would keep quizzing Tank until he admitted what he'd done.

'She's been quiet and withdrawn since I went out to get the fish and chips.' Smithy pressed on.

'Has she?' Tank was reluctant to say too much. He was probably worried he might trip himself up.

'Her eyes are red raw. She must have been bawling her eyes out for hours,' Smithy said.

'Don't you think most birds would cry if they were in her position?' Tank snapped. His composure was starting to slip.

'But she's more distraught now than she was when we first brought her here, which doesn't really make sense, does it?'

'It makes perfect sense to me. She's obviously worked out that nobody's coming to save her. I'm no psychologist, but I would have thought that feeling of hopelessness would provoke a pretty extreme reaction.'

Tank's words made my blood pressure soar. But I wouldn't let myself fall to pieces. I had to stay strong. I had bucketloads of grit and determination. I just had to find where they were lurking deep inside me.

'I get what you're saying, but I'm not buying your theory,' Smithy replied after a long pause.

I felt a rush of relief. I had a horrible feeling Smithy was going to fall for Tank's deflection technique.

'I reckon you'd be sobbing into your pillow, too, if you were in her shoes,' Tank laughed.

By the way he responded, it was clear Smithy didn't take kindly to Tank's comment.

'Don't speak to me like that, you little prick! You can deny it all you want, but I know something happened while I was out. Last night, she kept thrashing about and screaming, "Please, don't do this. Please, don't hurt me," over and over again.'

I felt my blood run cold. Tank was going to be furious with me, but I hadn't meant to drop him in it. I'd intended to keep my promise. How was I to know I was going to sleep talk?

24

MACKENZIE

'Word on the street is Carly's living in a run-down hostel at the edge of the town centre, near the station,' I said when Roscoe answered my call.

'Good work, MacKenzie,' Roscoe replied.

'Don't get too excited. I haven't had a chance to check it out yet, but the info came from a reliable source.'

'That's good to hear. Can you pay her a visit asap? Don't rattle her too much. She's only a young girl. I don't want her hurt. I just want my money back,' Roscoe instructed.

I swore under my breath. I hated this kind of job. Intimidating women, especially ones still in their teens, didn't sit easily with me. Roscoe and I were cut from the same cloth in that respect, which was why he was sending me to do his dirty work. He didn't have the stomach for it, either.

'Not a problem. Consider it done, boss,' I replied, hoping my reluctance wasn't as apparent as it felt.

Roscoe had been good to me. He'd given me a job and put a roof over my head when I'd turned up out of the blue. No questions asked. Then he'd saved my arse when Samson's hound was baying for my blood. He treated me like the son he'd never had. Roscoe was a living legend in my eyes. I had huge respect for him, so I wasn't in any position to refuse his request, no matter how much I wanted to.

I had a habit of being economical with the facts if the situation warranted it, but I wasn't lying when I said I had a lead. The part I was unsure about was that it came from a reliable source. I was new to the area, so I'd got the tip-off through a friend of a friend. I wouldn't want to put money on it being right. It might end up coming to nothing.

In hindsight, I probably should have done some more digging before I'd gone back to Roscoe. But I was going around in circles trying to find Carly, and this little nugget was the only glimmer of hope I had to offer. I didn't want him to regret sticking his neck out for me. If he cut me adrift, I'd have no protection from Samson or the Albanians.

25

SAMSON

Lily and Daisy had been pulling in the punters since they'd started singing at Eden's. But the act was dead in the water, so I'd have to pull the plug on it and find a replacement before Tuesday night, which was going to be a massive ball-ache I could happily do without. But it had to be done. I didn't want boozed-up customers asking awkward questions. It didn't take a lot to put the rumour mill into overdrive. I had enough to deal with without attracting any unwanted attention. The only way forward was to find something even better than a pair of drop-dead gorgeous twins. Yeah, right! I hated to say it, but I was fucked with a capital F.

'Des, it's Samson. I'm just phoning to tell you I'm terminating the girls' contract with immediate effect.'

I steamrolled in with the purpose of my call before the mouth almighty could talk the legs off me. He thought he knew everything about the music business and didn't have the sense to keep his trap shut.

'Sorry, did you say you were terminating their contract?' Des questioned.

'That's right.'

'But why? I don't understand.' Des clearly couldn't believe his ears.

'It's a management decision. I'm not at liberty to discuss the details with you,' I replied, fobbing him off.

'You can't do that,' Des whined.

'I can do whatever I want. It's my club, and I make the rules.'

'But they signed a contract.' Des was still fighting their corner.

'It's not worth the paper it's written on...'

My solicitor had made sure of that years ago. In my experience, people rarely bother to read the agreement properly, if at all. Their heads were in the clouds when they were given the opportunity to sign on the dotted line. They never questioned the terms. They couldn't write their name quickly enough.

'We'll see about that! I'll sue you.'

That was fighting talk if ever I heard it. Des was a little runt in the flesh, but he had a warrior's spirit. I'd have admired him, if he wasn't such an annoying fucker.

'Be my guest,' I replied, knowing full well he wouldn't have the balls or the money to follow through with the threat.

'You think I'm bluffing, but I mean it,' Des continued, determined to fight tooth and nail.

I had to give credit where credit was due, Des was quite an actor when he put his mind to it. He almost had me convinced, but there was an undertone of desperation that had crept into his voice which gave the game away, filling me with a huge sense of pleasure.

'You'll be throwing money away on a case you'll never win. If you take a look at the fine print, you'll notice a clause stating that the management reserves the right to terminate an act without any notice. That's show business, baby,' I laughed.

'You must have a screw loose if you think cutting Lily and Daisy is a good idea.'

I didn't think it would take long for Des's stroppy attitude to make an appearance.

'You're getting right on my tits. Who the fuck do you think you're speaking to? Don't you dare use that tone with me, you ginger tosser!'

I bellowed down the phone. He was very lucky I couldn't put my fist through my mobile's screen. Otherwise, it would have been connecting with his jaw right about now.

'I apologise if you think I'm coming on strongly.'

Des had suddenly found his manners. His tone was a lot more polite than before. If he was expecting me to accept it, he'd be waiting a long time.

'It's just I really think you're making a mistake. My girls have been drawing the crowds. You'd have to be mad to pull the plug on them.'

I should have known the change in attitude wouldn't last long. Des was a well-practised, pushy parent. He'd had years of experience. But I despised people like him. I was the one in the power seat, and I didn't take kindly to somebody trying to railroad me into something. And besides that, I wasn't pulling the plug on anything. Lily had been kidnapped and Daisy had done a runner so their act no longer existed.

'That's your opinion, and you're entitled to it, but I'm not interested in what you think. I've launched enough careers in my time to know what works and what doesn't.'

My comments seemed to temporarily silence Des which was a blessing as my ears were ringing from listening to him rabbit on.

'I can assure you I'm not trying to be disrespectful, but I'm absolutely gutted, and I know the girls will be devastated when they find out.' Des's attempt at a guilt trip was pathetic.

'Look, Des, business is business, and when things aren't working out, the best thing to do is sever all ties.'

I wasn't usually this soft, but I needed to cut Eden's association with Lily and Daisy asap. Parting on bad terms was never a good thing. People held grudges. I had a sneaking suspicion a man like Des could hold one longer than most. He'd be lingering in the background, waiting for an opportunity to get even for years to come. But I'd keep him on my radar, so if he tried something, he'd be mincemeat.

'Is there anything I can say to make you reconsider?'

I shook my head and blew out a loud breath. I thought he'd got the message. But instead of dropping the matter and jogging on, Des was making a last-ditch attempt to get me to change my mind. I didn't bother to answer him.

'Please, can you keep them on for a little bit longer and see how things go?'

Des wasn't going to give up any time soon. I'd tried to let him down gently, but he wasn't taking the blindest bit of notice, so it was time to cut the fucker off. I'd spent too much time on this call already.

'The trial period is up. And this conversation is over.'

I spelt it out nice and clear before I hung up.

It had never been my intention to cancel Lily and Daisy's act. I'd had high hopes for the pair of them. Des was right; Eden's takings had gone through the roof on the nights the girls performed, and I could really do with the money right now. It seemed like I was cutting off my nose to spite my face, but things hadn't worked out the way I'd been expecting, so I didn't have a choice in the matter. Sometimes life dealt you a huge pile of steaming shit, and there was nothing you could do about it apart from suck it up and get on with it.

26

DAISY

I felt myself inwardly groan when I saw Dad's name come up on my phone's display. I was very tempted to not bother picking up the call, and let it go to voicemail, but that was just going to end up prolonging the agony.

'Hello.'

'Your mum and I need to speak to you urgently. Can you come over to the house?' Dad's tone was assertive. Demanding. Which immediately got my back up.

'Can't you just tell me over the phone?'

I didn't fancy having to do a four-hour round trip to hear whatever it was he had to say.

'No, Daisy, I can't. We want to speak to you in person. Get here as soon as you can,' Dad's voice boomed down the phone. Then he hung up.

'Are you OK?' MacKenzie asked as I stomped into the living area.

'My dad's such a dickhead,' I seethed.

'What's he done now?' MacKenzie laughed.

I was glad the frostiness between us had thawed. It was good having somebody on hand to listen to me rant.

'He's insisting I drive all the way back to London because he can't possibly tell me what the problem is over the phone,' I fumed.

'What a pain in the arse. I'd offer to go with you, but Roscoe's sending me on a job,' MacKenzie replied.

I was surprised Roscoe was sending MacKenzie out. He told us not to leave the apartment for our own safety.

'I think I might have found where Carly's living, so he wants me to go over and give her a rap on the knuckles.'

'At least you've tracked her down. I'm still no closer to finding Lily. I could really do without my dad summoning me home. I'd planned to spend the rest of the day looking for possible leads, not stuck in traffic on the M20.'

'Why don't you ask Bernice to go with you?' MacKenzie fixed his beautiful eyes on me.

'I'd prefer to go on my own.' Dad was such an arsehole to her last time. I wouldn't put her through that again.

'I don't think that's a good idea. Roscoe won't be happy if he finds out you've put yourself at risk.' MacKenzie sounded concerned.

'What he doesn't know can't hurt him.' I flashed MacKenzie a look, warning him that this conversation needed to stay between the two of us.

'Don't worry, I'm not going to say anything. My lips are sealed, but I'd feel a lot happier if you went with somebody,' MacKenzie replied.

'Well, I'm not going to ask Bernice. She's done enough already,' I insisted.

'I'm sure she wouldn't mind. She's taken a real shine to you.' MacKenzie flashed me one of his winning smiles as he tried to talk me round.

'That's sweet. I like her, too, but I can't expect her to drop everything because my dad's being his usual unreasonable self. I don't want to impose on her.'

'But how are you going to get there?' MacKenzie asked, realising his efforts were in vain.

'I'll drive. Lily's car's still parked outside The Castle. The sooner I get this over with, the better.'

'I might as well go with you. I've got to pick up my wheels from the pub, too.'

The Old Flour Mill was only a mile from The Castle, but the weather conditions were so bad lately it made the relatively short walk a torturous experience. The moment we stepped outside, a gale burrowed beneath the edge of the golfing umbrella I was trying to shelter under. I had to hang on for dear life as it dragged me along the pavement. I thought it would never end, but finally, the beach was in sight. As we walked towards it, waves barrelled out of a steel grey sea and crashed on the shore. The white cliffs loomed out of the pebbles like ghostly figures. This was nature at its wildest. Relentless. Unforgiving. I couldn't wait to get out of the icy downpour and behind the wheel of the car.

'Wish me luck,' I said as I unlocked Lily's Fiat. My fingers were trembling so much that I had trouble putting the key into the slot. But I'd have to push my fear aside and front it out before MacKenzie noticed. I didn't want him to know I was terrified of going to London alone.

'Likewise,' MacKenzie replied.

The rain lashed against the windscreen as the wind howled around me. Lily's car was being battered by the elements and I had to grip the wheel hard as I fought to stay on course. The glass kept misting up, distorting my vision, so I had to drop my speed. I hadn't been on the M20 long when an accident a couple of junctions ahead closed the road.

The alternative route I was forced to take crossed the Kent Downs. I was sure the rolling hills and quaint villages were lovely on a bright summer's day, but I couldn't admire the view. I had to keep my eyes on the road as it wound around the landscape. Low-hanging hedgerow scraped at the side of the car like witches' fingers as I sped along the narrow country lanes. I turned the radio up, trying to block out the sound of the wind as it tore through the bare branches of the trees high above me. I hoped Lily's car was reliable. I wouldn't want to break down out here. It felt like I was passing through the middle of nowhere. A small cluster of houses sprang up every so often, followed by acre upon acre of fields. I was beginning to regret not taking the train or bringing Bernice for company. It was going to be a long, lonely drive.

27

MACKENZIE

'Hello, darling.' Bernice flashed her veneered smile when I walked into The Castle.

She was pulling a pint of Guinness for an old boy sitting on a bar stool at the end of the counter. I was surprised to see her working, but Roscoe was short-staffed with myself and Carly being unavailable, and she was a natural, so I supposed it made perfect sense. Bernice used to manage The Beehive before she married Roscoe. It had been his local when he lived in East Dulwich. Their eyes met over the beer pumps and that was the start of their love story.

'What are you doing here?' Bernice asked.

'I was hoping to have a quick word with Roscoe, if he's about.'

'He's in his office,' Bernice replied.

'Cheers,' I said.

I walked across the planked dark wood floor, out of the door at the side of the bar and into the corridor. Roscoe's office was at the far end on the left. He was sitting in his leather chair with his legs up on the desk when I poked my head inside.

'Sorry to disturb you, boss. I just wanted to have a quick word if that's OK.'

'Of course, it's OK, come in, son.' By the smile lighting up his face, I could tell Roscoe was pleased to see me.

'I'm going to check out that address now and see if Carly's staying there.'

'That's great. I don't mind telling you, I was gutted when I realised she'd shafted us. She seemed like such a nice girl. I thought I could trust her, but it just goes to show, no matter how good a judge of character you think you are, there are always people out there who take you by surprise.' Roscoe shook his head. 'So, what can I do for you?'

'I just wanted to find out a few more details before I confront Carly. How much money did she take?'

'A couple of hundred quid.'

I was shocked that Roscoe would bother recouping such a small amount of cash. It wasn't as though he was on the bread-line or anything. He was doing well for himself, as far as I could see.

'I know it's not a lot of dosh, but it's the principle. Being mugged off leaves a bad taste behind. It's embarrassing to think a guy like me who's been around the block a few times was done over by a little slip of a girl barely out of school.' Roscoe threw out the palms of his huge hands.

'Don't beat yourself up about it. It happens all the time. I've said it before, and I'll say it again. It's always the people you least suspect who end up getting away with things.'

'True, but it doesn't make me feel any better. Carly's made a fool out of me, so I can't let that go. I've got my reputation to think about.' Roscoe's tone had angered.

It was human nature to leave your guard down around people you thought posed no threat, so I understood why Roscoe was so pissed off, but I still wished I wasn't the one having to track Carly down.

'Leave it with me. I'll see if I can find her,' I said as I walked out of Roscoe's office.

* * *

Less than ten minutes later, I pulled up outside the hostel. I peered through the misty windscreen as the rain pelted on the roof of my car. The place was a dump. I was amazed anybody was living there, so I checked the address on my mobile, and it confirmed I was at the right place. The outside walls were crumbling and discoloured. It looked as though they'd once been white, but they'd turned grubby from neglect. There was multicoloured graffiti scrawled along the bottom of the left-hand side of the guest house, and two of the letters were missing from the hostel sign. It didn't have any kerb appeal whatsoever. You'd have to be pretty down on your luck to consider staying there.

I pulled up the hood on my jacket and ran over to the front door, trying not to get soaked in the meantime. I rang the doorbell three times in quick succession, then gave the glass panel a good rap with my knuckles for good measure, hoping my impatience would be rewarded quickly. While I waited, I stared at the flaky paint on the front door. First impressions counted. The building looked derelict, so I knew the place was going to be a shithole before I even stepped over the threshold. And when I did, it didn't disappoint.

A dark-haired woman who looked to be in her early thirties opened the door. 'Please come in,' she said.

If the weather hadn't been so foul, I'd probably have stayed on the doorstep, but going inside had to be the lesser of two evils. Maybe not, I thought as the smell of drains shot up my nostrils as soon as I entered the hall. It was putrid. It almost took my breath away, but the woman seemed unfazed by it.

'Are you looking for a room?' she smiled.

Her manner was warm and friendly, much more inviting than the surroundings. I wasn't sure where she was from, but judging by her strong accent, English wasn't her first language.

'Actually, I'm looking for a friend of mine. I believe she's staying here. Her name's Carly Andrews.'

By the expression on the woman's face, I knew I was in the right place. She looked mildly panicked, as though she'd been caught out.

'You from the police?' Her brown eyes narrowed as her thick, arched eyebrows bunched together.

I knew undercover cops never looked like the Old Bill, but it was taking things to another level suggesting I was in that line of work. The corners of my lips twisted as I tried to stifle a smile.

'No, I'm a friend of hers.'

That wasn't true. I'd only met her on a couple of occasions, but the woman seemed suspicious of me, and I didn't want to be shown the door before I'd done what I came here to do.

Her features softened. 'If you wait here, I'll see if she's in her room.'

'Thanks.'

The woman turned her back on me and walked up the flight of stairs at the back of the hall. As she moved, her long, wavy hair swayed from side to side. It was hypnotic. My eyes were glued to it as her footsteps faded into the distance. While I waited, I glanced around the dimly lit passageway. It was a depressing sight. I supposed you couldn't expect budget accommodation to be kitted out like The Ritz, but it was grotty even by cheap hotel standards. The stained patterned wallpaper peppered with mould had peeled away from the walls in large sections. The vinyl floor was covered in cigarette burns and had lifted along the edges of the yellowing skirting board and by the front door. I wasn't an expert in building structures by any means, but it looked to me like the place was riddled with damp.

I glanced up when I heard two sets of footsteps walking down the squeaky staircase, drawing closer. Carly froze mid-step when she spotted me standing in the hall. She looked nervous and hesitated for several seconds before she began to move again.

'Hi, MacKenzie, what are you doing here?'

Carly deserved an Oscar for her performance, pretending to be surprised to see me.

'Could we have a quick chat in private?'

The woman who'd opened the door to me was lurking behind Carly and I didn't want to accuse her of being a thief while she had an audience. Carly looked over her shoulder to where the woman was standing.

'Would it be OK if we go into the guest lounge for a few minutes, Zerina?'

'Of course, would you like me to bring you some tea or coffee?'

'No thanks,' I replied.

Carly led the way into a room at the front of the hostel, which overlooked the busy main road. It wasn't exactly what I'd call plush. There was a cathode-ray tube TV in front of the window. I hadn't seen one like that with the huge hump on the back like a camel for years. I was surprised there were any still in existence. I thought they went out with the ark. When I managed to tear my eyes away from the relic, I cast them around the rest of the space. A selection of mismatched chairs and sofas lined the other three walls like a waiting room. All of them looked equally uncomfortable and had seen better days.

'Roscoe asked me to come and see you,' I said once Carly had closed the door.

Her eyes started darting around the room as though she was looking for the best escape route. I felt bad for her. She must have been in dire straits to be desperate enough to nick a couple of hundred quid. Her pale green eyes misted over as she stared up at me. She looked like she was going to burst into tears. Please don't let her start crying, I said to myself. I hated seeing a woman upset, and it made things ten times worse if I was the cause of their tears. Carly had a vulnerability about her. I could see she was terrified, so I just wanted to get this over and done with.

'Roscoe wants to know why you cleaned out the till.'

I very much doubted it, but she might have had a good reason, so I didn't want to accuse her of stealing without giving her an opportunity to explain.

Carly swallowed the lump that had formed in her throat before she began to speak. 'I'm sorry. I'll pay back every penny.' Her voice cracked.

She looked distraught, so I wasn't going to put the thumb screws on her. I decided to take a different approach.

'Are you in some kind of trouble?'

Carly's eyes widened. Then she dropped onto the nearest lumpy-looking sofa and buried her head in her hands. I knew she was crying even though she wasn't making a sound when I saw her skinny frame begin to tremble. I sat down next to her, draped my arm around her bony shoulder, and pulled her towards me.

'Hey, don't cry,' I said, doing my best to soothe her. 'Haven't you got any family that could help you?'

Carly sat up straight and turned her tear-stained face towards me. Then, she slowly began to shake her head.

'Why don't you tell me what's wrong? I can't help you if I don't know what I'm dealing with.'

Carly looked so innocent. So childlike that I felt compelled to offer my assistance, but I had a horrible feeling I'd just opened a can of worms.

28

DAISY

I'd set off around one thirty, but it was dark by the time I arrived outside our semi-detached in Camberwell. The journey had taken twenty minutes longer than before because the route I followed took me miles out of the way.

'It's so kind of you to grace us with your presence. You took your sweet time to get here,' Dad said when I opened the front door. He was standing in the hallway with a mug clenched in either hand and a scowl resting on his freckled face.

I felt like turning around and walking back out, but I was here now, so I might as well get this over and done with.

'You might not have noticed, but the weather's atrocious, and I've just had to drive all the way up from Dover...'

'What the hell were you doing in Dover?' Dad cut me off impatiently. His head snapped around like it was on elastic. His manner was abrupt. Rude.

'It's a long story.' I had no intention of elaborating. I hadn't come here to answer questions, so I needed to refocus the conversation before Dad started one of his grillings. 'What did you want to speak to me about anyway?'

Dad's face reddened, but he didn't reply, so I followed him into the living room. Mum was sitting on the sofa, snuggled into her dressing gown, looking like death warmed up. Dad perched on the seat next to her and put the hot drink down on the table in front of her.

'There's a nice cup of tea for you, love. You didn't bring your friend with you today then.' Dad flashed me a sarcastic smile. 'How do you know her?'

'MacKenzie works for Bernice and her husband now.'

'I might have known he'd have something to do with all of this,' Dad huffed.

What the hell was that supposed to mean? I wasn't going to ask. I didn't have time for this now. Take a deep breath and let the snide remark float over your head, I told myself, while battling the natural instinct to get into an argument with him.

Dad tilted his head to one side and started pulling strands of his ginger beard through his fingers. 'So MacKenzie's new job is in Dover, is it?'

'Where MacKenzie's working has nothing to do with you. I thought you needed to speak to me urgently about something important,' I fired back, unable to hold my tongue.

'While you've been gallivanting with him, your mum's been crying nonstop. She's been inconsolable. I bet you haven't given your sister a second thought, have you?'

Dad didn't need to state the obvious. Mum's eyes were red and swollen. Her cheeks blotchy.

'Seriously? We're doing this now, are we?'

Dad glared at me as silence hung in the air between us.

'Have you heard from Lily?' Mum asked. Her dark brown eyes glued to mine as she fixed me with a look of concern.

I shook my head. Did she seriously think I wouldn't have told them if I had any news? But at least she'd managed to steer the conversation away from MacKenzie.

'Your sister's missing and you were the last person to see her. Why aren't you trying to find her?' Mum's eyes narrowed.

Anyone would think I'd planned the whole thing.

'We can't just sit here doing nothing. It's absolute torture. We'll have to call the police, Des,' Mum said. She was having trouble accepting that her daughter was gone.

'I know it's hard, but we've talked about this. I can't get the Old Bill involved. Warren's watching me like a hawk. If he drives by and sees PC Plod parked outside, he'll go nuts. Then there'll be consequences. Serious ones. You know as well as I do that snitches get stitches. Involving the authorities isn't an option, so you need to get that idea out of your head.'

I was taken aback by his attitude. He never usually spoke to my mum like that. And she wouldn't usually tolerate it if he'd dared to. She'd rip his spine out as quick as look at him. But Dad seemed agitated and it didn't take a lot to push his buttons. I knew that better than most.

I was in two minds whether to tell them I would have been looking for Lily if I hadn't been summoned here. But I decided against it. I didn't want to get caught up in a back-and-forth, which would achieve nothing apart from prolonging my visit. I kept my mouth shut, aware that every second wasted could spell disaster for my twin.

The sound of somebody pounding on the front door halted their conversation. The contents of my stomach dropped and my pulse soared. I wished I'd listened to MacKenzie. He'd told me not to take the risk. Told me not to come here on my own. Did I listen? Of course not. I was my own worst enemy. Samson wanted my head, and I'd just handed it to him on a plate. My tears were threatening to fall, but bawling my eyes out wasn't going to save me.

Bang. Bang. Bang. The vibrations on the front door were so loud they came through the wall. Dad leapt out of his seat, but instead of heading out into the hall, he dashed over to the window. Being a professional curtain twitcher, he couldn't resist pulling back the nets. But seconds later, he dropped the fabric as though a hot pan had scalded him, and the colour drained from his face.

'We're not expecting anybody. Who's at the door?' Mum was as weak as a kitten, but she managed to push herself away from the back of the sofa. She craned her neck and peered out of the window. She obviously couldn't see anything from where she was sitting, so she started questioning my dad again. 'Who's out there, Des?'

Dad didn't reply. He'd flattened himself against the wall and was standing as still as a statue staring straight ahead. His feet were slightly apart, and his arms were hanging down by his sides.

'Who is it, Des?' Mum's voice was louder this time.

Dad still didn't answer. He lifted his right arm and pressed his forefinger to his lips, warning us to stay quiet. He was barely daring to breathe, let alone speak. He was usually full of bravado and acted like a Rottweiler trapped inside a Chihuahua's body. I'd never seen him shy away from anything, especially somebody being so disrespectful to his house. So I knew we were in big trouble.

When the hammering on the door started again, Dad's eyes darted around the room. His Adam's apple bobbed up and down in his throat. He looked petrified. The way he was behaving was alien to me.

'What's going on? You're scaring me, Des.'

Terror was written all over Dad's face, so Mum looked over at me for reassurance. Her brow was furrowed, but there was nothing I could say to put her mind at rest. I was too busy shitting myself at the thought of whoever was banging on the door.

29

SAMSON

Gary was still licking his wounds, so I'd driven down to Dover alone. It wasn't a problem. I didn't need backup. Roscoe wasn't much of a threat. He was no threat at all. And Gary was proving to be more incompetent by the minute. He'd be more of a hindrance than a help. If you wanted something done right, you had to do it yourself.

By the look on her botoxed face, Bernice nearly shit herself when I burst through the door of Captain Pugwash's watering hole. The place was a dive, crammed to the rafters with tacky seaside memorabilia. I couldn't bear cheap tat. I always pushed the boat out when I kitted out a place. How could anyone enjoy a pint while lobster pots and fishing nets dangled inches above their bonce?

If Bernice was hoping to conjure up an image of a serving wench with her big plastic jugs pushed up in her customers' faces, she needed to rethink the idea. The only vibe I was getting from her was washed-up old sea hag. It was time she retired her skimpy outfits and passed them on to a bird half her age.

'Where's MacKenzie?' I shouted as I stormed up to the bar with a sawn-off shotgun clenched in my right hand.

'How am I meant to know? I can't remember the last time I saw him,' Bernice replied, her tone was stroppy.

I didn't like her attitude. She had an air of defiance about her. She needed taking down a peg or two. A good clatter would do her good. If I'd had more time, I'd have been happy to oblige, but I had to focus on the purpose of my visit.

'I'm going to ask you one more time,' I said, lifting her chin with the gun's barrel. 'Where's MacKenzie?'

'I've already told you; I don't know,' Bernice replied, throwing the palms of her hands out.

She looked me straight in the eye, but I knew she was lying, so I glared back at her with a killer stare. Roscoe hadn't rushed to her rescue. She must be here alone. It was clear she wasn't going to talk, so I turned on my heel and walked out. I didn't want to have a wasted journey, though, so I blew out the windows of Roscoe's crappy little pub as a parting gesture.

30

DAISY

A rush of dread ripped through my insides when the sound of the front door giving way filled the room. Before any of us had time to react, a man wearing a long leather trench coat, flat cap and jeans burst into the room. Judging by the commotion going on in the hallway, he wasn't alone. Whoever was out there was trashing anything they came into contact with. They'd smashed the mirror and made firewood of the table.

'You haven't been returning my calls, Des and I don't like being ignored. It hurts my feelings. It's extremely bad manners. Didn't your mother teach you any?'

I'd never seen the man before, but his presence in our living room made Dad's face turn grey and take on a waxy appearance. I could see him visibly shaking from where I was sitting on the far side of the room. Even though the guy clearly posed a huge threat, I was overjoyed to see it wasn't Samson and his anger wasn't being directed at me.

'I-I'm s-sorry. We've been dealing with a f-family em-emergency s-so I've been a b-bit distracted,' Dad stammered, assuming the role of the underdog.

It was weird to see him behaving like this. He was a nervous wreck and looked close to tears. I was only familiar with his aggressive side. He ruled our house with an iron fist and made a pastime out of bullying me.

'And you're about to have another emergency to deal with,' the man grinned. As his lips parted, I caught sight of his heavily discoloured, overcrowded teeth. They were all different shapes and sizes. Jagged. Like broken bottles. I only managed to tear my eyes away from them when the two meatheads that had been trashing our hall stormed into the room. They stood side by side like Tweedledum and Tweedledee directly behind their boss.

'P-please give me a ch-chance to explain. My d-daughter...' Dad spluttered before the man spoke over him.

'Shut the fuck up, Desmond. I didn't come here to listen to any more of your pathetic excuses. I want the money you owe me.'

As the words left his mouth, the penny dropped. This had to be Warren Jenkins unless Dad had been stupid enough to take out another loan from an equally shady character. Borrowing from one gangster to pay off another would be a foolish move even by his standards, but desperate people resorted to desperate measures, didn't they?

'Eden's had some technical problems with their bank transfers over the Christmas period. But we've been told it will be sorted out soon, and then we'll be able to pay you,' Mum said, finding the strength to try and divert the attention away from Dad.

That was news to me. But our wages were paid directly into Dad's bank account as he was our manager, so it could very well be true.

'Oh, fair enough. I understand. Thanks for letting me know. I'll just sit tight and wait until Eden's sorts their cash flow out, shall I?' Warren turned away from Dad and spoke directly to Mum.

'The money should be coming through any day now,' Mum added for extra reassurance.

She'd either chosen to ignore his sarcastic tone, or she hadn't noticed it.

'Any day now. That's good to know.' Warren started looking around the room with a big grin on his face. A moment later, he switched. 'Do you think I'm running a fucking charity? Who the fuck asked you to pipe up anyway?' Warren shouted, getting up in Mum's face.

She glared back at him, so he lunged forward and grabbed hold of a clump of her long, dark brown hair, which was hanging over her shoulders in a mass of tumbling curls and wrapped it around his fist. He yanked it with all his might, pulling her onto her feet. Onto her tiptoes. Mum was pretty tall, but Warren was the size of an ogre, so he dwarfed her.

'Who the fuck do you think you are, looking at me like that, you brazen bitch?' Warren spat the words into Mum's face.

My heart started galloping in response. It wasn't in her nature to back down, but I was willing her to fight the urge to lash out.

'I'm sorry,' Mum said in a tiny voice barely above a whisper.

Relief swept through me. Not only had she wound her neck in, but she'd gone one step further and followed up with an apology, which was the most sensible thing she could do even though I knew she didn't mean it.

Warren Jenkins was an animal. Anyone could see that my mum wasn't well. But he'd attacked her over the way she'd looked at him. Watching him drag her around like a rag doll was hard to stomach. I'd huddled into the chair, holding my breath, not knowing what to do for the best. There was nothing I could do apart from stay quiet. Stay out of it.

If I'd tried to get involved, I'd become the focus of his attention, and selfish as it may sound, I wasn't prepared to martyr myself. I didn't want to see either of my parents get hurt, but if the roles were reversed, I wasn't sure they'd wade in to defend me. Nothing I did was good enough. My efforts fell short every time. So I did what Lily, the golden girl, would do. I retreated into my shell and kept my mouth shut. Right about now, Mum and Dad were probably wishing they'd never had favourites.

'Please let Tara go. She's not the one who owes you the money,' Dad suddenly blurted out.

There was no sign of the stammer that had affected his speech earlier. It seemed to have evaporated into thin air as he rode in on his white horse to try and save the day.

'Maybe not, but I don't like her attitude. She's a mouthy bitch, and I didn't appreciate the way she was eyeballing me. She needs a good slap.'

When Warren twisted Mum's hair tighter, she let out a yelp, and my heart began to thunder in my chest.

'Warren, please don't hurt her. She said she was sorry. What more do you want her to do?' Dad's voice cracked with desperation as the brave face he was wearing started heading south.

Why the fuck did Dad just say that? Talk about putting ideas in his head. I could just picture Warren's depraved mind going into overdrive. The man was a raving lunatic. My heart went out to Mum. I wouldn't have wanted to be in her shoes.

'Now that you come to mention it.' Warren laughed.

He suddenly let go of Mum's hair, and she staggered backwards. My breath caught in my throat as I watched him slowly unzip his fly. Oh my God, surely he wasn't going to get his cock out. I felt the contents of my stomach shift as visions of Christmas Eve came barrelling towards me. Samson's breath on my neck. The overpowering smell of his aftershave. The feeling of his fingers forcing their way inside me. Rough. Painful. Violating. I had to clamp my tongue between my teeth to stop myself from screaming.

Mum's big brown eyes were wide with terror. She started backing away from him, but she'd only taken a few steps when the sofa hit her behind her knees, folding her legs like a collapsible table. She fell onto it but continued to stare up at Warren, unable to tear her eyes away from him while she waited to see what he was going to do.

Dad rushed towards Mum. Despite the danger, he was willing to put his life on the line to protect his queen, which was very commendable, but by the way Warren was towering over Dad, I had a horrible feeling it might just come to that.

Warren didn't seem like the kind of man you could reason with. It suddenly dawned on me why Dad had been so desperate for Lily and me to get the gig at Eden's. I'd resented the way he'd gone about it, but now I understood what he was up against. What an impossible situation he'd got himself into. But I couldn't feel sorry for him. This was his own making. And he'd dragged his family into this because of his own selfishness.

Warren was at least a head taller than Dad and had a massive frame. Dad was short and slight. The odds were stacked against him. He didn't stand a chance. He was no match for Warren, without throwing the two bruisers he'd brought along with him into the mix. A feeling of impending doom started crushing my chest. I could sense this wasn't going to end well.

'You should learn to keep your woman under control.'

Warren spat the words into Dad's face, then he glanced over his shoulder to where Tweedledee and Tweedledum were standing. No words were exchanged but they instantly stepped past him and took up positions on either side of Dad. They each took hold of one of his arms and bent them up behind his back. Dad let out a groan of displeasure.

'Hold him still, boys,' Warren said, and his face stretched into a smile.

Dad immediately started bucking and thrashing about as he struggled to break free. Warren stepped towards him, took off his flat cap and brought his prominent forehead down on the bridge of Dad's nose. My dad cried out as blood started running out of his nostrils. Mum let out a whimper, too, as though she could feel his pain.

'You've fucked me about once too often, Kennedy, so now I'm going to teach you a lesson.' Warren's voice had a dark edge to it. It was threatening. Menacing.

Dad's blue eyes grew wide with fear. Mum clamped her hands over her mouth, to stop herself from screaming out loud as Warren pulled something metal out of his trench coat pocket. My pulse started racing in my wrist when I saw the light bounce off the shiny object. At first, I thought it was a knife, but when I looked closer, I realised it was a screwdriver. Not the sort you'd have in a regular toolbox, an industrial-sized one. Warren had the heavy-duty handle gripped in his palm like a dagger.

'Are you going to take your punishment like a man, or are you going to scream like a fucking pussy?' Warren asked.

'Oh my God,' I said under my breath.

Mum looked absolutely terrified as one of Warren's goons pushed Dad onto the seat next to her. The men pinned my dad down, having turned his face to one side. Warren loomed over Dad, who continued to wriggle and move around, making himself a difficult target to strike. Nothing could have prepared me for what came next. I'd never experienced brutality like it. I seriously thought Warren was just trying to scare the shit out of Dad. I honestly didn't think he'd be sick enough to take things any further. How wrong could I have been?

Warren lifted his arm up and then drove the long screwdriver into Dad's ear over and over. Mum let out a blood-curdling scream as chunks of flesh and gore hit her in the face. The sight was so gruesome I thought I was going to lose the contents of my stomach. Now, it was my turn to cover my mouth with my hands. Tears started rolling down my cheeks when my dad's head lolled backwards. Mum sat next to him, frozen to the spot. She stared into the middle distance, numb with shock.

Warren looked like a crazed lunatic as he stood over my dad's lifeless body, panting like he'd just run a marathon with the blood-stained screwdriver gripped in his right hand. Rivers of red ran down the handle and seeped between his fingers.

'Right, let's go. Our work here is done,' Warren said.

The blood-spattered men released their grip on Dad. Then Warren bent down and spat in my dad's face before the three of them walked out of the house. I waited until I saw them walk down the path before I leapt out of my chair and raced over to where my dad was slumped on the sofa with blood pouring down the side of his face. His eyes were open, but there were no signs of life.

'Phone an ambulance,' I screamed at Mum.

But she just sat there rocking backwards and forwards with tears rolling down her cheeks. The desperate urgency I was trying to convey went straight over her head. She was too distraught to help. I'd have to deal with this alone. I wanted to fall apart like her, but where would that leave Dad? Hard as it was, I had to keep my shit together.

I was all fingers and thumbs as I tried to find a pulse. Tried to see if he was breathing. But I was wasting precious time. So I rushed over to where I'd left my bag on the other side of the room. I yanked it off the floor and sank my hand inside, scrambling around, searching for my mobile. Once I got hold of it, I keyed in the three numbers that had been drilled into me since childhood. Nine. Nine. Nine.

'Emergency. What service do you require?' the operator asked.

'Ambulance, please.' I was breathless. My voice was shaky.

'Hold the line. I'm connecting you now,' the operator said.

'Ambulance service. Is the person breathing?' a woman asked.

'No. I'm not sure. I don't think so. Please hurry, my dad's been attacked.' I quickly reeled off the address.

'Help's on its way to you now. Do you know how to do CPR?'

'No.' My heart started thundering in my chest.

'That's OK. I'll talk you through it. Can you put your phone on hands-free?'

The woman was so calm. I was all over the place. I had trouble hitting the speaker button. My hands were trembling so badly.

'The ambulance should be with you any minute. I need you to check if your dad is breathing. Can you see his chest moving up and down?'

'No.' My voice was shaky. I was trying to stay composed, but panic was coursing around my body.

'OK. Put your ear near his mouth and nose and place your hand on the lower part of his chest. Can you feel him breathing?'

'Yes, but it's very shallow,' I replied after a short pause.

'Try not to worry. Help will be with you soon.'

Worry? That was an understatement. I was beside myself. Dad and I had never seen eye to eye, but witnessing him being butchered and left for dead changed everything. I wished I could turn back the clock. Wished I could do more to help him. I didn't want this to be the end. I wanted to put things right between us. After everything that had happened, I realised life was too short to fall out with your nearest and dearest.

What the hell had Lily and I been dragged into? I'd never experienced violence like it. These people were on another level. There were no boundaries. Nothing was off-limits. I was seriously concerned for our safety.

31

MACKENZIE

When I pulled up outside The Castle, my heart started hammering in my chest. All the windows at the front of the pub had been blown out. Some of them had shattered into tiny pieces, while the others bore the telltale sign of bullet holes. I felt a shiver run down my spine. I'd never forgive myself if something had happened to Roscoe and Bernice.

I jumped out of the car and rushed up to the entrance. I had to slow my step when I got closer, treading carefully as I crunched over shards of glass littering the pavement. The pub seemed eerily quiet. But I couldn't rule out whoever had done this might still be inside. Reluctant as I was to come face to face with the culprit, I couldn't afford to bottle it, so I took a deep breath and pushed open the door. I was bricking it, scared of what I might find.

Roscoe was standing in front of the driftwood mantelpiece staring at the open fire when I walked in, but he turned away from the roaring flames to face me. He had a tumbler of dark spirit clamped in his right hand. A half-full bottle of Courvoisier sat on the wooden barrel table closest to him.

'Thank God you're all right. What the hell happened?' I asked.

'Samson took it upon himself to threaten Bernice with a sawn-off shotgun, and when she didn't give him what he wanted, he turned the shooter on my boozer,' Roscoe said, and then he downed the contents of his glass.

'Jesus. Is she hurt?'

Roscoe shook his head. 'She's a bit shaken up, but that's understandable. She'll be as right as rain in no time. She's a strong woman.'

I felt a wave of guilt wash over me. Roscoe hadn't gone into details, but you didn't need to be a genius to work out who Samson had come looking for.

'So did you find Carly?' Roscoe asked, changing the subject.

I was surprised he was pushing the incident to one side as though it was nothing, but that suited me just fine. No doubt Roscoe had a plan to get even.

'Yeah. My source was right. She's living at the hostel,' I replied.

'What did she have to say for herself?'

'She said she was sorry, and she promised she'd pay back every penny,' I replied.

'Too right she will. She should count herself lucky I'm not adding interest! Did she say why she took it?' Roscoe pulled out a chair, reached for the bottle and topped up his glass.

'No, and I know this doesn't excuse what she did, but I got the impression she's in some kind of trouble.'

Roscoe put his drink down on the barrel and straightened his posture. 'Why? What did she say?'

'She didn't say anything, but she'd have to be pretty desperate to bother nicking a couple of hundred quid. It's not worth the aggro. And the place she's living in is an absolute dive. You'd be hard pushed to find anywhere worse,' I reported.

Roscoe shook his head. He seemed troubled to hear that she was so down on her luck.

'Carly was so distraught, I didn't want to push it. I tried to get her to open up to me, but once I started digging, she clamped her mouth shut. She wasn't having any of it. Not in a defiant way, she seemed scared of something,' I continued.

'Or someone.' A guilty look settled on Roscoe's face. 'I hope it's not me. I wasn't trying to put the frighteners on her...'

'I know you weren't. I promise you, I didn't go in all guns blazing. I took the softly-softly approach,' I replied to put his mind at rest.

I'd only met Carly on a few occasions, but she seemed too young and vulnerable to be living away from home. She was only seventeen.

'I don't like the thought of her staying in a flea pit when I've got properties lying empty. Do you think I should offer her a place to crash?' Roscoe asked. I could see he was worried about her, too.

'I wouldn't. You might scare her off. And if she runs, she could end up anywhere. I'll try and work on her, offer her a friendly ear and see if I can get her to confide in me,' I suggested.

'That's a good idea,' Roscoe replied.

'I know you told me not to leave the apartment, but maybe I should pop over to the hostel from time to time to keep an eye on her.'

'Fair enough, but don't put yourself in danger. Samson's on the prowl, and he's making his presence felt.'

Roscoe fixed his eyes on me. The Castle had borne the brunt of Samson's frustration this time. But we both knew those bullets were meant for me.

'Do me a favour; when you see Carly, tell her to forget about paying back the money. Tell her she can keep it. She obviously needs it more than I do.'

Roscoe's words brought a smile to my face. He was generous to a fault. Then relief swept through me. I wasn't cut out to be a debt collector.

'Hello, darling. It's good to see you again so soon. Twice in one day. I'm honoured,' Bernice said.

Her full red lips stretched into a grin when she walked through the door marked private and took up position behind the bar. She breezed in as though she didn't have a care in the world. She didn't look like she'd just been threatened by a violent maniac.

'It's good to see you, too. I promise I'm not stalking you. How are you feeling?' I asked.

'I'm fine,' Bernice replied.

'Roscoe told me what Samson did. You must have been terrified.'

'How's Daisy?' Bernice asked to divert the attention away from herself.

I'd been hoping she wouldn't ask me that. My mind began racing as I watched her pull her long ponytail over her shoulder and stroke it with her fingertips. I didn't know what to say without giving the game away.

'She's good, thanks.' I'd decided to keep my answer vague.

'Are you going back to the apartment now?'

It was an innocent enough question, so I replied without hesitation.

'Yes.'

'Would you mind if I go and see Daisy for a while?' Bernice asked Roscoe.

I clenched my arse cheeks together to stop myself from farting. My guts always started rumbling when I was in a stressful situation.

'Of course, I don't mind, doll. MacKenzie can give you a lift, and then I'll come and pick you up in a couple of hours when Harvey starts his shift,' Roscoe replied.

'Thanks, darling. I won't be a minute. I'll just get my coat and bag,' Bernice said, flashing me a smile with her ultra-white teeth.

I felt my bowels start tuning up again, so I clenched tighter. I'd promised Daisy I wouldn't tell them that she'd driven back to London on her own, but Bernice had backed me into a corner, so I had no other option but to come clean. I felt beads of sweat break out on my forehead and the palms of my hands before I began to speak.

'I wasn't going to say anything because I didn't want to get Daisy into trouble.'

Bernice glanced at Roscoe as the words raced out of my mouth as though they were galloping towards the finish line in the Grand National with a huge bet riding on the win. I couldn't finish the sentence quickly enough. I wanted to get the confession over and done with. I felt the weight of the secret resting on my shoulders. I knew Roscoe wouldn't be happy that Daisy had put herself at risk. I felt responsible that I'd known what she was doing but I'd stood by and let her go.

Roscoe was holding the glass up to his lips, but he put it back down on the table without taking a sip and trained his disfigured face on me. His stare was unnerving. My Adam's apple started bobbing up and down.

'I think you better slow down, son and tell us what's going on,' he said in a calm manner.

You could have blown me down with a feather. I'd been expecting him to start shouting and roaring, smashing glasses and tipping tables over as he battled to contain his temper. Daisy hadn't listened to his warning, so he was bound to feel pissed off about it. His unemotional reaction took me by surprise. I was used to Samson blowing his top over the slightest thing, lashing out at the person closest to him. The way Roscoe and Bernice were acting, you'd never think Samson had peppered their pub with bullet holes after threatening the landlady with a sawn-off shotgun a short while earlier. Their poker faces were up there with the best. They were hard to read. A couple of closed books.

'Daisy's gone to London...' I said as an opener.

'She's what?' Roscoe pushed his chair back and got to his feet.

His cool demeanour suddenly vanished into thin air. I felt my blood pressure spike in response.

'Her dad called and insisted she come home straight away. Apparently, he had something really important to tell her, and he wasn't prepared to do it over the phone.'

'Do you think they've found Lily?' Bernice asked.

'Why did you let her go on her own?' Roscoe ignored her question and turned his attention to me.

A huge lump was stuck in my throat, and I had trouble swallowing it. 'I had to go to the hostel. You told me to go and see if Carly was living there.'

'Don't you dare blame me for this! It's your fuck up, so own it,' Roscoe shouted, batting away my pathetic excuse.

'I'm sorry. I tried to stop her, but Daisy wasn't having any of it.'

'You should have told me straight away. I would have gone with her.' Roscoe let out a loud sigh.

'What are we going to do? She could be in real danger.' Bernice steepled her fingers as she locked eyes with Roscoe.

'It'll be all right, doll. I don't want you upsetting yourself. You've had enough to deal with for one day. I'll sort this mess out,' Roscoe replied, then he flashed me a filthy look.

32

DAISY

'Go and open the door, Mum, the paramedics are here!' I shouted, tearing my eyes away from my dad when the ambulance pulled up outside.

I was trying to jolt her into action, but Mum didn't move a muscle. She just sat, trembling from head to toe, staring into space as though she was in a trance.

'For fuck's sake,' I said under my breath as I raced out of the room and along the hall before throwing open the front door. 'He's in here. Please hurry. He's in a bad way,' I said with barely contained panic.

The two paramedics followed me into the room. The man rushed over to Dad, dropped to his knees and got to work on him. He was still breathing, but only just. His breaths were shallow. Laboured.

'Can you tell us what happened, please?' his female partner asked.

My mind went blank. My thoughts were scrambled. I was lost in the fog. Then, it started to clear. I had to navigate my way out and fill in the details without giving the game away.

'I'm not really sure. I think he was mugged. I walked in and found him like this a little while ago,' I lied.

I'd had to think on my feet. Come up with a feasible explanation in a split second. Throwing Warren Jenkins' name into the mix would have been a disastrous move. I was in enough trouble as it was with Samson without having another gangster joining the queue. I liked my facial features the way they were. I didn't want them rearranged. Pleading ignorance was the best I could come up with. Mum was in no condition to contradict what I'd said.

'What's the patient's name, please?'

'Desmond Kennedy.'

Relief rushed through me when the female paramedic asked the question. She must have believed my sketchy account.

'How old is he?'

I had to think about the answer. It didn't roll off my tongue.

'Umm, I think he's fifty-three.' I looked over at Mum for confirmation, but she was in a world of her own.

'And what's your relationship to the gentleman?'

'I'm his daughter.'

'Is that your mum?' the female paramedic asked.

'Yes,' I replied. Although, she was doing a great impression of a waxwork dummy.

'Is she injured, too?'

'No, I think she's just a bit shocked.'

'That's understandable. It's quite common to be dazed and confused if you've witnessed a traumatic event. In most cases, it's short-lived and passes quickly. Your dad's our main priority, but when you get to the hospital, if you're worried, you could always ask a doctor to check her over.'

'Thank you.'

'I need to ask you some questions about your dad's medical history.'

'Mum, I'm going to need your help,' I said, but I got no response.

'You might not know the answers, but just do your best. Anything you can tell me will be useful.' The female paramedic flashed me a sympathetic smile.

'I'll give it a go, but I'm not promising anything,' I replied.

'Is there anything we should know about your dad's health? Does he suffer from any conditions?'

'Not as far as I know.'

'Is he allergic to anything?'

'No. Not as far as I know.'

'Does he take any medications?'

'I don't think so. I'm not much help, am I?'

I felt like shaking Mum by the shoulders. She would have known all the answers. But instead of offering any assistance, she'd shut down and left me to deal with everything.

'You've been great,' she reassured.

A few minutes later, I watched as they lifted my dad off the red-stained sofa and strapped him onto a gurney. There was so much blood. Too much blood. Was it possible to bleed like that and live to tell the tale?

'We're taking him to King's College Hospital,' she said as they wheeled my dad out of the house.

It crossed my mind as I watched them loading him into the ambulance that he might never come back to this house again. I shook that thought from my head. There was no point in wasting precious time and energy on what-ifs. I had to stay focused. Stay strong. Mum had already lost touch with reality. I couldn't afford to join her.

As the ambulance pulled away from the kerb, I rushed back

into the living room, grabbed hold of Mum's wrists and pulled her onto her feet. I was tempted to slap her around the face to provoke a reaction. But I couldn't bring myself to do it. She was a shell of herself. The feisty woman who raised me was nowhere to be seen. She was buried deep beneath the surface. Lost. Numb. In a state of disassociation.

'Mum, we've got to go with Dad.'

She said nothing. Just stared at me as though I was a total stranger. I went to retrieve my bag from the other side of the room, then took hold of her hand and towed her to the hall. She followed on autopilot.

I lifted Mum's coat down from the hook behind the front door and shoved her arms through the sleeves like she was a reluctant toddler being forced to go out against their will. She didn't fight me, but she did nothing to help either.

* * *

The wait in A & E was unbearable. Torturous. Being surrounded by people with all sorts of illnesses and injuries wasn't for the faint-hearted. I'd seen enough blood to last me a lifetime. I wouldn't consider myself particularly squeamish, but the walking wounded we were sitting shoulder to shoulder with looked like they'd come from a battlefield.

At least they weren't contagious. I couldn't allow myself to think about the amount of airborne diseases that were floating around us, or I'd have run for the door. It would be a miracle if Mum and I walked out of here without catching something. People were sneezing, coughing and spluttering. I was scared to breathe. The whole place had to be crawling with bacteria. That wouldn't usually concern me. What the hell was happening to me? I was turning into Lily.

Hours after Mum and I had taken seats on hard plastic chairs, we got called through to speak to the doctor.

'I'm sorry to say Desmond has sustained life-threatening injuries.'

The doctor's words weren't unexpected, but hearing them said out loud rattled me.

'We'll know more when he's been for a CT scan. It's impossible to say at this stage whether he'll survive the attack. He's critically ill. The next forty-eight hours will be crucial. He's lost a lot of blood, and he sustained some horrific injuries to his ear canal.'

My head was spinning. There was a lot to take in.

'Would you like to see him?'

'Yes, please,' I replied.

I needed to get the image of him butchered and covered in blood out of my head and replace it with one of him looking more peaceful in case he didn't survive. His life was hanging in the balance. Even though our relationship was complicated, I was devastated to see him like this.

It was hard to compute; one minute, we'd been having words, and the next, he was close to death. I couldn't get my head around it. The speed at which it happened was mind-blowing.

As Mum and I approached the bay, Dad lay motionless in the bed, hooked up to machines. He was deathly pale. Barely clinging to life.

* * *

After what felt like an eternity, the doctor reappeared. Judging by the solemn look on his face, the news wasn't good.

'Desmond suffered a penetrating brain injury during the attack, which was most likely caused by a foreign object, possibly a screwdriver or something similar. The weapon passed through the right zygomatic bone and caused significant damage to internal structures all the way to the posterior cranial fossa.'

The doctor's words swirled around me. I didn't have a clue what he was talking about.

'It's not a common injury. And because of its rarity, the treatment will be complex and non standardised. I have to warn you that intracranial injuries carry a high risk of mortality. Even if our initial attempts are successful, he could develop a serious infection such as meningitis or suffer from cerebrospinal fluid leakage in the coming days,' the doctor continued.

Mum and I stared at him like a couple of zombies.

'We're admitting Desmond to ICU. You'll be able to visit him once he's settled. You should know his condition remains unchanged. He's still in a coma. If he does pull through, he may have long-term problems to deal with such as vertigo, paralysis of the face, permanent hearing loss...'

I began zoning out as the doctor reeled off the list.

'I know it's a lot for you to take in. Do you have any questions?' the doctor asked.

'No,' I replied.

I couldn't concentrate on anything. My head was scrambled. I wouldn't have been able to think of a question if my life depended on it.

Dad was hanging on by a thread. It was surreal to imagine him not being around. He'd been perfectly fine a short while ago. If he died and Lily never came back, Mum and I would be the only two left. I wasn't sure how I felt about such a drastic change to our family dynamics. Picturing a future without them was weird. Worrying. How would we cope? I didn't need the added pressure, so I pushed the idea out of my mind. I already had too much on my plate to deal with.

33

MACKENZIE

It should have taken around one and three-quarter hours to get to Daisy's house, but Roscoe shaved off fifteen minutes by putting his foot to the floor. When he pulled up outside, the place was in darkness. Lily's car was nowhere to be seen. I didn't know what to think. Daisy wasn't answering her phone or her texts.

'I'll go and check it out,' I said, unclipping my seat belt.

'Be careful, son,' Roscoe replied, making eye contact with me in the rear-view mirror.

I leapt out of the car and raced up the drive. I noticed the front door was slightly open even before I reached it. That wasn't a good sign. Nobody in their right mind would go out and leave the house like that. I pushed the edge of the door with my fingertips and it groaned as it creaked open on buckled hinges.

'Daisy, it's me,' I called from the doorway.

When she didn't respond, I stepped inside and flicked on the light to expose anyone lurking in the shadows. The only thing that greeted me was destruction. Somebody had upended a wooden table and smashed it to pieces. The landline, pens, paper and sets of keys lay in a jumbled heap. The large mirror behind the front door was hanging at an angle. Some shattered glass remained in the frame, the rest of the fragments were scattered all over the wooden floor. The place was a mess. I didn't need to go any further to know that something bad had happened in here.

My fingers searched for the light switch before I walked into the living room. My breath caught in my throat when I saw the blood-stained sofa. It shocked me to the core. Having my fears confirmed rattled me, but I forced myself to check all the rooms in the house just in case Daisy was hiding somewhere. Once I ruled that out, I hot-footed it back to Roscoe's car.

'I take it Daisy wasn't in there,' Bernice said when I reappeared alone.

'The house is deserted, but the front door is hanging off its hinges, and somebody's smashed up the hallway.' I paused for a moment, to catch my breath before I continued. 'Something terrible must have happened. The sofa's covered in blood.'

Bernice gasped, and Roscoe slammed the palms of his hands down on the steering wheel.

'Why the fuck did she come back here on her own. I knew this would happen,' Roscoe said.

'Where's the nearest hospital?' Bernice asked.

'King's College,' I replied.

'How far is it?' Bernice quizzed.

'Five minutes at the most.'

'Do you know the way?' Bernice's blue eyes bored into mine.

'Yes.'

'What are you waiting for, Roscoe? Start the car. MacKenzie will direct us.' Bernice had sprung into action.

'I know the way. I don't need MacKenzie to direct me. What makes you think she's at the hospital? Samson wants her dead, so his goons are hardly going to call her an ambulance,' Roscoe snapped.

I'd never seen him speak to Bernice like that before. He was clearly feeling the pressure like the rest of us. She was only trying to help. He didn't need to bite her head off, but I supposed we all handled stress in different ways.

'I know it's probably a long shot, but I still think it's worth a try. Unless you have a better suggestion?' Bernice's voice was calm. She hadn't taken offence.

When she reached over and rubbed Roscoe's hand, he turned to face her, and his features softened. 'I'm sorry I jumped down your throat.'

'That's OK.' Bernice's voice was soothing.

'I can't believe this has happened. I should have realised he'd already got to Daisy when he turned up at the pub looking for MacKenzie. They were both on his hit list...' Roscoe shook his head from side to side.

The contents of my stomach flipped upside down.

'I suppose we might as well try the hospital. It's as good a place to start as any,' Roscoe said, coming around to Bernice's way of thinking.

Bernice and I scoured A & E while Roscoe waited in the car. Daisy was nowhere to be seen. We briefly considered asking at the counter if Daisy Kennedy had been admitted, but the queue was massive, and I wasn't sure they'd give out information like that anyway because of patient confidentiality, so we didn't bother hanging around.

We'd almost made it back to Dover when my mobile started to ring. I scrambled to pull the phone out of my pocket and answer the call before it rang off.

'Hi, MacKenzie,' Daisy said.

The sound of her voice sent a wave of relief crashing through my body. 'Are you OK?'

'Not really. My dad's in ICU. He's on life support.'

Even though Daisy and her dad had a troubled relationship, she sounded distraught.

'Jesus! What happened?'

Bernice turned around in her seat. I could feel her blue eyes boring into mine like lasers as she tried to listen in to the conversation. She was desperate to know what was going on, but I'd been waiting ages for Daisy to make contact, so I didn't want to cut her off mid-flow. Breaking away from Bernice's intense gaze was virtually impossible as I tried desperately to focus on what Daisy was saying.

'Warren Jenkins broke into my mum and dad's house not long after I arrived and attacked Dad with a screwdriver. He kept driving it into his ear over and over. There was blood everywhere. Dad's in a coma. The doctors aren't sure whether he's going to make it or not.' Daisy's voice cracked as she finished the sentence.

I paused for a moment to allow Daisy's words to sink in. I didn't want to tell her that I'd been to her house and seen the state of the sofa in case she tore a strip off me for poking my nose into her business. I knew only too well how feisty Daisy could be.

'I'm sorry to hear that. Where are you?'

'At King's College Hospital.'

'Are you on your own? Do you want me to come and keep you company?'

Roscoe glanced into the rear-view mirror, and my eyes were drawn to his.

'Mum's with me. Thanks for offering to come, though. I appreciate it, but there's nothing you can do. We've just got to wait and see how Dad responds. Anyway, I'd better go. I don't want to leave Mum on her own for too long. She's in a right state. I just wanted to let you know what happened. I'm sorry it took me a while to call you back.'

'No need to apologise. I get it. You've been up to your eyes in it. Please keep me in the loop if you can,' I said.

'I will,' Daisy replied, and then the line went dead.

'What's going on?' Bernice asked the minute the call ended.

I blew out a loud breath. 'The name means nothing to me, but have you heard of a guy called Warren Jenkins?'

Roscoe nodded. 'He's a loan shark. Well, at least he was last time I crossed paths with him, but that must have been almost twenty years ago.'

'Daisy said he broke into their house and repeatedly forced a screwdriver into Des's ear. The poor bastard's in a coma. The doctor said it's touch and go.'

Bernice's fingers flew up and covered her mouth. 'Oh my God, that's awful!'

'That sounds like the kind of thing Jenkins would do. He's a nasty piece of work. A vicious bastard,' Roscoe replied.

'Is Daisy OK?' Bernice asked.

'She sounded a bit shaken up.'

'She must have been terrified,' Bernice added.

'I offered to stay with her at the hospital while she waits for news, but she's with her mum,' I said.

'Poor Daisy. That's a lot for a young girl to deal with. First Lily, and now Des. It never rains, but it pours,' Bernice said.

My heart went out to her, too. The Kennedys were having a bad run. The family seemed to be lurching from one disaster to another. I felt partly to blame for the trouble they were in. It was my fault Lily had been snatched. I hadn't intentionally dragged her into this mess, but she'd still become a pawn in the game.

'I totally understand why Daisy wants to be near her dad, but I'm not happy about her being in London. I can't protect her if she's not on my patch. I'll leave her be for now, see if Des makes it through the night, but I'll have to bring her back to Dover tomorrow whether she likes it or not,' Roscoe said. Concern was carved into his features.

I was worried about her, too. Daisy was in a vulnerable position. So was I, for that matter, but at least I wasn't on Samson's doorstep. The sooner we got her back to the coast, the better.

34

SAMSON

Crystal Tits and some other slappers were busy entertaining the punters, stripping down to their birthday suits, when a couple of Jack the Lads decided to join in. They were acting like a bunch of clowns, making a nuisance of themselves with the girls.

Igor had eyes on them. He stepped out of the shadows and appeared at the side of the stage. 'Hey, hey, hands off the dancers, or I'll show you the door,' he shouted, gesturing with his hand in case they couldn't hear him over the music.

It was club policy that nobody from the audience was allowed on the stage. That got punters ousted. I knew Igor was intending to eject them from the joint before anything kicked off. But the plan spectacularly backfired.

Igor and Jermaine waded in, showing no fear when the fuckers chose to ignore the verbal warning. My doormen wouldn't ask twice and wasted no time manhandling the blokes down from the platform. It should have been over as quickly as it started. But the geezers had backup.

As my bouncers were marching the scum towards the exit, all hell broke loose. At least eight guys leapt into action, throwing punches and smashing bottles over innocent bystanders' heads. Leroy and Caleb were quick off the mark. They tried their best to restore order, but they were badly outnumbered and were struggling to contain the bunch of hooligans wreaking havoc on the dance floor.

I'd been watching from the sidelines, but it was time to get my hands dirty. I made sure I got out of the CCTV field before I let loose on the mouthy fucker baiting me in the Adidas T-shirt. He thought he was big and mighty because he was fuelled by drink. He was about to be on the receiving end of my temper.

'Get out of my club before I call the police,' I bellowed in the cocky little shit's ear.

The mention of the filth usually worked wonders even though I had no intention of involving them. I'd deal with the wanker in my own way, and by the time I was finished with him, he'd be begging for a night in the cells. I had zero tolerance for anyone with a bad attitude.

As I hauled the scrawny little runt towards the door, I used my free arm to rain punches down on him. Giving him digs to the body and head. He was bleeding from the nose and mouth, and his left eye was starting to close by the time we reached the street.

My guys were skilled scrappers. You had to be handy with your fists to do their job. But even they were being tested tonight. This group of louts were making their presence felt. It was two-on-one. The odds were not in my bouncers' favour.

While all of us were dealing with the bedlam, trying to contain the brawl, Caleb was dragged to one side. I glanced over in his direction. He looked rattled. Three of the guys had him surrounded. They were doing a bit of posturing, but nothing he couldn't handle.

'Step the fuck away from me right now,' Caleb yelled, trying to front it out as best as he could.

The next time I looked, they'd managed to get him down on the ground, and before any of us could help, one of the fuckers pulled out a blade and sliced off his ear. Caleb started squealing like a pig as blood ran down the side of his head. It shocked me to the core how quickly the fight had got out of hand. We were in danger of losing the battle if we didn't step things up a gear.

I headbutted the fucker I was expelling, and he fell in a heap at my feet, so I booted him a couple of times in the gut as a parting gesture before I went to help Caleb. The guys were trying to flip him over to get at his other lughole. He was thrashing about on the pavement like a beached whale. Having discreetly pulled my shooter out of the waistband of my suit trousers, I grabbed hold of the guy with the knife and dug it into his back.

I leant forward and whispered in his ear, but what I said wasn't sweet nothings, I just didn't want all and sundry earwigging. 'Unless you want me to insert this gun up your arsehole, you'll get those fuckers off my guy right now.'

He let out a series of whistles and snapped his fingers over and over like he was a member of the *West Side Story* cast. His men instantly froze and looked over in his direction like a pack of well-trained Border Collies waiting for the farmer's instructions.

'Let's go,' he said with a sense of urgency in his voice.

'I'll call an ambulance,' Igor said as he raced over to where Caleb was writhing in agony on the floor.

'I don't ever want to see you fuckers darken the doorstep of my club again. Understand?' I bellowed at their retreating backs.

Arben Hasani was getting right on my tits, sending his guys over to cause trouble at Eden's to try and throw his weight around. He was wasting his time. He wasn't going to intimidate me. My reputation preceded me. I was a mean fucker. If the Albanian wanted to play the power game, there would only be one winner. And it wasn't going to be him.

35

LILY

Saturday 3 January

I jolted awake from a fretful sleep. Everything was quiet. No chatter. No radio. No sounds of life coming from below. I listened intently. There was nothing. Something had happened. Something was different. Something had changed. Smithy and Tank never both went out at the same time. Had they abandoned me? Was it a trap? There was only one way to find out.

'Help. Help,' I yelled.

I held my breath and waited for a response. Silence. Stillness. Emptiness. No echoey footsteps or voices. I was completely alone. The thought made me elated but also made me panic. My heart started racing. My mind was muddled. Confused.

I'd tried to be on my best behaviour. Used my manners. Stayed quiet. Stayed submissive. That wasn't hard for me. It came naturally, but where had it got me? Nowhere. I had to make the most of this opportunity. Who knew when they'd be back? If they'd be back. Time was of the essence. I couldn't afford to weigh up the pros and cons. I needed to act.

I was being held against my will, but I'd been given a chance to end this nightmare. Only a matter of metres separated me from help, but the space felt like an ocean. Memories of what happened the last time I tried to escape came barrelling towards me. Terrifying me. But I had to fight the fear. A sudden burst of bravery came from somewhere deep within me. I'd had enough of waiting. I yanked at the shackle over and over, but it didn't budge. I just ended up hurting my wrists in the process. I slumped back on the sofa. I could feel the desire to free myself begin to ebb away. It was leaving as quickly as it had come.

I'd been pinning my hopes on Daisy raising the alarm, but it looked like she hadn't bothered. She was my twin, but we didn't have a bond. It was fractured. Broken. She wouldn't be pining for me. She was probably glad to see the back of me. The thought of that broke my heart. I wanted things to be different between us. I wanted us to be close. I wanted my sister to love me the way I loved her.

But why was nobody else looking for me? Where were my mum and dad when I needed them most? Why had they deserted me? Surely, they missed having me around. The pain of abandonment seared through my body. Burnt into my flesh. It would leave scars behind. Scars that would probably never heal.

This was a hopeless situation with no end in sight. The thought of dying all alone suddenly brought my fighting spirit to the surface again, and the survival instincts that were hard-wired into human DNA kicked in. I slammed the chain against the metal bedframe. The sound was loud. Reverberating. With any luck, the waves would be carried some distance through the air. Picked up on somebody's radar. Arouse their curiosity enough to make them investigate where the noise was coming from.

I kicked out at the wall repeatedly until my bare feet ached. Then I went back to welting the chain against the bedframe over and over. Screamed blue murder at the top of my lungs until my voice gave out. I did everything in my power to raise the alarm. Nothing worked. Nobody came.

I was physically and mentally drained, so I dropped down onto the bed and lay on my side with my back to the door. I pressed my face into the pillow, curled into a ball and let the tears fall. They came slowly at first, and then I cried like a baby. Big, angry, heartbroken sobs. Hopelessness had got the better of me, and I allowed myself to crumble.

36

SAMSON

Sunday 4 January

'I'm sorry to disturb you, boss, I've got some bad news.'

Nobody in their right mind wanted a wake-up call like this. 'What the fuck is wrong now, Gary?' I bellowed down the phone, hoping to burst his eardrum for disturbing my beauty sleep. He knew damn well not to bother me before mid-afternoon at the earliest.

'I've just had a call from the driver. He said the shipment's been nicked.'

It wasn't even lunchtime, and my day had already gone down the pan.

'What do you mean it's been nicked? What about the tracker?'

I always insisted Bluetooth trackers were attached to my shipments in case a situation like this arose. It wasn't uncommon for a rival gang to try and intercept the drugs when they were on the last leg of their journey after we'd done all the hard work getting them into the country. The tracker wirelessly connected to Gary's mobile phone. He should be able to geolocate the cocaine around the clock, following it every step of the way until it reached its destination.

'It's been disabled.' Gary said.

His voice was barely above a whisper, but there was nothing quiet about my reply.

'For fuck's sake!' I roared.

I'd had a feeling something else would go wrong even before Gary called. The shipment had been doomed since it left Ecuador. It got stuck in a storm, and the ship had to divert three hundred miles to avoid the worst of it. Then, it got caught up in the backlog the storm had caused. When it finally was unloaded, the Dutch authorities had threatened to search it.

I thought we'd seen the last of the delays until a pointless police investigation stopped everything in its tracks after some cocaine collectors suffocated to death in mysterious circumstances. I'd done mankind a favour by ridding the world of the low-life scum, and yet the media circus surrounding the event turned the crooks into martyrs. Instead of sweeping it under the carpet, Joe Public wanted justice for them, so the authorities were forced to look like they cared about the untimely deaths. The probe had taken weeks and turned up nothing.

I'd never had any issues importing cocaine while I'd been buying my gear from Vincenzo Lombardi's stock. But the minute I cut him adrift, all hell broke loose. I hadn't let him get away with trying to stitch me up, though. Some of his workforce met a grisly end as payback. That should have been the last of it. Was he at it again? Or was someone else responsible?

'The shipment must have been tampered with. Trackers don't just disable themselves. How did the driver let that happen?'

'I don't know, boss,' Gary replied.

'Do you know how pathetic you sound?' My temper was reaching boiling point.

Gary didn't reply.

'When did you first realise you'd lost contact with my gear?'

My temples were throbbing in time with my heartbeat. Patience wasn't my strong suit. I was ready to blow my top. After what felt like an eternity, Gary began to stutter his reply.

'U-umm. U-umm.'

'You sound like fucking Porky Pig from *Looney Tunes*. Just spit it out, you half-wit.'

'I only noticed when the driver called me to say the van had been nicked.'

Heads were going to roll for this.

'You're meant to keep track of the coke all the time it's on the move. That's why we fit the Bluetooth devices.'

'I know that. And I usually do, but this time I fucked up...' Gary's sentence trailed off.

'Fucked up is an understatement. You should count yourself lucky you're not within striking distance. If I could get my hands on you right now, I'd beat the shit out of you.'

I was absolutely livid. There was no way I was going to stand back and let Lombardi turn me into a laughing stock.

'Tell me the driver's full account. And don't leave anything out,' I bellowed down the receiver.

'He's not sure what happened. He said the first part of the operation went to plan. Some guys at the port loaded the cocaine into the back of the transit in Rotterdam, and he boarded the ferry to Felixstowe shortly afterwards. The journey was uneventful until he went to the bog to have a slash not long before the ferry reached land. Somebody must have followed him in and hit him over the back of the head with something while he was at the urinal. A member of staff found him collapsed on the toilet floor after the ship had docked. He'd been out cold. Whoever attacked him stole his keys, his wallet and his passport, too,' Gary said.

Fuck me. I know I told him not to leave anything out, but I wasn't expecting him to rattle on like that. I didn't think he was ever coming up for air.

'This wasn't a random attack. Whoever walloped the driver on the nut in the shitter knew he had a van load of gear. They must have been watching him from the minute he got behind the wheel. What's the number plate of the van?'

'I'm not sure. I can ask the driver, but I doubt he'll know. I think they come from a fleet. He just takes whichever transit he's allocated,' Gary replied.

'The ferry company must have a record of the plate,' I said, barely able to contain my rage. It was bubbling under the surface, ready to make an appearance.

'You're right. I hadn't thought of that; leave it with me, boss. I'll get onto them now.'

Of course, I was right. I was always right. I was beginning to wonder what I paid Gary for. Why did I always have to think of everything? His incompetence was outweighing his usefulness these days. It would put a huge dent in my wallet, but I'd have to get my source inside the force on the case.

'The sooner DC Boyd puts a trace on the van, the better. Make sure you do it straight away, Gary, it's urgent.'

'Yes, boss.'

Whoever was responsible had a death wish. If they thought they could nick my gear and get away with it, they had another think coming.

* * *

'Boyd, it's Samson. Samson Fox.'

'Well, well, well, now there's a blast from the past,' Boyd replied. 'How are tricks?'

That was a moronic question if ever I'd heard one. I wouldn't have been phoning the money-grabbing arsehole if everything had been hunky-dory. But I didn't want to get off on the wrong foot. I hadn't spoken to the man in ages, and I needed his help, so I'd have to mind my manners.

'Not great, as it happens.'

'I'm sorry to hear that.'

Boyd's tone was upbeat and didn't match his sympathetic words. My misfortune was his gain. I could picture the pound signs in his eyes. Greedy bastard. He was always on the take.

'I've had one of my shipments nicked.'

'Dear, dear, dear. What's the world coming to? How did that happen?'

Boyd was making all the right noises, but I knew he didn't give a flying fuck about the finer details of the robbery. He was only concerned with how much he could fleece me for this time.

'Some dickhead knocked the driver out when he went into the bogs for a leak. The cheeky fucker stole the keys and went off with a whole van load of gear.'

'So it wasn't a random attack. Somebody had to be tailing the driver. They knew exactly what you had concealed inside the van,' Boyd said.

Talk about stating the obvious and telling me what I already knew. But I had to let him have his moment in the spotlight. Let him think he was imparting his wisdom on a lowly member of the public who had no idea how a criminal mind operated. He was pathetic. Listening to him droning on was getting my back up, but I had to keep the charade going for a little bit longer.

'I've got the registration. Can you put a trace on it for me, please?' I made sure to say the magic word even though he was getting right on my tits.

'Not a problem. Leave it with me,' Boyd said before ending the call.

I had a bunch of cretins working for me, so it was impossible to keep control of everything.

37

MACKENZIE

MACKENZIE

How's everything going?

I typed out a message and then hit send before I changed my mind again. I'd spent the last fifteen minutes trying to compose a text to Daisy. I wanted to open the lines of communication, but I didn't want to ask her how Des was doing in case he'd popped his clogs. I needed to choose my words carefully so that I didn't upset her, and I decided the best approach was to keep things vague.

I'd been hoping Daisy would reply straight away, but two hours had passed before she responded. When my phone eventually pinged, and I saw Daisy's name come up on the screen, my heart started beating like a drum. I could see the beginning of the message, but it wasn't clear whether Des was still in the land of the living or not, so I scrambled to open it.

DAISY

My mum's in bits. She's absolutely heartbroken. She's convinced Dad's going to die. But he's somehow managing to hang on. Stubborn to the last... The doctor saw him earlier and he said he's not out of the woods. It's still early days.

I blew out a sigh of relief. Daisy had enough on her plate right now without her dad dying on top of everything. Twenty-three was too young to lose a parent. Even a useless one like Des. I know I probably shouldn't speak ill of him while he was at death's door, but he was a jumped-up little prick with an evil temper. Maybe a near-death experience would do him some good. It might make him take stock of his life and change his outlook, soften some of his rough edges.

MACKENZIE

I'm glad to hear he's holding on. Keep your chin up. He's a fighter. If anyone can get through this, he can. Let me know if there's anything I can do.

I sent the text and then gave Roscoe a call to fill him in on the latest development.

'I've just had a reply from Daisy,' I said.

'What did she say?' he asked.

'Des is alive, but it's touch and go.'

'I'm not trying to sound callous, but this could drag on for ages, and there still might not be a good outcome. The sooner we get Daisy away from London, the better. It won't take Samson long to get wind of what's happened to Des, and then she'll be a sitting duck,' Roscoe warned.

'That makes two of us.' If I'd been behind the bar when he came calling, I wouldn't be breathing now.

'That's why I've decided to keep you on the move. You'll be

more vulnerable if you stay in one place. Samson has spies every-where,' Roscoe replied.

A tremor shot through my insides, but I did my best to hide my fear.

'Text Daisy and tell her you're coming to collect her. That's non-negotiable. I'll send one of my guys with you as backup.'

I should have known that job would land at my feet. I didn't want to send that message. Daisy wouldn't take kindly to being bossed around.

'No worries. I'll let you know when I hear back from her, but just so you know, she's not responding to messages quickly.'

'Keep the pressure on, son. Her safety's riding on it.'

MACKENZIE

> Roscoe's not happy about you staying in London. He wants me to bring you back to Dover straight away.

DAISY

> Tell Roscoe I'm not going anywhere. My mum's heartbroken. She's totally devastated. There's no way I'm leaving her.

Daisy's reply was instant. Roscoe wasn't going to like it but I admired her loyalty and the fact that she wasn't holding a grudge against her mum and dad. But she'd picked a bad time to become the model daughter. I couldn't help feeling she was underesti-mating how much danger she was in.

'I can't say I'm surprised,' Roscoe said when I broke the news to him. 'Bernice and I expected she might refuse to come back, so we're not going to mess about; we're going to implement a plan.'

My temples started to pound. I wondered what he had in store for me.

'As Daisy's digging her heels in, I don't want to drag her back kicking and screaming. Bernice is going to go to London instead to lend her support and help out with practical things. Tara and Daisy still need to eat, so she'll cook their meals and ferry them backwards and forwards to the hospital. Stuff like that. She's going stir crazy sitting here waiting for news,' Roscoe said.

I breathed a sigh of relief. At least the plan didn't involve me.

'Bernice's presence will be a lot more subtle than if you or I turned up and started hanging around like a bad smell. She's more than capable of watching Daisy's back. She's a force to be reckoned with, my missus. If Samson steps out of line again, she'll have his bollocks for earrings,' Roscoe laughed.

'Do you want me to text Daisy and let her know?'

'No, she'll probably tell Bernice not to bother, so it's better if she turns up unannounced. Lily's still on the missing list, so we're going to be up to our necks trying to track her down,' Roscoe replied.

He wouldn't hear me complaining. Finding Lily should take priority over everything.

38

DAISY

I knew Roscoe's intentions had come from a good place, but the last thing I needed right now was him sticking his beak in. I'd spread myself thin enough, trying to keep everyone happy without him joining the bandwagon. I already felt suffocated by the situation. It had been an ordeal and there was no sign of it ending any time soon.

'I'm just going to get some air,' I said to Mum.

I needed a break from the bedside vigil. Watching and waiting was getting me down. Dad was hooked up to all sorts of equipment, which let out alarms and bleeps at regular intervals. They were giving me a headache.

'Don't go too far!'

Mum seemed horrified that I was stepping outside. I wasn't used to her being so needy. Being shackled to her morning, noon and night was stifling. Draining. I was doing my best to support her, but she was splintered. Broken. Consumed by grief. It was a lot to cope with.

'What are you doing here?' I asked when I spotted Bernice breezing along the corridor.

She was wearing thigh-high black patent boots, skin-tight black Lycra trousers, a black polo-necked jumper and a cream-coloured fake fur jacket. Her face, as always, was fully made up. She seemed too dressed up for the hospital setting. Mum and I had been wearing the same clothes since yesterday. We hadn't even brushed our hair or teeth. I felt like a bag lady, but it seemed shallow to be concerned about my appearance at a time like this.

'I came to offer you some moral support. I'm sorry about your dad.' Bernice wrapped her arms around me and planted a kiss on my cheek. As she did, I got a lungful of the cloud of perfume surrounding her.

'Thanks,' I replied.

Bernice's heavily made-up eyes searched my face. 'It must have been awful for you to witness something so horrendous. I'm worried about you, darling.'

'I'm OK.'

I managed to force out a smile of reassurance, but every detail of the attack was tattooed on my brain. I wanted to scrunch my eyes shut to block out the vision of Warren Jenkins and the blood-covered screwdriver. It all happened so quickly. I was struggling to process it. My thoughts were scrambled. Disjointed. None of this seemed real.

'Well, you don't look OK. You look exhausted.'

I wished I wasn't so easy to read. Wished I could choose whether to reveal my innermost thoughts. But I found it impossible to hide what I was thinking. My face made announcements without my permission. There was nothing I could do about that.

'Let me take some of the strain off you,' Bernice said.

Her voice was soothing. Oozing empathy. I could feel my bottom lip begin to tremble in response. I didn't usually cry at the drop of a hat. That was Lily's department. But Bernice's sympathetic manner set me straight off. I'd done my best to stay strong and managed to put on a brave face in front of my mum but the floodgates had opened. I'd been bottling up my emotions and now that Bernice had loosened the cork, there was no way to stop them pouring out.

'Shush. Shush. Everything's going to be OK. I'm here to help you.' Bernice took both of my hands in hers and gave them a reassuring squeeze.

'I'm sorry. I don't know what got into me,' I said, pulling my hands free and frantically wiping my tears away with my fingertips. I was embarrassed that I'd broken down in front of her.

'There's no need to apologise. You've been through so much.'

'Disaster seems to be following me wherever I go at the moment,' I replied.

'I know, darling. You've really hit a bad patch, haven't you? How's your dad doing?' Bernice fixed me with a look of concern.

'There's no change. He's still unconscious. Mum's sitting with him but I needed a break. It's horrible seeing him like that...' I let my sentence trail off.

'I'm sure it is,' Bernice said.

'I've been trying to hold it together for Mum's sake, but it's hard. Waiting for something to happen is torture. Time moves so slowly when you're sitting on a hard plastic chair for hours on end. Every now and again, I have to step outside. But when I do, Mum starts to panic. She won't leave his side. The only time she tears herself away is to use the toilet.'

Bernice reached for my hand. 'Did you stay here all night?'

I nodded. 'Yeah. We've been at the hospital since Dad was brought in yesterday. At least I think it was yesterday. I've lost all track of time.'

'I can imagine.' Bernice gave me a sympathetic smile. She paused for a moment as though she was trying to choose the right words before she continued speaking. 'I know you want to be there for your dad, but you'll make yourself ill if you carry on like this. You need to get some rest; you look dead on your feet. Why don't I take you home for a bit? You can have a nice soak in the bath and grab a couple of hours sleep. I'll make you something to eat then I can drive you back again. What do you think?'

I agreed with Bernice wholeheartedly, but how could I leave? Dad was fighting for his life and Mum was a mess.

'It doesn't matter what I think. My mum's in bits, so I can't abandon her.'

'You've been here since yesterday and there's been no change in your dad's condition. He could stay like this for days or even weeks. What you're doing isn't sustainable. I know you want to be with him in case anything happens, but you won't be any use to your dad if you make yourself ill in the meantime. The doctors will call you if anything changes.' Bernice's eyes were pleading.

She'd already won me over, but a warped sense of duty was tethering me to my parents. I wasn't really sure why. I'd been on the receiving end of Dad's temper more times than I cared to mention. It seemed hard to believe it was the same man in the hospital bed. The man who'd tormented me my entire life was nowhere to be seen. He was a shell of himself.

Dad and I had shared a lifetime of tension and butting heads. We'd been sparring partners for as long as I could remember, constantly at each other's throats. But watching him stare death in the face, had changed my perception. What if he died? We'd never be able to right the wrongs. Why couldn't things have been different? Regret began to simmer under the surface. I was an emotional wreck. I wished I could cut myself adrift from all of this. But I couldn't do that to Mum. She needed me. I was the only person she had to lean on.

'Look, darling, I don't want to speak out of turn, but I don't understand why you're digging your heels in. You've always been second best in your parents' eyes. Everyone knows having favourites is wrong, but the way your dad treated you was despicable. He should be ashamed of himself. He doesn't deserve your loyalty...'

Bernice let her sentence trail off. I sensed there was a lot more she wanted to say, but she was holding back, aware that I was feeling overwhelmed by everything. What she'd said was true, but listening to her slag him off while he was on his deathbed stabbed at my conscience. Allowing her to openly criticise my parents seemed wrong somehow. Maybe it was because Dad's future was uncertain. I couldn't explain it. Normally, I'd be the first one to bitch about them. Bitch about him. But they were my family, which gave me the right to do it.

I suddenly felt my volcanic temper spike. Anger rumbled inside me. Began creeping through my veins. A second later, I was ready to blow my top. I was desperate to vent my frustration. The desire to let it out was overwhelming. I had to fight the urge to unleash my fury, which was bubbling beneath the surface.

My emotions were running high. It would be very easy to say something I'd end up regretting. And the last thing I wanted to do was to have words with Bernice over her telling me some home truths. She was only trying to look out for me. Protect me. The best thing I could do was let it slide.

'I know you're right, but there's no way my mum will agree to that,' I said.

'Let me talk to her.'

I'd been expecting Mum to bitterly object when Bernice ran it past her, but she didn't answer. Instead, she glared at me in silent protest, then bowed her head, looked down at her lap, and began wringing her hands together. Resentment was seeping out of every pore in her body. Her response made my stress levels rise. My shoulders were full of knots. My head was pounding. I knew

Mum's heart was breaking. She was drained. Exhausted. But so was I. And I was slowly being suffocated by her emotions. My emotions. I couldn't take any more of this.

'I'll be back before you know it,' I said before I headed for the door. Sometimes, you had to be cruel to be kind.

39

SAMSON

'Samson, it's DC Boyd. We've found the van.'

'That's fantastic news.'

I'd been expecting him to say the thieves had changed the plates and it had disappeared without a trace.

'Don't get too excited,' Boyd said.

I felt the smile slide from my face. Where was the silver lining? Every cloud these days contained a big pile of horse shit.

'The van's been abandoned in the car park of a service station on the A12. It was open and there was nothing inside, so whoever nicked it must have transferred the shipment to another vehicle.'

'For fuck's sake,' I shouted down the phone.

'I know this must be frustrating for you.'

'Have you checked the CCTV footage?'

'There was no point. The cameras don't cover that area.'

Boyd couldn't have sounded less interested if he tried. I despised him with a passion. He always managed to rub me up the wrong way. But I needed his help, so I'd have to mind my Ps and Qs. Losing my rag at this precise moment wasn't an option.

'Jesus Christ, you couldn't make this shit up. Did you dust it for prints?'

'Again, there didn't seem much point.'

'Of course, there's a point,' I said through gritted teeth.

I was one step away from unleashing my fury on the useless fucker, spouting a tirade of abuse in his direction. Boyd was getting right on my tits. What the hell did I pay my taxes for? I might as well not bother. Truth be told, most of the time, I didn't bother. Robbing the taxman blind was one of my favourite pastimes.

'I know this wasn't the outcome you were hoping for, but I'm sorry to say I think we've reached a dead end.'

It was clear he didn't give a flying fuck about my missing cocaine. I wonder if he'd be as quick to wash his hands of the matter if I told him I'd adopted a no-win no-fee approach. I had a good mind to call his bluff. Bent coppers were the scum of the earth. I preferred to deal with career criminals any day of the week. But I needed his expertise in this situation, so I'd have to wind my neck in.

'Surely there's something you can do.' I softened the tone of my voice, but it grated on me to almost have to plead with the bastard.

'I wish there was, but in all honesty, whoever nicked your gear is long gone.'

Why did Boyd sound so fucking smug? Had he helped himself to my coke? It wouldn't surprise me in the slightest. He was a slimy fucker. Always on the take. And that would explain why he wasn't prepared to do anything to stop the trail going cold. You couldn't trust anyone where money was concerned. Boyd had better hope my theory wasn't correct. Double-crossing me wasn't compatible with life.

'That may be so, but I need to find the shipment. Do me a

favour see if you can lift any prints. Just humour me for old time's sake.'

I shouldn't even have to ask him to do that. It was basic police work routinely carried out at a crime scene. What was the world coming to when you had to tell a copper how to do his job? The level of service was diabolical. Boyd considered himself a pillar of the community, but he was nothing more than a professional con artist.

'No can do. I'm already back at my desk.'

Boyd attempted to dismiss me, but I wasn't having any of it. He should have known better than to try and fob me off with a load of old flannel. He wouldn't be the one dusting surfaces looking for clues, so it made no difference whether he was back at his desk or not. I could do without him trying to wind me up. My pulse was already galloping without him adding to the stress.

'Correct me if I'm wrong, but I didn't think that was your department. Don't the forensic team usually lift the prints?' Now, it was my turn to be smug.

If we were about to have a dick swinging competition, he should know I had the upper hand. Mine was bigger and better, so naturally, I'd win every time. Boyd let out a large, exaggerated pantomime sigh. I didn't need to rub the tosser's face in it. He knew when he was beaten.

'OK, OK. I'll send a unit over as soon as one becomes available, but honestly, mate, take my advice. There's no point in winding yourself up about this. You win some. You lose some. You might as well kiss this shipment goodbye. It's sailed off into the sunset. It's already halfway to Spain by now,' Boyd laughed.

He was highly amused by his own joke. The fucker was very lucky I wasn't within striking distance right now, or I'd have grabbed him by the throat and squeezed the life out of him.

'Anyway, I'd better go. I've got another call coming through,' Boyd said, cutting me off before I had a chance to respond.

Like hell he did. That was the biggest load of bullshit I'd heard in a long time. The useless fat fuck went out of his way to avoid work. He sat in his car eating slice after slice of pizza straight from the box, or any other takeaway he could get his chubby little mitts on, for hours on end while pretending to do surveillance. The only covert movement he was interested in was how long the queue was in the kebab shop.

40

DAISY

I stood outside the front door for several seconds, paralysed by fear, before I plucked up the courage to push it with my fingertips. I took in a long breath as I stepped inside. Splinters of glass crunched under my feet, making me wince. The house that I'd grown up in had an ominous feel to it. I slipped off my jacket and slung it over the banister. Then I tiptoed over the debris that littered the hall floor.

'Sorry about the mess,' I said as though a couple of children's toys were littering the floor when an unexpected guest had arrived.

'Don't worry about it, darling.' Bernice gave me a sympathetic smile intensifying the laughter lines at the corners of her eyes.

As I drew closer to the lounge, my step faltered. I grabbed onto the door frame and peered inside the room. My muscles felt like they'd seized up when my eyes homed in on the blood-soaked sofa. I wanted to look away but I was glued to the horrific sight.

'Why don't you go and get some rest while I have a tidy up?' The feeling of Bernice's fingers on my arm broke the spell I was under.

* * *

I'd only slept for a couple of hours, but I already felt like I could function better. It was amazing how quickly your body responded when you allowed it to rest.

'Hello, darling. How are you feeling?' Bernice asked when I walked into the kitchen.

'Almost human,' I replied.

Bernice's eyes searched my face. 'That's good to hear. You definitely look a lot brighter.'

I hadn't set the bar very high, though. 'It would be difficult to look worse than death warmed up,' I said, trying to keep my tone light.

Bernice gave me a half smile and then steered the conversation in a different direction.

'I wasn't sure what kind of food you like to eat, so I've rustled up some sausage, mash and onion gravy. It's Roscoe's favourite!' Bernice said.

'Ooh, thank you. That sounds lovely.'

My stomach started growling as my nostrils filled with the smell of home cooking. I hadn't realised how hungry I was until Bernice put the plate down in front of me. As I started to eat, she poured me a large glass of chilled white wine and then sat down opposite me.

Since she'd come into my life, she'd been watching over me like my guardian angel. I couldn't think too much about the kindness she was showing me, or I'd end up breaking down in tears. So I concentrated on the plate of food in front of me. I didn't come up for air until I'd eaten and drunk the lot. Then, I slumped back in the chair and rubbed my hands over my stomach.

'Thanks for that. It was so nice. I'm not surprised it's Roscoe's favourite!'

'Aww, I'm glad you enjoyed it, darling. Would you like some more?' Bernice pushed her chair back and stood up.

'No, thanks. I'm absolutely stuffed.'

'That's what I like to hear!' Bernice's full lips stretched into a smile.

'I wouldn't say no to another glass of wine, though.'

'Coming right up!'

Bernice walked over to the fridge, took out the wine and brought it over to the table. She filled my glass and then put the bottle down in front of me.

'Thank you,' I said.

'My pleasure,' Bernice replied.

We hadn't known each other long, but we'd already become very close. From the moment we'd met, she'd showered me with the kind of affection I didn't get at home.

'I've been thinking about this a lot. Do you mind if I ask you something?'

'Of course. You can ask me whatever you want.' Bernice grinned.

'You'd have made a great mum. Why didn't you have any kids?'

The booze had gone straight to my head, and the alcohol had loosened my lips. Drunk words. Sober thoughts. I should have had the sense to keep them to myself, but I'd been desperate to know the answer. I'd wanted to ask her more about it when she'd told me she didn't have a family, but the opportunity passed before I had the chance to question her.

I shouldn't blame the wine, but I tended to say stuff when I was drinking that I would never say otherwise. When I saw the smile slide from Bernice's face, I instantly regretted asking such a personal question. She'd been so happy. Now, she looked awkward. Uncomfortable.

Bernice marched across the kitchen, opened one of the

cupboard doors and reached for a glass. She brought it back to the table and emptied the rest of the bottle into it. I could see her eyes had misted up when she held the wine up to her lips and downed half of it in one swallow.

'Forget I said that. I'm sorry. I didn't mean to pry. It's none of my business...' I let my sentence trail off.

Now, it was my turn to feel awkward. I picked up my drink and glugged a huge gulp of wine. I'd well and truly dropped myself in it, and no amount of back-peddling was going to make the situation better. I should have realised it was a deliberate move when she'd gone off on a tangent the last time the subject came up. She'd obviously had good reasons to kick my curiosity into touch.

'I was no spring chicken when I met Roscoe. I was in my mid-thirties. He came into my life unexpectedly, like a whirlwind and turned everything upside down. I'd been through a tough time, and the last thing I was looking for was love. But he swept me off my feet. Put a ring on my finger six weeks later. Neither of us were getting any younger, so we started trying for a baby straight away...'

Bernice's voice cracked, and she reached for her glass. Dread started to rise up from my stomach. I wished I'd never brought this up now. I could see her hands shaking as she sipped her wine to steady herself. I felt like an arsehole for putting her through this.

'Why don't we leave this to another time,' I said, reaching across the table for her hand.

Bernice shook her head. 'The months rolled by, and I still wasn't pregnant, so we went to the doctor, and they sent us for tests. Roscoe's a proud man. He was expecting the doc to confirm he had a higher-than-average sperm count full of strong swimmers...' Bernice paused for a moment and took a couple of deep breaths to compose herself. I could see this was distressing her, but she seemed determined to continue. 'He never imagined in his wildest dreams that he was firing blanks. We'd both thought the issue lay with me, given my age. When the doctor confirmed he was sterile, he didn't take the news well. He was crushed and rapidly went off the idea of having a family now that a natural conception was out of the question. It broke my heart. Nearly cost us our marriage, but the bottom line was he was just too proud to have IVF. There was no talking him round. I gave it my best shot, but he accused me of nagging and gave me an ultimatum. Either I accepted his decision, or he'd walk away.'

Bernice's words made a huge lump form in my throat. It was so large it hurt to swallow it. It seemed to lodge itself in my chest, but I forced out a sympathetic smile for her benefit. Guilt welled up inside me. I felt bad that my nosiness had forced her to relive the ordeal she'd clearly worked so hard to bury.

'I'm so sorry. I had no idea. That must have been such a hard decision to make,' I said.

'It was,' Bernice said.

She pushed her chair back, got to her feet, picked up my plate, knife and fork and took them over to the sink. Then she turned around to face me with a smile pasted on her face, having dusted herself off.

'Do you want some pudding, love? I picked up a trifle from the Co-op while you were asleep.'

'Maybe later,' I replied.

Bernice was a legend. It was early days, but something told me I was going to learn a lot of life skills if I stuck with her. She might not have kids of her own, but she was like a surrogate mum to me.

41

SAMSON

'Gary, get your arse over here right now. I've just spoken to Boyd and the van's been abandoned at a service station on the A12. According to him, it's empty, but he wouldn't be able to find a rotting carcass if it was tied to the end of his nose. I want to check it over myself.'

Knowing Boyd's limited attention span, he probably hadn't thought to look in the underfloor compartments, or the fake wall panels. I dare say he just stuck his beak in the back and gave it a cursory glance to get me off his case. There was too much riding on this to take the useless tosser's word for it.

* * *

An hour and forty-five minutes later, Gary guided my black Range Rover into the space next to the van. It had been left unlocked in a quiet corner of the car park furthest away from the building housing the shops and fast food outlets.

Whoever had done this had planned it with military precision. We'd torn every inch of it apart, but nothing had been left behind.

Nobody stole from me and got away with it. If you tried to rip me off, I'd come back at you twice as hard. They might have thought they'd pulled one over on me, but I had contacts, so it was only a matter of time until I found the bastards responsible, and then I'd make them pay good and proper.

Gary and I were on our way back to London when my mobile started to ring. 'Yep,' I said, only narrowly resisting the urge to bellow, 'What the fuck do you want now?'

'I sent the forensic guys around to look at the van, and they've managed to lift some prints from the passenger side. We're checking them against the national fingerprint database. I'll let you know if they come up with a match, but don't hold your breath. Somebody's probably shifting your gear on the street as we speak. Adios,' Boyd said and then hung up the call before I had a chance to ask any questions.

I slammed the palm of my hand down on the dashboard. Boyd needed to watch his step. He was only my go-to person because of the loyalty he showed my dad when he got banged up. But he was a lazy, fat fucker. There were no two ways about that. He was skating on thin ice. If he wasn't careful, he'd find himself cut from my payroll.

I'd barely parked my arse on my office chair when my mobile started ringing again. I felt like firing the poxy thing across the room. Every time I answered it, I seemed to get more bad news. I let out a long, slow breath before I picked up the call. 'Hello,' I begrudgingly said.

'Don't sound so glum, Sam,' Boyd said.

I hated people shortening my name. I saw it as a high level of disrespect, so he'd got my back up straight away. I'd just about had enough. I'd been dealing with crap since I'd opened my eyes this morning.

'I haven't exactly got a lot to be happy about, have I?'

My voice had a sarcastic edge to it. But instead of taking things down a level, the DC carried on regardless.

'I'm not sure I'd agree with that!' Boyd sounded like he was on cloud nine while I was wallowing in my misfortune. 'I'd say it's your lucky day, Foxy,' Boyd chirped with the enthusiasm of a host from a TV game show.

Foxy? Who the fuck did he think he was talking to? I could feel my jaw twitching as I clenched and unclenched my fist. What I wouldn't give to ram it in his face right now...

'How you've come to that conclusion is a mystery to me,' I said through gritted teeth while wondering what planet he was on.

'Well then, let me share the good news with you. I've just spoken to the lab, and they've confirmed they've got a match on the set of prints they lifted.' I could tell by the tone of Boyd's voice that he was grinning from ear to ear.

Fuck me! Now, he had my undivided attention. I'd been expecting him to feed me another pile of bullshit. I leapt to my feet and started pacing around the room.

'Don't keep me in suspense. Is it anyone I know?'

'I doubt it. They're a pretty insignificant petty criminal. They've been arrested before on a few occasions for selling weed and shoplifting, but they've never been convicted. They're low down the food chain. Just a small cog in the machine. In fact, I'm surprised they were even involved in an operation like this. You weren't robbed by amateurs,' Boyd concluded.

Talk about telling me something I didn't already know. Boyd was getting right on my fucking tits.

'If you ask me, they've probably been brought in as a scape-goat. As I said earlier, the prints were on the passenger's side. The rest of the van was clean. It was dusted inside and out, and they didn't find a thing. The prints may well have been planted there to send us on a wild goose chase.'

The way Boyd was talking, anyone would think the police were actually investigating this crime. I couldn't stomach listening to the bloke any longer. He was doing my head in.

'Can you email me the report so that I can take a look myself?'

'Don't you trust me?' Boyd laughed.

He'd hit the nail on the head, but I wasn't going to share that nugget of information with him. He'd just proved that he still had his uses. A few moments later, the email landed in my inbox.

I opened the attachment and stared at the mugshot. It was grainy. And, like a typical passport photo, it probably looked nothing like the person it belonged to. But having said that, the face did look slightly familiar. There was something about the sad eyes and hollow cheekbones that rang a bell even though I couldn't put my finger on where I knew the person from. The name meant nothing to me. But that didn't surprise me. I had enough trouble trying to remember who worked for me, let alone someone I may or may not have crossed paths with years earlier.

I met a lot of people in my line of work. And besides that, random strangers always shoved their business cards into the palm of my hand. Sometimes, I didn't even bother glancing at them before I tossed them into the bin. I'd always been better with faces than names. The mug was definitely sparking a small glimmer of recognition, so it warranted further investigation. Although, I didn't hold out too much hope. Boyd was right. There was no way this person had masterminded the stunt.

But it was the only lead I had, so I'd have to get Gary to do some digging and see what he could come up with before the trail went cold. Once my coke disappeared up people's noses, it would never be seen again.

42

MACKENZIE

Monday 5 January

My eyes had started bugging out from being glued to my iPad screen, so I'd taken a well-earned break. I'd been lying on the bed savouring the coke coursing through my veins when my mobile sprang to life. I stretched my hand over to the bedside cabinet and picked it up.

CARLY

I'd really like to talk to you if you're not too busy

I was surprised to see the message was from Carly.

MACKENZIE

Never too busy

I typed and then hit send.

Any excuse to get away from sifting through Google looking for the elusive warehouse. I'd taken up the slack since Daisy was preoccupied with her dad, but so far, the search for Lily had been fruitless.

* * *

'Thanks for coming.' Carly said when she opened the hostel door.

'No worries,' I replied, reluctantly stepping inside the seedy-looking dive. It was a real house of horrors.

The first thing I noticed when Carly let me in was how dilated her pupils were. She had a bottle of Henry Weston's 8 per cent cider gripped in her hand, but I doubted that was the cause. Don't get me wrong, that stuff would blow your head off, and she was well on her way to being trollied. But I was pretty clued up on these things, so I'd be amazed if she hadn't taken something along with the booze.

'I hope I haven't dragged you out of your way,' Carly said.

'Nah. I've got an apartment in the Old Mill House. It's not far from here.'

'Lucky you.' Carly smiled before she bounded down the hall like the Duracell bunny. 'Follow me,' she called over her shoulder as she led the way into the guest lounge and closed the door behind me. 'Do you want a drink?' Carly asked, downing the dregs of the bottle.

'No thanks,' I replied.

I wouldn't usually turn down the offer, but I didn't want to ponce off somebody so skint.

Carly put her hand in a small black bag sitting on the wooden sideboard covered with mug rings and nondescript stains. She took out another bottle, held it up to her mouth and removed the cap with her teeth. I was stunned. I'd never seen a woman do that before.

'You sure I can't tempt you?' Carly jiggled the bottle in front of me.

'I'm sure.'

'Suit yourself,' Carly replied, then she put her hand in the pocket of her tracksuit, pulled out a bundle of notes and held them towards me. 'This is for Roscoe. Can you give it to him and tell him I'm really sorry I let him down?' Carly's green eyes looked sad.

'He doesn't want it back.'

'I know, but I'm flush at the moment,' Carly smiled, waving the notes at me.

'You need it more than he does,' I replied, shoving my fingers into the front pockets of my jeans so that she couldn't force the cash into the palm of my hand.

'Seriously, mate, you should take it while I've got it. Money tends to burn a hole in my pocket. I've never been good at economising. Once I get it, I spend it. There's no point in worrying about tomorrow; you might never see it. I prefer to live in the moment.'

'Why don't you treat yourself to a slap-up meal?'

Carly didn't look like she'd eaten recently. She was small and skinny, with bones jutting out from every angle. She looked malnourished.

'Nah. It would be wasted on me. I don't have much of an appetite. I probably shouldn't be volunteering this, but I've had a drug problem for years.' Carly tilted her head to one side, tucked her chin down and looked up at me through her eyelashes as she gauged my reaction.

I couldn't say that surprised me. Carly was skin and bone. She had a washed-out complexion and dark circles all around her eyes like a panda, which made her look permanently tired. Her brown hair hung limply over her shoulders. It was dull and lifeless.

'What do you take?' I asked.

Carly laughed. 'I'm honestly not fussy. I snort, pop pills or inject anything that crosses my path, mate. It depends on how broke I am, but I have to make do with spice most of the time.'

I'd given most things a go, but even I'd stopped short of trying the zombie drug. I liked my gear to be naturally occurring, not something synthetic manufactured in a lab. Getting high was one thing. Being in a semi-comatose state was another.

'I can't trust myself where money is concerned. I tend to be a bit light-fingered. I'm not proud of it, but I've been living from hand to mouth for the last three years, so when temptation's put in my way, it's virtually impossible for me to resist. I'm not trying to make excuses, but feeding a habit is expensive.'

She didn't need to tell me that.

'I hope you don't mind me asking, but where did you get the cash? You didn't rob a bank, did you?' I laughed.

I was fully expecting Carly to zip her mouth closed, but she couldn't get the words out quickly enough. I'd thought twice about whether or not I should ask, but judging by her response, she was dying to share the information with me.

'I sold some cocaine.'

My ears pricked up. 'Where did you get that from?'

I'd got myself into this mess because I'd thought I was borrowing a kilo of cocaine from Arben Hasani to tide us over until Samson's shipment arrived from Rotterdam. But then the fucker decided to do some double-dealing and demanded I cough up sixty grand at short notice to buy it instead.

'From a guy I sometimes work for. He pays me in coke, so when I get a call from him, I jump at the chance. He gives me a much better deal than the hourly rate I get for pulling pints. The problem is he never gives me much notice.'

Carly was drunk and high, so the words poured out of her mouth like juice from a carton. I didn't like the sound of this. She thought she was onto a good thing, but she was too young and naive to see what a dangerous situation she'd got herself into.

Being the last link in the chain wasn't an enviable position. It was risky. I should know.

'Zerina called me the other night when I was working at The Castle and told me she had a job for me. But I had to get myself to Felixstowe straight away. That's why I left the pub unattended and helped myself to Roscoe's money. I needed to buy a train ticket and pay for a B & B,' Carly explained before taking a swig of her cider.

'Sorry, can you back up a bit? Did you say Zerina phoned you?'

Carly had lost me. I thought I'd been paying attention, but maybe I'd missed something. I had a lot on my mind at the moment.

'Yeah.'

So I hadn't been hearing things. 'Isn't that the woman who runs the hostel?'

Carly nodded.

'What's Zerina got to do with this?'

'She's the cousin of the guy I work for. He never contacts me directly. Zerina organises everything.' Carly was so trusting.

'What's his name?'

'I haven't got a clue, but he pays well, so I don't bother asking questions. What I don't know can't hurt me,' Carly grinned.

She wasn't wrong; discretion counted for a lot, but I couldn't help feeling she was being taken advantage of. The kingpins made a habit of staying in the background, but she didn't even know the guy's name and she was the one with her neck on the block.

I was going to ask her why she had to go all the way to Felixstowe, but I didn't want to come across too heavy in case she thought better of confiding in me. Then she blurted out the reason anyway.

'Zerina's cousin had a shipment coming in from Rotterdam, and he wanted me to travel with the driver to Dover. Apparently, a van's less likely to be stopped by the police when there's a woman sitting in the passenger seat.'

I hadn't really ever thought about that, but I wasn't sure she was right. I reckoned somebody had fed her that line, and she'd swallowed it down without questioning it. She was a teenager, barely out of school. She probably didn't realise how much trouble she'd be in if the Old Bill had pulled the van over. She'd have most likely been banged up with the driver, even though her part in the operation was minimal.

'So you brought the gear to Dover?'

'Yeah. Zerina's storing the coke at the hostel until I can shift it. I'm under strict instructions to sell it cheap and flood the market, so that's exactly what I've been doing,' Carly replied.

I wondered if Roscoe knew he had serious competition in such close proximity. He hadn't mentioned anything to me about a rival gang operating on his patch, so my guess was this was going to be news to him.

'How often does Zerina receive shipments?'

Carly shrugged and held my gaze. 'I'm not sure – it's the first time I've done a job like this.'

'I thought you said you'd worked for the guy before.' I felt a frown settle on my face.

'I have, but that was when I lived in London.'

'You lived in London? What part?'

'Camberwell,' Carly replied.

'No way! That's where I grew up.' I didn't bother adding *and lived until very recently* because I didn't want to answer any awkward questions.

'I left home when I was fourteen and ended up living at Springfield Lodge.'

'Is that the Salvation Army place on Grove Hill Road?'

'Yeah. Anyway, I don't want to hold you up. I just wanted to give you this dosh before I end up blowing it,' Carly said, putting an abrupt end to our conversation.

As I walked back to my car, I called Roscoe. 'Hi, it's MacKenzie. I've just been around to Carly's place. She said the reason she left you high and dry the other night was because she got a call from Zerina, the woman who runs the hostel, telling her to go to Felixstowe because she was needed on a job. Zerina's cousin had a shipment coming in from Rotterdam. From what I can work out, the guy's usually based in London.'

'Who is he?' Roscoe didn't sound happy.

I shook my head. 'Carly doesn't know his name. She gets her instructions from Zerina. Her job was to escort the driver down to Dover and now the shipment's being stored at the hostel until she flogs it. Zerina's cousin pays her in gear so she wasn't making a lot of sense, but I thought you should know.'

'How much coke are we talking about?' Roscoe sounded concerned.

'I'm not exactly sure. She didn't say, but I know she's already sold some of it. She was waving wads of cash around and was desperately trying to give me the money she stole from you.'

'Tell Carly she's not to sell coke on my patch under any circumstances. I don't care what her orders are. Can you stake out the hostel and make sure she doesn't do anything underhand? Be discreet and phone me if she makes a move,' Roscoe said before he hung up.

Why did I always get given the crappy jobs? I didn't want to get involved in this. Carly wasn't likely to listen to me if I waded in and threw my weight around. Her boss was a big player. She'd be a fool to cross him. And if I started interfering, I could end up with a bounty on my head.

43

DAISY

'What's the matter, darling?' Bernice asked.

The question was uncomplicated. But I didn't know how to answer it, so I shrugged.

'You know you can tell me anything, don't you?'

I nodded. Bernice wasn't going to judge me for staying away from the hospital, far from it. She'd been encouraging me to keep my distance. She wasn't my parents' biggest fan and had been pretty vocal about them. But her scathing words had come from a good place. She was just looking out for me. She cared about my welfare and had been hugely maternal to me.

Bernice was a good listener, but she wouldn't understand any of this. Our family dynamic was complex. Full of inconsistencies and intricacies that weren't easy for others to fathom. Unravelling the different genetic threads that made us function as a group would blow most people's minds.

Dad and I had never seen eye to eye, but that didn't stop me from feeling guilty that I'd taken myself out of the equation. Seeing him hooked up to machines, making no progress, while

Mum sat beside him, lost in her own private world with grief hanging over her like a shroud, was depressing.

My mum wasn't impressed that I'd deserted my post, but we didn't both need to watch Dad clinging to life by his fingertips twenty-four hours a day. I couldn't handle it. It made me feel helpless. I had to do something constructive. Diverting my attention back to finding Lily had to take priority. Dad's condition hadn't changed since he'd been admitted. There was a long, bumpy road ahead with no guarantee he was going to pull through.

I couldn't just abandon my twin. She needed my help, and I wanted to be there for her. I regretted all the times I'd locked her out of my life. I'd spent too long being bitter and twisted. Jealousy was an ugly trait.

But in my defence, we should never have been raised in competition with each other. It had caused bad feeling. More than that. It had made our relationship toxic. Always being the loser had left its mark on me. I'd gone through life as my sister's understudy and I resented living in her shadow. We were identical. But she was a better version, apparently. I pulled off the look less well.

I could see by the way she was staring at me that Bernice wanted me to confide in her. But I was scared to open up while my emotions were all over the place. I didn't want her pity. And I definitely didn't want to make a fool of myself.

'Come and have a look at this,' Bernice said, realising she was wasting her time.

I sat down at the pine kitchen table next to her, and she turned her iPad around so that I could see the screen.

'I didn't want to say anything before because I didn't want to get your hopes up. But this caught my eye. It must be a new development of sorts. These warehouses are too bright and white to be old ones,' Bernice said.

I peered at the screen. 'Oh my God, the pictures look exactly like the ones in the clips.' My heart started palpitating.

'They do, don't they? The more I look at them, the more I'm convinced this is the right place.' Bernice beamed, and her blue eyes shone like sapphires.

'Does it give the address in the listing?' My eyes scanned over the advert.

'Unfortunately not, it just mentions the site has good access to Central London and that it's in close proximity to excellent rail and road networks, which it says are essential for product distribution,' Bernice replied.

The thought of Lily being the product sent shivers down my spine. I hoped we weren't too late to save her before she was distributed to some god-forsaken place in the middle of nowhere.

'I tell you what, let me give the estate agent a call and see what I can find out.' Bernice picked up her mobile and dialled the number. 'Good evening, I'm interested in viewing a commercial property that I've seen on your website. Could you please give me a call back to arrange a viewing? My name's Bernice Allen,' she said in her best telephone voice.

'I take it they're closed for the evening.'

Bernice nodded. 'I'm afraid so, but the recorded message said they open at nine in the morning.'

I wasn't sure where Bernice was going with this. I couldn't imagine Lily was being held in a property an estate agent had the key to. She must have seen the look of doubt clouding my face because it prompted her to speak.

'We might be barking up the wrong tree, but it's got to be worth a try. Don't you think?' Bernice fixed her eyes on me and tilted her head to one side.

'The interior certainly looks very similar to the one in the videos, but...'

'I've spent a long time searching, and I haven't found anything else that fits the bill,' Bernice cut in before I had a chance to finish my sentence. 'If I get the full address from the agent, we can check it out for ourselves. Deal?'

'Deal,' I replied.

44

LILY

My stomach started having cramps again. I'd barely eaten for days, so I balled my fists and pushed them into my flesh to try and stop them. But they kept coming. I knew they'd pass in time. They always did. But the hunger pangs never truly left. They came and went. Some were more ferocious than others. My hope was fading fast along with my waistline.

My breath caught in my chest when I heard the sound of footsteps bouncing off the metal steps. A painful memory I'd tried to bury stirred within me. It clawed its way to the surface. Raised my blood pressure. Raised my heartbeat. Made my palms sweat. I backed myself against the headboard and squeezed my eyes shut as I heard the door swing open.

'It's about time you were fed and watered,' Smithy said.

I let out a sigh of relief and opened my eyes.

'I'm going to get a Chinese takeaway. What do you fancy?'

He looked irritated when I didn't reply and began tapping his foot impatiently. I couldn't concentrate. Thoughts were whirring through my head. I didn't want him to go out. I didn't want him to leave me alone with Tank.

'Make up your mind. I haven't got all night.' Smithy's tone was abrupt.

'Don't go to any trouble on my account. I'm not hungry,' I said, hoping he'd stay put.

'Suit yourself,' Smithy replied as he left the room.

I listened to his footsteps as he walked back down the stairs, but they didn't stop at the bottom. They kept going. A moment later, the warehouse door opened. A car door slammed, an engine roared to life, and then faded into the distance. My heart skipped a beat when I heard another set of footsteps approaching.

'What the fuck do you think you're playing at?' Tank roared when he burst into the room.

My bottom lip started to tremble, so I sank my teeth into it and hoped he wouldn't notice. But the whole of my body began quivering when Tank marched across the room. I tried to duck out of the way as he lunged at me, but I was backed up against the headboard with nowhere to go, so he was able to grab hold of me. The skin on my upper arm burned as he dug his fingers into my flesh.

I yelped and then quickly whimpered, 'I'm sorry.' I wasn't sure what I was apologising for, but I said it anyway. I didn't know what else to do. He was a sadist, so the last thing I wanted to do was anger him.

'I thought I'd made myself clear.' Tank's spit sprayed my face. I desperately wanted to wipe it away but couldn't move my hands. Who was I trying to kid? Even if they hadn't been tethered, I'd never have had the nerve to do it. 'I told you not to say anything.' Tank's eyes blazed as he raised his fist. His tone was deep. Menacing.

'I promise you, I never said a word.' I looked up at him with pleading eyes, and he glared back at me.

When Tank moved his arm back, I knew this was my moment of reckoning. My time was up. He was going to beat the life out of me. Once he started hitting me, he wouldn't be able to stop. He had no self-control. He'd keep going until I took my last breath. I was sure of it.

'I honestly didn't tell Smithy what happened. Please don't hurt me,' I begged.

'Well, you've been acting really weird around him, which has made him suspicious. The last thing I need is him breathing down my neck. If he tells tales to the boss, you're dead,' Tank threatened.

'I'm sorry I made him suspicious. I didn't mean to.' Tank lowered his fist, so I took advantage of his hesitation. I had a lot of grovelling to do. If I chose my words carefully, I might get out of this unscathed. 'I won't give Smithy reason to think anything's wrong between us.' I was doing my best to bond with him and form a connection so that he wouldn't hurt me. As if I'd be on good terms with my kidnapper. The idea was ridiculous. But if it pacified him, I was happy to go along with it. 'How does that sound?' I forced out a smile.

Tank smiled back. It seemed genuine until I saw his features suddenly change. Harden. My heart was in my mouth. I thought he was falling for the crap I was feeding him. But he was playing games, too. He was more intelligent than he looked.

'You think you're so fucking clever, don't you? But I know exactly what you're trying to do. I've seen that stunt on TV. You're trying to befriend me to save your own skin.' Tank's eyes bored into mine as he threw me a black look.

I started shaking my head as fear raced around my body at a rate of knots. 'I honestly wasn't trying to do that. You have to believe...'

My sentence stopped mid flow as a scream escaped from my lips. Tank had pulled my legs towards him and was pinning me down on the bed with one hand as he tugged at my jogging bottoms with the other. I was in a blind panic, which sent my pulse into overdrive.

'You need to be taught a fucking lesson,' Tank spat the words at me and then slapped me around the face.

My ears started ringing, and my cheek began pulsating like it had its own heartbeat. 'Please don't do this.'

'Shut the fuck up. If you don't co-operate, I'll finish you off,' Tank shouted.

'Please, please don't hurt me.' My voice cracked with emotion.

When Tank's lips lifted into a smile, I started struggling with all my might. If I died trying to break free, so be it. I had an over-whelming desire to fight. I couldn't lay here and do nothing. My screams became louder. More urgent. More ear piercing. So he silenced me by forcing his forearm onto my windpipe. I gasped for air. Desperate to claw at his skin, lash out at him, but my wrists were bound. I tried to wriggle out from under him, but I was anchored by his weight.

'Get off her, you fucking bastard.'

I'd felt myself drifting away, but the sound of Smithy's voice began to bring me back to reality. I could feel it pulling me towards it like I was being towed on a lifeline. A moment later, the pressure on my throat released. Smithy grabbed Tank by the back of his top and hauled him off me. I was like a baby taking its first breath. Gasping. Swallowing. Chest heaving. Fighting to try and fill my lungs. When I managed to, I wished I hadn't bothered. The overpowering smell of garlic hit me right at the back of the throat. I thought I was going to gag.

As soon as I was strong enough to move, I scrambled toward the headboard. While I tried to come to terms with what had just happened, I watched Smithy manoeuvre Tank with ease. The huge monster of a man weighed a tonne. I'd been powerless to stop him. Thank God Smithy arrived in the nick of time and stepped in before Tank tried to rape me again.

When they squared up to each other with fists clenched like two heavyweights in a ring, I tucked my legs under myself. My chest felt heavy, as though a boulder was weighing down on it. My heart was racing and my pulse was galloping at the side of my neck. I was struggling to regulate my breathing. But I knew I was lucky to have escaped being assaulted. If Smithy hadn't walked in when he did, there would have been a different outcome.

'What the fuck were you doing to her?' Smithy shouted. His eyes were blazing.

'Why are you so bothered? She's just a bit of skirt.'

Smithy's features hardened. 'Look at the state of her.' His head snapped around in my direction. I could feel the intense weight of the men's eyes on me. Penetrating. Fear inducing. 'She's terrified of you. You're a fucking animal.'

'And you're such a gent!' Tank fired back before he let out a laugh.

'You were going to rape her, weren't you?'

'So what if I was,' Tank challenged.

'You're a sick bastard. No wonder she's been acting strangely. You've done this before, haven't you?' Smithy pushed Tank in the chest with the palm of his massive hand.

It didn't take a lot to provoke Tank, so he was riled up and ready to do battle in the blink of an eye.

'Don't you dare put your fucking hands on me,' Tank roared.

I dropped my head, rounded my shoulders and hugged my knees.

'What are you going to do about it?' Smithy puffed out his chest. He was determined not to let the matter go.

I tried to push myself further into the headboard, but I was as far back as I could get. I hated confrontation and didn't want to witness their fight, but there was nowhere I could go, so I screwed my eyes shut to block out the sight of them. Seconds later, my eyes sprung open when I heard the sound of a car coming this way. I wanted to scream at the top of my lungs, but Smithy and Tank were standing metres away from me, so my cries for help would have been short-lived.

'I'll stay with the girl. You go downstairs and see what's going on, and make sure you're discreet,' Smithy said.

This was it. The moment I'd been waiting for. Help was coming. Tank darted out of the room and charged down the stairs. Shortly afterwards, I heard the sound of muffled voices, and then the car drove away.

'Who was it?' Smithy asked when Tank walked back into the room.

'It was the boss. There's shit going down, so he might need backup at short notice. He wants us to stay tooled up and ready for action,' Tank said.

I was shocked by how civil they were being. They were carrying on as though they hadn't been at war with each other moments ago. The whole thing was surreal.

'Are you hungry?' Smithy asked, holding up the carrier bag of food.

I shook my head. I couldn't trust myself to speak in case I burst into tears. I wished I could be brave. Be strong. But that didn't come naturally to me. I was a wreck.

'We'd better get some down our necks before we're called out,' Tank said, then the two men walked out of the room and I dissolved into floods of tears.

45

MACKENZIE

Tuesday 6 January

I'd been out for the count, thanks to the weed and booze I'd had earlier, when I suddenly felt a weird pressure on my neck. I tried to take a deep breath, but something was crushing my windpipe. My eyes flickered open. My vision was blurry, so it took a moment for it to register what was going on. I froze when I realised Arben and two of his guys were hovering over me.

Arben flicked the light switch next to the bed. I squinted, then blinked a couple of times until my eyes focused and adjusted to the brightness. I recognised his entourage, dressed in Adidas puffer jackets, instantly. They were the men who'd been sent to collect the money he'd demanded from me for the coke. The guy holding the machete to my throat was the nutter desperate to practise his carvery skills the last time we'd met. I'd never forget his face or the evil glint in his cold killer's eye.

How the hell did he find me? I'd cut and run to put some distance between us, reasoning I'd be easier to track down if I'd stayed in London. I never expected Arben to sniff me out in

Dover. Let alone break into the Old Mill House in the middle of the night without triggering the alarm or me hearing a sound.

Arben gestured to his guys with a flick of the head. The knife wielding maniac moved the machete away from my throat, so I took a gasp of air. Before I'd fully inflated my lungs, they ripped the quilt off me, dragged me out of the bed and hauled me down the corridor to the kitchen. The ticking clock on the wall filled the silence, counting down the time before one of us was forced to speak.

'I had such high hopes for you, MacKenzie,' Arben said.

I didn't know how to respond. I was worried I might say the wrong thing, so I opted to keep my mouth shut while fixing my eyes on his to show I was giving him my full attention. He moved away from me and switched on the ceramic hob. Moments later, it began glowing red. I felt my guts rumble.

'What made you think counterfeit notes were an acceptable form of currency? I told you there would be consequences, didn't I?' Arben's dark brown eyes bored into mine, and my Adam's apple started dancing in my throat.

'I honestly don't know how that could have happened. I checked the notes myself, and they were genuine,' I babbled. My choice of words were a gamble.

'So what are you trying to say? Are you accusing me of lying?' Arben's features hardened.

'Of course not. I'm just saying there must be some sort of misunderstanding.'

'There is no misunderstanding. The notes were fake.' Arben narrowed his eyes and glared at me.

'What, all of them?' The words leapt out of my mouth before I could stop them.

Arben didn't look impressed that I'd questioned him, so I kept my thoughts to myself. If the odd dodgy fifty had slipped through sixty grand's worth of cash, I could have believed it. But there was no way the whole lot of them were forgeries. I handled money every day of the week. I could spot a fake a mile off, and there was no way I'd have intentionally passed any on to the Albanian. I didn't have a death wish.

'Yes, all of them. I'm getting a bit fed up of your attitude. I don't appreciate you implying myself or anyone who works for me is dishonest.'

Arben's eyes shifted sideways, and my heart began to race. A split second later, two of his goons dragged me over to the hob.

'I'm going to give you a little taster of what's in store for you,' Arben said.

Then the guy who'd been holding the machete to my throat wrenched my arm up and started to force my hand down on the glowing ring. I bucked and thrashed around as I tried to break free, but the hold the men had on me was too strong. I let out a blood-curdling yell as I tried to pull my hand away.

Pain shot through my body when my skin made contact with the red-hot surface. The smell of burning flesh filled the air around us. I'd reached my threshold. I was in a bad way. I'd never experienced agony like it.

'Please let me go,' I begged. I was embarrassed that I was having to grovel, but I was desperate.

I turned my face towards Arben. He was grinning from ear to ear. Then he gave his guys the nod, and Machete Man and his sidekick released their grip on me.

I had to wrench my hand off the hob. It had stuck to the plate like steak on a griddle. I was trembling from head to toe. I gripped my right wrist with my left hand to try and stop the throbbing before I turned my hand over to survey the damage. My palm was charred black. The entire surface was thickened and had a dry, leathery appearance. The pain was unbearable. My legs felt like jelly.

'I suspected you'd be a pussy. Your taster punishment only lasted a couple of seconds. How are you going to cope when we really get stuck into you?' Arben grinned.

I felt my blood run cold.

'I'll give you exactly a week to come up with the money. If you don't pay up, you're going to suffer.'

I was already suffering, so I took the threat seriously. But if I had to cough up for gear I hadn't managed to shift a second time, I might as well let him snuff me out now and save myself a week of turmoil.

'Sixty grand is a lot of money. I'm going to need more time than that,' I replied, my face contorting as I spoke through the pain.

Arben shook his head and laughed. 'What makes you think you owe sixty grand? You're late paying, and the debt carries interest. I want one hundred grand by next Tuesday, MacKenzie.'

'A hundred grand?' The shock of what I'd just heard made me temporarily forget the agony I was in.

Arben nodded. 'If Zerina hadn't told me where you were hiding, you'd owe a hell of a lot more.'

My heart sank. I'd made a rookie mistake. Everyone knew walls had ears. I could kick myself for telling Carly where I was living. Daisy and I wouldn't be safe here now that Arben had found out.

46

LILY

'Here's your breakfast,' Tank said when he walked into the room.

I shifted in my seat and edged away from him when he put the glass and plate down on the table, which made him smile.

'I don't care if you're not hungry. I'm not going anywhere until you finish the lot,' Tank threatened.

My pulse started racing in my wrist. I looked at him warily. Even though I could hear Smithy moving around downstairs, I still felt uncomfortable being alone with him. I couldn't trust him. Not after what he'd done to me.

'Hurry up. I haven't got all fucking day.'

Tank's booming voice made me jump out of my skin. He laughed. I wanted to burst into tears, but I managed not to. I didn't want to give him the satisfaction of seeing me break down.

'Do as you're fucking told.' Tank raised his fist, and I cowered.

'Please don't hurt me,' I begged, suddenly engulfed by a feeling of desperation.

I was pathetic. Disgusted with myself. But I didn't know how else to react. His behaviour was outside my control.

'If you don't get that down your neck right now, there'll be consequences. And don't start fucking blubbering, or I'll give you something to cry about,' Tank grinned.

'I'm sorry. I'm going to eat it right now,' I said apologetically.

I eyed the plate through a veil of tears. The sight of the slightly burnt white toast swimming with butter made nausea start to well up inside me. I liked healthy, nutritious food, so the thought of eating worthless carbohydrates that would spike my blood sugar and insulin, along with a generous helping of fat, made panic rise up in me. It was going to take a Herculean effort on my part to get through the whole slice. I wasn't at all confident I could do it. But I had to force myself to try.

My limbs were stiff from underuse, so I moved like an eighty-year-old woman. Slow. Cautious. I was frail from lack of food. Weary from lack of sleep. Weepy from the helplessness of the situation. But I somehow managed to reach across and pick up the glass of orange juice. I could tell by the smirk on his face that he'd put something in the drink. I wasn't stupid. I locked eyes with him. I wanted him to know that I knew. But I followed his instructions like I'd been brainwashed.

I didn't know what he'd put in the juice. It was probably better not to know what I was drinking. I wouldn't dare disobey him. I was scared to death of him. I'd witnessed what he was capable of, so I knew I had to stay on his good side. I couldn't take much more of this. I was losing hope. Losing my mind. Losing the will to live. There was nothing else I could do but comply. I switched on autopilot and took the path of least resistance. Showing fearlessness didn't come naturally to me. I liked to retreat inside my shell until it was safe to come out.

I bit into the slice of buttered toast, which had gone cold and soggy, and started to chew. It was repulsive, so I started washing big chunks of it down with the bitter-tasting juice to get it over and done with sooner. I felt myself shudder as I wiped away the greasy film covering my lips with the back of my hand. The minute I put the empty plate and glass back on the table, Tank picked them up and walked out of the room.

As soon as he'd closed the door behind him, I lay down on the bed, closed my eyes and focused on the sound of my heartbeat pounding in my ears while I waited for the drugs to take effect. It didn't take long for me to zonk out. I drifted in and out of sleep. Bad dreams kept jolting through me. Every time I woke, my eyes strained as I tried to focus. I kept forgetting where I was until the clink of the chain forced reality to the forefront of my mind.

47

DAISY

'I've just spoken to a nice young man at the estate agents. I told him I'd changed my mind and wanted to check out the area before I arranged a viewing. He very kindly gave me the address and a bit of background info. The units have only just gone on the market, and all of them are still available apart from one.' Bernice smiled.

'That's fantastic news.' I grinned back at her.

'I know, darling, and what's even better is the place isn't far from here. The industrial estate is off Battersea Park Road.'

After the relief came the uneasiness. Bernice's words made the contents of my stomach flip. I felt my features lock as the smile slid from my face.

'It looks like our hunch was right. Samson must be behind all of this. The warehouse is slap bang in the middle of his territory,' Bernice said.

I was inwardly seething. He'd tried to convince me that MacKenzie or Arben were responsible to keep the heat away from himself. I despised him more than I would have thought was humanly possible. I wasn't going to let him get away with taking my sister. He needed to pay for what he'd done to Lily. For what he'd done to me. I wanted revenge. And I was going to get it.

'With any luck, all of this will be over soon.' The sound of Bernice's voice brought me back to the present.

'Is Roscoe on his way?'

Bernice shook her head. 'I haven't told him we think we've found the property.'

'Why not?'

'It'll take Roscoe hours to get here, so I'm going to take matters into my own hands.'

My temples started to throb. 'You're not suggesting we go on our own, are you?' I questioned as dread started rising up within me.

'That's what I had in mind.'

'I'm not keen on that idea.' I steepled my fingers in front of my lips.

'Don't look so worried, darling.'

My mouth dropped open when I saw Bernice take a handgun out of her Chanel handbag and push it into the waistband of her wet-look PVC spray-on trousers. Her high ponytail and figure-hugging clothes reminded me of Lara Croft. Albeit an older version.

'Honestly, darling, it's no big deal. You'll be in safe hands with me. I'm armed and dangerous. I'm not afraid to take on a man, so those guys had better take cover.' Bernice laughed.

She was trying to make light of the situation, but I wasn't amused in the slightest. I was terrified. She might look every inch the glamorous badass, but I wasn't convinced she'd be able to pull off the role if things turned ugly. I'd seen the blokes who'd snatched Lily. They were huge. Dangerous. I had a horrible feeling the two of us were going to be out of our depth.

'Shall we hit the road?' Bernice asked.

I held her gaze, but I didn't know what to say. I stood in the middle of the kitchen floor, paralysed by fear. Bernice caught hold of my hand and weaved me through the house. She took no notice of my reluctance, which was probably a good thing. Lily needed help. We couldn't afford to wait hours for the cavalry to arrive.

Once we were inside her car, she kept the conversation going to distract me from what we were about to do.

'I'm sure I don't need to tell you I'm no shrinking violet. Blending in with the crowd never appealed to me. I like to stand out, which is why I have waist-length hair extensions, lip fillers, Botox and a boob job. I'm on a quest for eternal youth and fully intend to grow old disgracefully.' Bernice let out a belly laugh.

I forced out a smile, trying to mask my discomfort. But she saw through the front I was putting on.

'I'm not walking into this blindly.' Bernice tore her eyes off the road to glance at me. 'I know a lot about how this business operates. I've lived a colourful life. Before I married Roscoe, I was the trophy girlfriend of a powerful gangster. His work was dangerous, and he didn't want me to be vulnerable, so he taught me how to fire a gun and look after myself. We were living it up in Spain back then, but I came back to England after he was gunned down in broad daylight by a rival gang.'

'Oh my God, that's awful.' I was genuinely taken aback by what she'd just told me.

Bernice let out a slow breath. 'I'd planned to put the lifestyle behind me. And I had. I was running a pub when Roscoe walked in one day and blew me away. He was such a gent. He literally swept me off my feet. I wasn't looking for love, but I fell for his charms anyway. I was powerless to resist. Fast forward a year, and I'm caught in the web again. What can I say? Working-class neighbourhoods are riddled with crime. I resigned myself to the fact that violence would always be a part of my life.'

I knew where she was coming from. Since Lily and I had started working at Eden's, we'd seen our fair share of trouble, and something told me there was a lot worse to come. I couldn't help thinking we were going to have a wasted journey. My fear was that Lily had been auctioned as a sex slave on the dark web right after she'd been kidnapped, and we weren't going to find any trace of her no matter how hard we tried. Logic told me to reserve judgement and not go jumping to conclusions. But I was impulsive, and lifelong habits were hard to break.

48

LILY

I could see from the skylight above that it was daylight when I woke. I had no idea how long I'd been asleep. Time was distorted. Could it have been twenty-four hours or more? Who knew, but my head still felt groggy from whatever Tank had given me. I almost begged him for some more so that I could block all of this out. When I drifted off, I was plagued by bad dreams. I'd always been highly strung, but at this stage, my hysteria was barely contained. Now that I was stuck in a never-ending nightmare.

I wasn't sure how long I'd been here now. Time crawled by. Seconds, minutes, hours, days. They all blurred together. There was nothing to do during the periods of isolation apart from stare at the four walls and watch the sky change from day to night.

Dark thoughts constantly surrounded me as my mind ran away with itself. Hopelessness was my only companion while I waited for help that I wasn't sure was coming. It was almost impossible to stay positive. The desire to curl up in a ball and stop breathing was overwhelming. I rocked backwards and forwards as my emotions poured out of me. Silent tears so nobody else would hear.

What was going to happen to me when the men left? Would they free me first or leave me chained to the wall? Were they going to keep giving me stuff to knock me out? Or did they have something else in store for me? I knew too much to be able to walk away, even if I promised not to breathe a word of my ordeal to anyone. And I would commit to that if they'd let me go. I'd never snitch on them. I'd be too scared to break my promise. But they'd never agree to that. They were never going to let me survive.

This whole situation was bizarre. I was the one being held prisoner, but I was a real threat to their freedom. No criminal would jeopardise that. I was doomed. Death was a certainty. I was convinced of that. Waiting for it to happen was drawn out. A different kind of torture.

Trying to second guess what was in store for me was doing my head in. I bit down on my bottom lip to help me focus. It wasn't working. I was still attempting to figure things out when I thought I heard a noise in the distance. I tilted my head towards the exterior wall and listened. There it was again. A very subtle sound in the background, like white noise. A low drone you almost didn't notice. Was it a car? I couldn't be sure. It was too far away. It had stopped now, whatever it was. But I may well have imagined it.

I was on high alert. Oversensitive to things going on around me. Constantly on guard. Tank posed a threat that was never far away. At least Smithy treated me with a bit of respect. He'd saved me from Tank. Saved me from being sexually assaulted a second time. The thought of that sent a shiver down my spine.

The memory was so fresh. So clear. I felt dirty every time I thought about what he'd done to me. Wished I could shed my skin like a snake. Have a fresh start. A new beginning. That was a pipe dream. I was scarred for life after the horrific, terrifying ordeal. I didn't want to accept it, but I had to face facts. This would change my entire world forever.

I knew I'd never get over it. I just hoped it wouldn't happen again. I wouldn't be strong enough to cope if it did. So far, I'd survived being kidnapped. But this was far from over. I couldn't allow myself to think about that now. I needed my mind to shut down. To stop my fear from taking over. To stop my thoughts from racing. To stop myself from losing hope. My dreams of freedom were shattered.

49

DAISY

'The estate agent said all the units were empty except one. But the industrial estate looks deserted. Why don't we leave the car here and check it out on foot?' Bernice suggested.

That could take hours. The place looked vast. White corrugated buildings stretched as far as the eye could see.

'I know it seems like a daunting task, but if Lily's being held here, we don't want to tip off the kidnappers by driving up to the door, do we?' Bernice had obviously read my thoughts.

'I see what you mean.' Whether I liked it or not, she had a point.

We'd been wandering around for an eternity, and there was no sign of activity at any of the warehouses. My feet were beginning to throb, and I was wearing trainers. Bernice had to be a good thirty years older than me, and she was striding along, her ponytail swishing behind her in a pair of sky-scraper patent boots. I was amazed she wasn't hobbling.

I was beginning to think the estate agent had made a mistake, and that all the units were empty when I spotted a black SUV in the distance parked outside the very end lock-up. A shiver ran down my spine as I had a flashback to the night Lily was snatched.

'Daisy, are you OK?'

I felt Bernice's fingers touch my arm and suddenly realised she'd stopped walking and was looking at me. I was frozen to the spot, staring straight ahead, my eyes glued to the SUV.

'I can't be 100 per cent sure, but I'm fairly certain that's the car the kidnappers were driving when they snatched Lily,' I said with a tremor in my voice.

Bernice's blue eyes started to shine. 'That's fantastic! We're one step closer to finding her. Let's take a look.'

'Don't you think you should call Roscoe and let him know?'

Bernice shook her head. 'No way. He'll tell me to wait for back-up, and it'll take hours for him to drive up from Dover.'

My pulse started racing. Bernice was digging her heels in, but instead of helping Lily, there was a real chance we could end up becoming her cellmates. This could be a disastrous move. Nobody else knew we were here.

Silence spread out between us. Unspoken words lay just beneath the surface. Desperate to claw their way out. I was fighting to keep them inside. Keep them to myself. Tact and diplomacy didn't feature highly on my list of character credentials. But I couldn't just go along with this without voicing my opinion.

'I think it's a terrible idea,' I blurted out.

Bernice looked at me steely-eyed. She attempted to raise her perfectly arched eyebrows, but they only moved a fraction of a millimetre thanks to the Botox filling her forehead.

'Why? You want to get your sister back, don't you?'

'Yes, but what happens if we get captured too? You haven't even told Roscoe what we've found out so we could disappear into thin air like Lily did? He wouldn't know where to look for us. I think it's a stupid move to—'

'I've got no intention of putting us in danger. I just want to get a better look. You can go back to the car if you're uncomfortable with that,' Bernice cut in, stopping me mid-flow.

I felt like Bernice had pushed my concerns to one side as she slapped me down to size. I couldn't stop her from going ahead without me, but I didn't want to go back to the car on my own either. Maybe I should text Mum and tell her we were looking into a possible lead and give her the address so that somebody knew our whereabouts. Surely, it wouldn't hurt to reach out. I was still mulling over what to do when Bernice started striding off without me, so I scuttled after her. My decision was made.

As we approached, we could see the shutters were pulled three-quarters of the way down, so it was impossible to look inside. We had no idea if Lily was in there. If she was, there was no way of knowing how many people were holding her.

'Let's take a look around the back. There might be another door,' Bernice whispered.

I followed two steps behind her. The cube-shaped structure, covered in corrugated steel, was enormous. It looked impenetrable, like an armoured box. There wasn't a single window, but there was another door to the rear. The shutters were only raised a little bit, no doubt, to keep prying eyes out.

I had no idea what was going through Bernice's head at this precise moment, but I hoped she wasn't planning to storm the building. It would be a risky move. It wasn't as though the two of us were highly trained paratroopers.

I let out a sigh of relief when Bernice said. 'OK, I've seen enough. Let's go back to the car.'

We walked to where Bernice had parked her cherry-red sporty Jaguar XE in silence. There was a bit of an atmosphere between us since I'd spoken up, but I was trying not to dwell on it. Hopefully, it would all blow over. We were both strong characters used to doing things our own way, so it made sense that sometimes we'd clash.

'I'm not trying to force you into anything, but I'm just telling you what I'm planning to do. It's getting late now, and dusk is the burglar's best friend. It takes a while for people's eyes to adjust to the changing light, so I'll take advantage of that. I'll wait for darkness to start falling, and then I'm going in,' Bernice announced.

My mouth dropped open. Bernice had nerves of steel. I was shocked that she was prepared to wade in on her own. Much as I thought she was making a terrible mistake, I couldn't let her go alone. The prospect of freeing Lily was exciting but terrifying. This was the opportunity I'd been waiting for. I just wished I wasn't scared stiff.

50

SAMSON

I'd been spending every waking moment at Eden's, not out of choice, out of necessity, since that scrawny little fucker MacKenzie shot through. I never usually darkened the doorstep regularly. I liked surrounding myself with an air of mystery. Being a hands-on boss wasn't my scene at all, but somebody had to stop the ship from sinking. Protecting my business interests had become my top priority.

MacKenzie had done a disappearing act and left me in the lurch on New Year's Eve without paying back the money he owed. Did he seriously think I'd forget about that? Wiping the slate clean wasn't on the cards for him. I always held a grudge against people who wronged me. Harbouring resentment and bitterness long after somebody had done the dirty came naturally to me.

I wouldn't rest until I made MacKenzie suffer. He was a chancer. A waste of space. Scum of the earth. I'd be doing the world a favour when I stuck a bullet between his eyes. He knew the ins and outs of how my business operated, so he couldn't just walk away. I'd be up to my neck in shit if he blabbed. I wasn't going to follow in my old man's footsteps and do time. Life was too short to get banged up. MacKenzie had to go. I couldn't take the risk.

MacKenzie reckoned he had a way with words. Fancied himself as a sweet talker. I'd seen him in action. Some people fell for the crap he spouted. I didn't doubt he'd promise me till he was blue in the face that he'd keep his trap shut. But the long and short of it was I couldn't trust a word the scruffy wanker said. He'd proved that to me a hundred times over, so he'd only have himself to blame when he was six feet under.

I'd been sitting in my office, sipping a single malt on the rocks, fantasising about the best way to torture and kill MacKenzie, when there was a knock on the door. 'What's up?' I called from my leather chair.

'Sorry to bother you, boss, but a guy from the council's asking to see you,' Jermaine said from the open doorway.

I was livid. My jaw began to spasm. What the hell did he want? Tuesdays had been dead since I'd cut the twins' act. He'd be lucky if we had twenty people across the threshold. And more to the point, why hadn't Boyd tipped me off? So much for having 'friends' in the force. He was meant to warn me when there was a check in the pipeline so I could make sure the officials didn't find anything when they came sniffing around.

They say bad luck comes in threes, and I was inclined to agree. I'd had my fair share of it recently. I'd been losing valuable drug trade since MacKenzie's departure. Then there was the problem with my shipment of cocaine, and the twins' career hitting the skids, all in a short space of time. So, I was overdue an upturn in fortunes.

I'd thought employing Crystal Tits and a couple of other slappers to do some exotic dancing would keep the punters rolling in. But the pervs they were attracting were only interested in wanking off in the bogs. They weren't buying any gear and were the type of geezers who sipped the same warm pint all night. If they pushed as much cash through my tills as they stuffed in the strippers' knickers, I might be in with a chance of making a profit.

'Did he say what he wanted?'

Jermaine shook his head.

51

MACKENZIE

I was shocked to find out that Zerina knew Arben. Was he the mysterious cousin Carly was working for? I had a horrible feeling he was. Blood was thicker than water, wasn't it? I didn't know Zerina from Adam so that would explain why she happily threw me under the bus. She must have overheard me telling Carly I was staying at the Old Mill House, which led Arben to my door.

Running away came across as weak. But standing my ground hadn't been an option. I was a grown man. Master of my own destiny. I knew I'd have to deal with the fallout when it inevitably came knocking. It was only a matter of time before Arben or Samson caught up with me.

If I'd had longer to hatch a plan, I'd have disappeared abroad. Maybe bought a van with false compartments like a magician's box and set up my own operation. Now that I knew a kilo of cocaine cost thirty thousand euros in Rotterdam, I'd have been able to pay back Samson in no time, doubling my money on the short ferry crossing. I had a feeling my debt with Arben would never be cleared. But fate had other ideas. Arben had tracked me down, so shooting through was out of the question. He'd have eyes on me. That was a given.

* * *

'What happened to your hand?' Roscoe asked when he walked into the living area.

'Arben and two of his guys paid me a visit in the early hours of the morning to deliver the latest ultimatum. I need to pay him one hundred grand by next week. This was just a taster.'

I held up my heavily bandaged hand. I'd been numbing the pain with coke and alcohol, but it was still throbbing like a bastard.

'Jesus Christ! How did they find you? I thought you'd be safe here.'

'You know I told you Carly's working for Zerina's cousin?' I said.

'Yeah.' Roscoe nodded.

'I'm not 100 per cent certain, but I think Arben's the mystery man. Carly said this was the first time she'd worked for him in Dover, but she'd previously sold gear for him in London.'

'I hate to say it, but I think you might be right,' Roscoe said. 'That fucker can't just set up shop wherever he feels like it. This is my territory. What are we going to do about it, son?'

I wasn't sure there was anything we could do to stop Arben. He had a powerful army behind him. Roscoe was no match for him.

'It's a good thing the girls are out of the way if it's all going to kick off. I'll text Bernice and see if there's any news. Encourage her to stay put.'

I couldn't think of anything worse than standing up to Arben.

Over the years, I'd learnt to express myself without having to use my fists. I was a talker, not a fighter. Roscoe was delusional if he thought we could take on the Albanians. They were big-time gangsters in a different league. We were going to be lambs to the slaughter.

52

DAISY

'Wish me luck,' Bernice said, turning to face me.

'I'm coming with you,' I replied, opening the car door before I had a chance to change my mind.

I pulled up the collar of my coat to block out the winter chill. It felt like it had dropped several degrees since we'd been waiting in the car. I glanced around to make sure no one was watching us as we began walking towards the unit at the furthest edge of the industrial estate. As we approached, I wondered how we were going to get inside. We could hardly just knock on the door and expect them to open up and welcome us in.

The front of the building looked the same as it had earlier, so Bernice and I made our way around the back. We stopped in our tracks when we spotted the shutters were open and made eye contact with each other but we didn't say a word. I held my breath when a man in his twenties came out for a smoke. He was tall and powerfully built. I instinctively flattened myself to the wall, closed my eyes and hoped he wouldn't see us. When I cautiously allowed my lids to open, I got the shock of my life. Bernice was standing behind the guy, digging a gun into his right kidney. A moment earlier, she'd been next to me. I hadn't heard her move. By the look of horror on the man's face, neither had he.

I hadn't expected Bernice to spring into action like Wonder Woman, but the second an opportunity had presented itself, she'd acted on it. I was shitting myself. There was no going back now. We had no idea what we were walking into. No idea how many people were in the warehouse. No idea how this was going to unfold. Everything was unfamiliar. I was out of my depth. I felt like running away. But I couldn't do that to Bernice. We were in this together. My confidence was evaporating into thin air. I had to compose myself. Had to pull myself together. Had to be strong. Lily needed me. I couldn't let her down.

By the way Bernice was holding the gun, I could tell she wasn't bullshitting. She knew exactly how to use it. I wasn't going to be much of a backup. I wasn't even armed. I'd never held a gun before, let alone fired one. I was an unskilled accomplice. I didn't know the first thing about situations like this. And yet here I was, wading in behind her. I was pretty sure I was going to be more of a hindrance than a help, but I didn't have time to dwell on that. I'd thought we'd be treading carefully. Not going into the lion's den all guns blazing.

'Keep your mouth shut and start moving. One word out of you, and I'll blow your head off,' Bernice said as she ground the barrel of the gun into the man's back.

I had to hand it to her. She had bigger balls than most men I'd met.

The first thing that struck me when I stepped inside was how enormous the space was. It was much bigger than it looked from the outside. My eyes jumped around the cavernous, double-height room, trying to take in all the details in a split second. Looking for clues. Looking for Lily. Light bounced off the walls and floors. Everything was immaculate. So white. So bright.

I stood level with Bernice, shoulder to shoulder. Putting on a united front. I wanted her to think she could rely on me. Even though I wasn't sure she could. But I was determined to dig deep and do everything in my power to assist her. I just hoped grit and determination counted for something.

'What the fuck's going on?' another guy suddenly roared when he spotted us.

He was standing on the far side of the warehouse in front of the shutters. He had a voice like a foghorn, which gave me the fright of my life. I thought my heart was going to break out of my ribcage, it was pounding so hard against it.

Bernice didn't answer his question. So I asked one instead. 'Where's Lily?'

The two men made eye contact with each other, and a silent exchange passed between them. I couldn't see my sister, but I could sense her. I didn't need their confirmation. We were in the right place. She was here somewhere. Out of sight, but close by. I was sure of it. My eyes scurried left and right as I searched for her.

'We know you're holding her. Why don't you make things easy for yourself and tell us where she is?' Bernice questioned.

The man standing over by the front shutters started laughing, and I saw Bernice bristle in response. Something told me he was making a big mistake underestimating Roscoe Allen's wife.

'I don't know what you're talking about, love,' the guy replied.

'I think you do, and if you don't start spilling the beans, I'm going to blow your friend's brains out.'

'Fuck me, my sides are splitting. Who d'you think you are? Gangster Granny?'

The guy let out a belly laugh, and the atmosphere changed in the room. A second later, the contents of my stomach somersaulted when I heard Bernice cock the trigger. The click barely had time to register before the sound of a gunshot filled the room.

It made me jump. My ears were ringing as the noise bounced around the empty room.

My breath caught in my chest. I'd been expecting to see the man she was aiming the gun at drop to his knees, but he stood where he was, rooted to the spot, staring straight ahead. His eyes were wide with fear. It took me a moment to realise Bernice had shot the other guy. The one who'd been disrespecting her. The penny only dropped when I saw him sliding down the wall. Then I noticed the back of his head was sprayed across the pristine walls like some kind of grotesque three-dimensional artwork.

I'd only ever seen the kind, caring side of Bernice. Who knew she could be such a badass? Her actions had taken me by surprise. Blindsided me. We'd spent a lot of time in each other's company lately. I thought I knew what made her tick. But the realisation hit me like a thunderbolt that I had no idea what was going on behind her eyes. Behind her smile. Never in my wildest dreams would I have imagined the woman who oozed compassion and surrounded me with love and generosity could have such a ruthless side.

'Now, unless you want to end up like your friend, you'd better make sure you speak to me in a respectful manner,' Bernice threatened. 'Who were you working for?'

I wondered why Bernice had asked the question in the past tense, but I didn't dwell on the matter when I heard the man's response.

'Samson Fox.'

Our suspicions had been confirmed, but it didn't bring me any comfort. Quite the opposite. I'd experienced first-hand what the depraved pervert was capable of. I just hoped Lily hadn't been subjected to the same treatment.

'I'm going to make this really simple for you. Tell me where Lily is, and you'll get to walk away without me harming a hair on your head. Do you think you can do that?' Bernice's tone was soft and gentle.

The huge man slowly shook his head.

Although I'd initially thought Bernice had been a bit hasty when she'd fired the gun, she clearly knew what she was doing. She was the puppet master and had complete control over the big oaf in front of her. She would have been no match for him strength-wise. He could have easily overpowered her, but he was in a robotic state. When somebody was pointing a gun at you, they had your total respect. Size meant nothing in a situation like this.

'I'll ask you one more time, and you'd better tell me the truth, or you'll have to face the consequences. Where's Lily?'

The man only had to look at his colleague's body lying slumped against the wall to know what would happen if he chose not to follow Bernice's orders.

'She's upstairs,' he replied, spitting the words out without hesitation.

'Now that wasn't so hard, was it?' Bernice's tone was calm. Collected. Then she cocked the trigger, moved the gun up to the base of the man's skull, and blew his brains out before he had a chance to reply.

The sound of my gasp took me by surprise. I covered my mouth with my right hand as the man collapsed in a heap on the floor. He keeled over almost in slow motion like a tree being felled. His body made a loud thud when it hit the floor seconds later. Fragments of flesh and bone rained down on him and settled on the glossy white tiles. He was lying face down with the cavernous hole at the base of his head on display for all to see. I tore my eyes away. I couldn't bear to look at the gruesome sight.

'Are you OK, darling?' Bernice asked, focusing her attention on me.

'I'm fine,' I replied, doing my best to front it out. Who was I trying to kid? I was a mess, trembling from head to toe.

'I'm sorry you had to witness that. I hadn't intended to kill them when I walked in. Killing somebody is so extreme. Taking a life is final. But that dickhead sealed his own fate when he started taking the piss out of me. I couldn't ignore it. I had to stand my ground. Men like that rile me up. I wanted him to know what I was capable of. Teach him a lesson.'

'I get that, but why did you kill the other guy?' He'd been putty in Bernice's hands.

'He was collateral damage. When you leave loose ends unfinished, they have a habit of coming back to haunt you,' Bernice explained.

'I'm surprised you shot him before you checked whether he was lying or not,' I said. If Lily wasn't upstairs, we might never find her now. Part of me wished Bernice had checked out his story before she'd pulled the trigger.

'I can assure you he was telling the truth.' Bernice's words were confident. She didn't have a shred of doubt.

I was more sceptical. He could have just said that to buy himself some time and tell her what she wanted to hear as a stalling tactic. More of the guys could be just around the corner. Four of them had snatched Lily. Only two were in the warehouse.

53

LILY

My head was groggy from the stuff Tank had given me. It felt like somebody had replaced my brain with cotton wool. My thoughts were fuzzy. Muddled. I'd thought I'd heard Daisy's voice. Thought I'd heard her saying my name. My ears pricked up. I listened. I must have been dreaming. There was nothing but silence. It felt tense. Threatening. It filled me with uncertainty.

A moment later, there was another sound. Something was going on down there. I got up from the bed. As I went to walk, I stumbled. My legs were weak. Bent like pipe cleaners under my weight. I steadied myself and staggered across the room as far as I could before the chain stopped me. I could just about make out a woman's voice. Was this the boss? Or had she come to save me? Free me. Was the nightmare over?

I didn't hesitate. I screamed, 'Help! Help me!' at the top of my lungs. I stopped shouting and listened. No response, so I started screaming again. A long, continuous cry until the sound petered out. My throat was hoarse. Croaky. Dehydration had taken its toll on me. I'd tried to raise the alarm, but I had a horrible feeling my vocal cords hadn't done a very good job. They were burning. Throbbing.

I waited, but nobody came. I wasn't sure anyone could hear me over the radio. But time was running out for me. I had to get myself noticed. Make some more noise. Cause a commotion. Somehow. Anyhow. I started to scream again, but my voice gave out almost instantly, so I banged the chain off the end of the bed over and over. Metal against metal. The waves reverberated around me. Somebody must have heard the racket. I tilted my head towards the door. Still nothing. Still no acknowledgement. I was about to start again when the unmistakable sound of a gunshot ripped through the silence. It filled me with horror. Left me feeling hollow. Empty. Alone.

54

DAISY

I was reeling from the enormity of the situation. Two men lay dead metres from me. The bright white space was no longer pristine. It was splattered with blood and grey matter. Battle-scarred. The vast room felt airless. Claustrophobic. My head was spinning, jumbled thoughts all over the place. My breathing was fast and erratic. I felt lightheaded. Before I knew what was happening, the contents of my stomach fired out of my body and landed at my feet.

'Aww, you poor thing, are you all right, darling?' Bernice asked as she rubbed my back with her fingertips.

'I'm OK,' I lied. The sight of all the blood was making me feel squeamish.

'Do you want to sit down for a minute?'

I shook my head. 'No, thanks.'

I couldn't believe how quickly Bernice morphed from a cold-blooded killer to a caring motherly figure. The transformation happened in the blink of an eye. But I wasn't scared of her. I was in awe. She was incredible. I was glad she was on my side, though.

Having seen what she was capable of, I wouldn't want to be her enemy.

The sound of Bernice's stiletto boots making contact with the steel steps caught my attention. I'd been so busy trying to compose myself I hadn't realised she'd wandered off. By the time I got to the bottom of the staircase, she was already halfway up. Bernice paused at the top and waited for me to catch up, then gestured for me to do the honours.

I reached for the handle. But something stopped me. I couldn't explain what it was, but it was a strange sensation, as if my subconscious was telling me not to open the door. My breaths came in short gasps as a wave of fear surged through me, tightening every muscle in my body. I was in two minds whether to press down on the handle or not. I was scared of what I was going to find.

Lily's eyes were wide with terror when I pushed open the door and stepped inside. She was sitting on a single bed at the back of the room chained to the wall. Her knees were pulled up to her chest, and her arms were wrapped over them. She blinked, but she didn't say a word. She just stared at me with disbelief written all over her face. She was shell-shocked and it was clear she couldn't process what was happening. She couldn't believe I was standing metres away from her. It was such a surreal moment. I was having trouble processing it, too. There was so much I wanted to say, but the words stayed static on my tongue. I didn't know how to begin.

'W-who's that?' Lily's eyes moved towards the open doorway as she tried to back away.

'Don't be scared, darling. I'm Bernice. I'm Daisy's friend. I'm not going to hurt you. I've come to help you.'

Lily fixed her gaze back on me, and her lips lifted into a smile. 'Thank God you're here. I thought I was going to die. There were times when I wanted to die. I wished I could slip away and end the misery.' Lily's words tumbled out of her mouth and made a lump form in my throat.

'It must have been awful.' I was careful to keep my tone neutral, aware that if I was too sympathetic, it might open the floodgates. Lily was dry-eyed for the moment, but I reckoned she was holding back a tidal wave of emotions that could sweep her off her feet if triggered.

'I could have sworn I heard you say my name a little while ago. I thought my mind was playing tricks on me. I wondered if I was hallucinating from lack of food or the drugs they've been giving me,' Lily said.

'They were drugging you? With what?' I was horrified and couldn't hide the way I felt.

'I don't know. They used to put something in my drinks,' Lily replied.

We fell silent. Lost in our own thoughts.

'I know you've been to hell and back, but you're safe now, darling,' Bernice said as she walked over to where Lily was huddled.

Concern oozed out of her. I felt the familiar stab of jealousy resurface when Bernice dropped down next to Lily and wrapped her arms around her. She held her close. Stroked her hair. Let my twin cry on her shoulder. Quietly at first, but then Lily found her stride and upped the tempo. She started to sob her heart out as though her life depended on it.

'Where are Tank and Smithy?' Lily asked, suddenly pulling away from Bernice.

They must have been the two guys Bernice had sent to meet their maker. I didn't fancy being the one to fill in the blanks, so I let Bernice do the talking.

'They can't hurt you now. They're dead,' Bernice replied, getting straight to the point.

Lily looked shocked. 'I wondered what happened. I heard the gunshots...'

Bernice shrugged. 'It was them or us.'

She was probably right, but she'd snuffed them out before we had a chance to find out. I didn't have an issue with that. It was always best to err on the side of caution and take preventative measures where thugs were concerned.

'Please, can we get out of here?' Lily's voice was coated in desperation.

'Of course we can.' Bernice gave Lily a sympathetic look. 'I just need to find something to cut the restraints. I'll be back in a minute.'

Bernice walked out of the room, and my eyes fixed on Lily. I stared at her, expressionless. I didn't know what to do. How to react. I was so pleased to see her. I wanted to hug her. Comfort her. Tell her everything was going to be all right. But we'd never been close. She might push me away. I didn't want to deal with her rejection. So, instead, I fought my instincts and did nothing. Bernice came back in carrying a pair of pliers, so I let her take the lead. Offer the sympathy. Offer the soothing words. She was better at it than I was.

'I'll have you out of those in a jiffy,' Bernice said. Then she cut the plastic restraints securing Lily to the chain.

My sister was free. The moment should have been euphoric. But it was shrouded in silence. Nobody said a word. Bernice and I watched relief spread over Lily's face before she rubbed at her wrists. There were angry red marks surrounding them. A reminder of the terrible ordeal she'd been through.

'Thank you so much,' Lily said, gratitude seeping out of every pore in her body.

I wasn't sure whether I should tell her about Dad or not. I weighed up how much she was capable of dealing with and then decided she'd reached her limit. I didn't want to be the one to deliver more bad news. More doom and gloom.

Lily stepped towards me, threw her arms around me and buried her face into my neck in a show of sisterly love. I mirrored the action. We both held onto each other as we tried to come to terms with the enormity of the situation in our own way. I was brimming over with happiness that Lily had survived. That we'd been given a second chance. It was hard to describe how incredible it felt to finally experience this long-anticipated hug. I'd heard it said that sisters made the best friends. I couldn't wait to put that theory to the test.

When I'd opened the bedroom door, I had no idea what condition we'd find Lily in. I had to say, she looked better than I'd been expecting. Dark shadows nestled under her eyes, black as rain clouds. She looked tired. A bit drawn. Paler than usual. And thinner. But all in all, not too bad, considering what she'd been through. I had a horrible feeling the wounds from the trauma ran deep. They were lurking out of sight. But not out of mind. Ready to resurface when least expected. They'd take a long time to heal. Some scars never truly faded. But she was alive, and that was all that mattered.

55

SAMSON

I knew MacKenzie had taken his drug paraphernalia with him when he'd shot through because I'd searched his office at the time, and there was no sign of it. But I'd have to hide my stash before I went to meet the Big Cheese from the council, just in case he started snooping around my office.

I'd kept the fucker waiting for ages, but I wanted to ram the message home. If you turned up unannounced, you'd have to wait until I was good and ready. My time was way more important than his. I was a busy man. That bottle of single malt wasn't going to drink itself.

I could see him looking at the memorabilia and photos hanging on the Hall of Fame as I walked along the corridor. He wasn't at all what I'd been expecting. I'd encountered a few different inspectors over the years, but the council's guys were usually one and the same. It was as though it was part of the job description to be approaching retirement age, with grey, balding hair and a large gut. Their swollen waistlines were from gorging on three-course meals funded by taxpayers' money that found their way onto expense sheets under the guise of business meetings.

The boys at Southwark Borough Council had definitely broken the mould with this bloke. He looked completely different; mid-thirties, dark-haired, swarthy complexion with a week's worth of stubble covering his lower face. He was dressed in a navy pin-striped suit. Even from a distance, I could tell it was made from cheap polyester, the type of fabric that sent sparks flying when your thighs rubbed together. I'd immediately taken a dislike to him, and he hadn't even opened his mouth yet. He looked like a hard-nosed son of a bitch.

He turned around as I approached and held out his hand. 'Mr Fox, I'm here to inspect your premises,' he said in a foreign accent.

I didn't know where the geezer was from. He had one of those English is my second language kind of voices that were ten a penny in a vibrant city like London. I was meant to be the sly one. Fox by name. Fox by nature. But he had a shiftiness about him that put me immediately on edge.

'Do you have any seized drugs in your amnesty box?' he asked.

'I have no idea. Eden's manager deals with things like that. He's not here at the moment, but I have a key, so we can take a look,' I replied, doing my best to give off *nothing was too much trouble* vibes.

I was pretty sure MacKenzie would have either hoovered up or sold on anything he'd confiscated, but I led the way to his office anyway. I had to show I was following protocol. A police and council clampdown stipulated that any drugs found on the premises had to be locked away, and the dealer's ID had to be photocopied and passed on to the police. As if that was going to happen.

We were compelled by the police and local licensing boards to stick to the rules and keep drugs out of Eden's. On paper, we were following orders, but the reality was very different. If I reported every lowlife attempting to smuggle gear into the club, it would be used against us. The police would more than likely shut Eden's down. When one of Igor's guys caught somebody carrying, he'd photocopy their ID and tell them the police would be notified. The photocopy was filed in MacKenzie's office. The drugs were seized, and that was the end of the matter. Notifying the Old Bill was a waste of resources.

Naturally, the wasters were refused entry. I didn't want scum like that trying to rip me off. The only dealing tolerated within the club was by my guys. I didn't care what the police and the council said; it was a necessary part of a working nightclub. All the measures we'd put in place wouldn't stop people using drugs. They didn't just want to get drunk. They wanted to get high, too.

I flipped the light switch on, walked into MacKenzie's office and over to his desk. The keys to the box were in the top drawer, so I pulled them out and opened it.

'Looks like it's empty,' I said after peering inside.

The official didn't take my word for it. He came to see for himself. What a nosey bastard!

'What happens to the drugs you confiscate at the door?' he narrowed his dark brown eyes and fixed them on me.

Obviously, I couldn't tell him we sold them on. It would be a shame to see them go to waste.

'We put them in the amnesty box,' I lied, then clamped my lips together to suppress a laugh. He was living in a fantasy world if he believed that.

'It seems very strange that you haven't confiscated any drugs recently. Are you sticking to the guidelines?' His eyes bored into mine.

'Absolutely. I'm offended that you're questioning my honesty,' I replied. Anger pulsed in my throat. I had to push it back down and show some restraint for once.

'Mr Fox, I'm not sure you're taking things as seriously as you should be,' the official said.

'What makes you say that? We do everything by the book.' I could feel my jaw twitching. That was never a good sign. It meant my anger was bubbling under the surface, ready to make an appearance.

'Why so defensive?' When I didn't reply, the cheeky fucker answered for me. 'Sounds like you're hiding something,' he grinned.

If he was trying to be funny, it wasn't working. He was getting right on my tits. I wanted to wipe the smirk off his ugly mug, but I somehow managed to resist the urge to raise my fist.

'I'm not hiding anything. I'm being totally above board. I don't appreciate you implying I'm flouting the rules.'

Eden's was one step away from being regulated into oblivion. The police targeted clubs that didn't introduce strict controls. There used to be other venues around here, but they'd all closed down. I'd done everything I could to avoid bringing in ID scans, breathalyser checks and physical searches, but there was no way around it if I wanted to remain open. And now this jumped-up little tosser was accusing me of not taking things seriously.

'I can assure you nothing underhand is going on. But we've made it so difficult for people to get in if they're carrying drugs, they've given up trying.' My tone was abrupt.

'I find that hard to believe.'

It was true; my punters usually knew better than to try and bring their own gear in.

'I've seen enough to know you're not following the regulations correctly. Failure to comply can result in a hefty fine or the closure of the club...'

'This has got to be a wind-up,' I interrupted.

My alter ego, Mr Nice Guy, had left the building and my tolerance for listening to crap had reached an all-time low. I was bored of the bullshit spilling from his mouth. It didn't take much to make me blow. He'd be on the receiving end of my temper quicker than he knew it.

Unlike the official's predecessors, he seemed hell-bent on dotting the i's and crossing the t's. He was a jobsworth. We'd never had an inspection this close to knocking-off time. The boys from the council were creatures of habit. There was something dodgy about this geezer. I could feel it in my bones.

'I'll be reporting my findings. You can expect a visit from my superior in due course,' the inspector said with a sneer.

I felt like slinging the dickhead onto the pavement by the scruff of his cheap suit, but I didn't want to give the smug bastard the satisfaction of seeing me lose my rag.

56

DAISY

Confusion flooded Lily's face when she spotted the carnage in the warehouse. Bernice had told her Smithy and Tank were dead, but it was clear she hadn't expected them to have met such a gruesome end. Her eyebrows knitted together before her eyes flitted away from the scene. I was desperate to leave but Lily was moving in slow motion. Her limbs were stiff. Her energy levels sapped.

'Are you OK, love? Do you want to rest?' Bernice asked.

Her kindness opened the lock on Lily's emotions, and she began to sob. My heart should have gone out to her after what she'd been through. But I felt a pang of jealousy stab my insides, which reached a new level when Bernice started buzzing around her like a blue-arsed fly. She used to do that to me until Lily had come into the equation. It was happening all over again. I was being pushed to one side in favour of my sister.

Irritation started clawing away at me as Bernice continued to fuss over Lily like a mother hen. Danger lurked all around us. Was I the only one who could sense the trepidation in the air? I wanted to be a million miles from the warehouse, not stuck in the middle of the melodrama surrounded by corpses. If that made me a bad person, so be it. No doubt Karma was waiting to bite me on the arse.

'I don't think we've got time for that. I really think we need to get out of here asap in case Samson turns up,' I said. I couldn't take any more. Lily could cry a river if she had an audience. She needed to cork her tearful display.

Lily stopped mid-blub and stared at me. Bernice was eyeballing me, too. I could tell by the look on their faces that my comment hadn't gone down well. I wasn't trying to be a bitch, but Lily's meltdown had to wait for a more convenient time. Our lives could be on the line.

'Samson Fox?' Lily quizzed.

'Yes. He was behind all of this,' I replied.

Lily looked horrified.

'Do you think you'll be able to make it to the car? It's about a fifteen-minute walk from here.'

Lily didn't answer Bernice's question. Instead, she tilted her head to one side and mulled it over. Anyone would think she had options the way she was carrying on.

'Otherwise, you two could wait here, and I'll go and bring the car back,' Bernice suggested, thinking she was being helpful.

'No way, José. I'm sorry, Lily, I can't stay here. I know you're struggling to walk, but I'll happily give you a piggyback,' I replied.

Silence spread out between us. It made me feel uncomfortable.

'Look, I'm not trying to tell you what to do. It's your decision. If you want to stay, that's fine, but I've got to get out of here. The place gives me the creeps,' I added as Lily seemed to have lost her voice.

When we stepped outside, a blast of cold air hit me in the face. A mixture of fear and excitement flowed through my veins as we inched our way back to the car. Bernice and I were on either side of Lily, linking her arms to stop her from stumbling. We still had a long way to go when suddenly my adrenaline spiked. I was sure somebody was coming up behind us. I could sense someone following us, but I didn't pause. I didn't turn around. I kept looking forward. Kept my worry to myself. I didn't want to scare the shit out of Lily. She was frightened enough without me making things worse. But my confidence was wilting with every pigeon step we took.

I didn't relax until we were all inside the car. I was glad I hadn't said anything now. Lily would have been beside herself. Imagination was a powerful thing. The threat had felt real, but it must have been my mind playing tricks on me. Or maybe it was the wind. It was racing past the metal units, distorting the sounds around us. Making things clang. Making things rustle. The warehouses were deserted, but the silence felt ominous. Loaded.

I let out a sigh of relief when Bernice locked us in the car. But the feeling didn't last long. I'd been looking down at my lap, fastening my seat belt, when a dark shape came into my field of vision. 'Oh my God, is that Samson?' I yelled as I pointed through the windscreen.

We all watched in horror as the car's silhouette moved closer. Nobody spoke or moved. It was like we were frozen in time. The Range Rover looked very similar to Samson's car. It had back and rear blacked-out windows, black alloy wheels with red brake callipers, and the glossiest wet-look paint I'd ever seen. It was very distinctive-looking. It had to be him. It was too much of a coincidence to be anyone else.

Bernice and I instinctively flattened ourselves against the front seats when the car turned the corner. Its lights shone out in front of it like panther's eyes when they were stalking prey. If he was about to ambush us, we were sitting ducks. I held my breath and hoped to God that Bernice's cherry red jag wasn't spotted. She'd parked in a discreet spot, but the colour was eye-catching, so it didn't blend into the background.

When the car was level with us, I could just about make out through the tinted glass that Gary was behind the wheel, and Samson was in the passenger seat. I felt my blood run cold. This could be game over for us.

57

SAMSON

The more I thought about it, the more I was convinced somebody was trying to stitch me up. The council did carry out spot checks without warning from time to time. But there was something odd about the smarmy wanker who'd just visited my premises. I wasn't convinced he was the real deal, even though he had what looked like genuine council ID. He'd gone above and beyond what was necessary. I didn't think I'd ever manage to extract the bastard from the club. He was in no hurry to leave.

Once I sorted out the useless fuckers I'd left guarding the warehouse, I'd phone Boyd and stick a rocket up his arse. He should have given me the heads-up that Southwark Council were about to start meddling in my life. I needed that like a hole in the head right now. It never rained, but it poured.

Gary and I had been heading to the industrial estate when my mobile had started ringing. I'd almost tossed the poxy thing out of the window. It was bound to be more bad news.

'I thought you'd like to know I've tracked down the owner of the prints,' Kyle had said.

He'd worked for me for donkey's years and was a trusted

member of my inner circle, so I'd given him the job of following up on the lead Boyd gave me. That had sounded promising. Maybe my luck was on the up.

'The little toerag's renting a room in Dover, and it just so happens somebody new has started selling coke in that exact location in recent days. In fact, I'd go so far as to say Carly Andrews has been flooding the market with cheap gear,' Kyle had continued.

I'd felt like I was going to blow a gasket. 'So much for Boyd's theory that she was brought in as a scapegoat, and that her prints were planted to send us on a wild goose chase. I'm beginning to wonder if he's got a fucking screw loose. He's not the sharpest tool in the box,' I'd replied.

'That makes two of them. Carly's got to be working for somebody. She wouldn't have the know-how to pull off a stunt like this. She's little more than a junkie,' Kyle had pointed out.

'Well, one name springs to mind. And he just happens to live in Dover, too,' I'd fumed. 'Are you in Kent?'

'Yeah. I'm staking out the hostel where Carly's staying so I can keep an eye on her,' Kyle had replied.

'Good. Don't move a muscle. We'll be with you as soon as we can,' I'd said before ending the call. Then I'd dialled Smithy's number to give him an update, but he didn't pick up, so I tried calling Tank. 'Why aren't that pair of arseholes answering their phones? I told them I'd be in touch.'

Had they forgotten who paid their wages? When I got my hands on them, they'd wish they hadn't blanked me! I gave them strict instructions to stay tooled-up and ready for action. The worst thing I could do was assume my employees were following orders. Assumption was the mother of all fuck ups. They were probably scoffing pizza and guzzling beer as I spoke.

I was fuming. I could feel my blood boiling. Murderous

thoughts raced through my mind as Gary drove past a row of empty warehouses. He parked my Range Rover in front of my unit next to the black SUV. I peered through the windscreen. The shutters were down. Nothing looked out of place.

We stepped outside and walked up to the front entrance. I hammered on the corrugated steel with my fist to get the guys' attention. Music was blaring inside. 'The dozy fuckers mustn't be able to hear me over the racket,' I said. Then I banged again. Harder this time for good measure, but there was still no response. 'Let's go around the back.' I could see Gary's shadow looming over me as we walked down the side of the building. He was one hell of a big lump. There was no denying that.

The minute I realised the shutter was raised, I knew something was up. I threw Gary a look, and we both pulled our weapons out of the waistband of our suit trousers. I couldn't believe what I was seeing when I stepped inside. The contents of Smithy's nut were splattered all over the white walls by the front door, and he was slumped against the wall with his eyes closed and his mouth hanging open. Tank was lying face down, spread-eagled like an overgrown starfish, with the back of his head missing. I didn't need to go any closer to know they were both dead.

I looked over my shoulder. Gary was standing inches behind me with a dumbstruck look on his face. 'Go upstairs and check on the girl, you big tart!' I bellowed.

I stood rooted to the spot surveying the scene as Gary sprinted across the floor and up the metal staircase. The sound of his size twelves making contact with the treads reverberated around me. It was hard to take in that two of my men had been snuffed out. It was a devastating blow to my team and one that I wouldn't take lightly. Heads would roll for this.

'She's not here, boss,' Gary shouted from the mezzanine level.

I'd suspected as much. Somebody had come into my warehouse without permission, executed two of my employees and stolen my property. No prizes for guessing who the culprit with the death wish was. Luckily for Roscoe Allen, I was feeling in a generous mood, so I'd be more than happy to make sure his wish came true.

58

LILY

I'd literally had to drag myself to the car. If Daisy and Bernice hadn't been supporting me, I don't think I'd have made it. Daisy was completely underestimating how terrible I felt. She had no idea what I'd been through. I'd barely eaten. Barely slept since I was kidnapped. I was running on empty.

Daisy's impatience was stressing me out, but I didn't want to do anything to rock the boat. I would never have got out if she hadn't freed me. So I'd be eternally grateful to her. And Bernice, of course.

When we finally made it to the car, I thought we were safe. I could taste freedom. It felt good. But things changed on a knife edge. Seeing Samson's car prowling close by sent me into a tail-spin. Fear took control and I started losing hope. There was no end to this nightmare.

I'd been over the moon when we'd signed the contract with Eden's. I'd thought it would be the making of us. Thought Samson was our saviour. How wrong had I been? Why had he done this to me? I'd only met him on one occasion, and he'd been singing my praises. Falling over himself to flatter me. But it was all an act. And I'd fallen for every word he'd spun me. More fool me.

Once Samson's car was out of sight, Bernice started the engine. She was gripping the steering wheel so tightly her knuckles had turned white. I was numb with shock. I sat in the back, hunched down. Trembling. Trying to stay out of sight. I couldn't go through it again. I wasn't strong enough.

'Are you OK, love?' Bernice asked as she made eye contact with me in the rear-view mirror.

I forced out a smile so small it was barely noticeable. I couldn't trust myself to speak. I needed to retain a small shred of dignity. Daisy would be unimpressed by an emotional display, so I dug deep and kept a lid on things. I wanted to build bridges. I didn't want to do anything to piss my sister off.

'You're safe now. But I'm sure you've been to hell and back,' Bernice said, giving me the green light to tell them what I'd been through.

I wrung my hands in my lap. I wanted to open up, but something was stopping me. What was I afraid of? I didn't want to be judged for not handling the situation right. And I wasn't sure I wanted to share the true horror of what had happened to me with anyone. I was still trying to come to terms with it myself. But suddenly, words came spilling from my mouth.

'It was horrendous. I can't even begin to explain how scared I was. Being kidnapped was one thing, but I had no idea how bad it was going to get.'

'Do you want to talk about it?' Bernice asked.

I swallowed down the lump in my throat. Maybe sharing the trauma would help me process it. 'I was terrified nobody was going to find me. The days were long and I didn't think I'd make it out of there...' I let my sentence trail off. How could I tell them that I tried to escape? I felt myself shudder at the memory of Tank assaulting me. It tortured me day and night. Haunted me. His weight. His smell. His roughness. I'd tried to put up a fight, but the attack was frenzied. Devastating. I'd never get over it. I wasn't ready to share it with anyone.

'You poor darling,' Bernice said before she took her eyes off the road and stared into my soul.

'I thought I was going to die in that room,' I said once I'd collected myself. 'I didn't give up. I nearly did. But somehow, managed to stay strong. The will to survive is the last thing that leaves you. It sticks with you all the way to the end. Even when you tell it to piss off.'

'I'm so sorry you had to go through that, but I want you to know, I started looking for you the moment they took you,' Daisy said.

She spun around in her seat and locked eyes with me as though pleading with me to believe her. I did. She had no reason to lie to me. As we stared at each other, a tear of gratitude rolled down my cheek. I'd been relying on Daisy. And she hadn't let me down. We were twins. We shared an unbreakable bond.

'Thank you. You'll never know how much I appreciate what you've done for me,' I replied.

Silence hung heavy in the air as Daisy and I shared a rare moment.

'When bad things happen, it's sometimes hard to get over them. I'm going to take you to the Old Mill House. You'll be safe there,' Bernice said, breaking the spell.

59

SAMSON

As we rounded the corner of Station Road, we passed Kyle's motor, parked with the lights off. He was in the driver's seat surveying the scene. I turned to look out of the passenger window and nodded an acknowledgement as we cruised by.

'That's Roscoe's Jag,' I said as we drew level with the hostel. It was within spitting distance.

'What do you want me to do, boss?' Gary asked, taking his eyes off the road for a second to glance at me.

'Block him in.'

I could see a car was wedged up behind Roscoe's, so when Gary stopped my Range Rover diagonally in front of the Jag, he sealed off any escape routes. It was time to make sure the gammy-eyed bastard never had the chance to pull a stunt like this again. You lived by the gun. You died by the gun.

'Keep MacKenzie in your sights. Don't let that little scrote slip through your fingers again,' I said.

I was concentrating all my efforts on Roscoe. I'd deal with his sidekick later. But I wanted him to have a front-row seat at his boss's elimination so that he'd know exactly what was in store for him. The treacherous fucker would be wishing he hadn't switched sides. As if I was going to tolerate him working for a rival.

I stepped out of my car, went around to the boot, and took out the Glock switch I had concealed there for just such an occasion. It was a small, illegal device that was my favourite weapon. It could go from semi-automatic to fully automatic in the blink of an eye and could pump out bullets like a machine gun but was a fraction of the size. I was itching to put it to use.

I calmly walked up to Roscoe's Jag and stopped in front of the driver's window. He turned to face me. We started eyeballing each other as he tried to establish the rules of the game. He was wasting his time. The usual ones were obsolete as far as I was concerned. I made them up as I went along.

He knew there was only one way this was going to end. Panic filled his eyes. But I didn't feel any empathy for him. Waves of hatred radiated off me. This day had been a long time coming. We'd been enemies for donkey's years. Now that I had him cornered, he was going to get what was coming to him.

I took a deep breath and started spraying the Jag with bullets. Roscoe's body jolted backwards and forwards as though an electric current was flowing through it. For each pull of the trigger, my Glock fired multiple rounds. It could fire twelve hundred per minute. Was it over the top to use all my ammo? It wasn't the most accurate weapon. It sometimes obliterated innocent bystanders and we were in a residential street. But a few extra casualties were the least of my concern. I wanted to make sure the fucker was dead.

When I finally stopped shooting, live rounds were scattered everywhere. I stared at the car riddled with bullet holes. Roscoe's lifeless body was slumped against the steering wheel. Blood, flesh and bone fragments ran down the windscreen. Inspecting my handiwork gave me a huge sense of satisfaction. I liked to keep things simple. And that was exactly what I'd done. There'd been no questioning. No time for explanations. No chatting bollocks. No trial. No deliberation. Just an execution. I wished I'd done it years ago.

60

MACKENZIE

The sound of gunfire stopped as abruptly as it had begun. Roscoe had been crying out in pain. Now, he was silent. I knew what that meant, but I was scared to look.

'Get down, son,' Roscoe had said before the sound of the shots rang out.

I'd buried my head in my hands and curled into a ball to make myself a small target. It all happened so quickly. I followed his order on autopilot and didn't have time to reply.

Samson was wearing his trademark grey suit, black shirt combo, and an air of superiority when he walked up to Roscoe's Jag. I'd always know he was a callous bastard, but this was extreme even by his standards.

When I eventually plucked up the courage to look over at Roscoe, I could see he was peppered with bullet holes. His eyes were open, and a look of horror was on his face. It was a terrible end for such a great guy. I wished I could have told him how much I loved and respected him. Samson had robbed us of the chance to say goodbye. Any last words Roscoe had were left unspoken.

He'd taken them to the grave with him. Bernice was going to be devastated when she found out.

My head was spinning. I was struggling to process what had just happened, so I didn't notice Gary wrench open the passenger door until it was too late. Seconds later, he reached inside and dragged me out of the car. I stood shellshocked on the pavement, still reeling from the traumatic event which had left my boss dead, while Gary gripped the back of my jacket in his fist.

I couldn't believe I'd escaped unscathed. I'd been sitting inches away from Roscoe. I knew it wasn't a lucky coincidence. Samson only had Roscoe in his sights. He'd finally settled the score. My time was coming. I was sure of that. Not only had I betrayed his trust, I'd witnessed something that would send him down for a long stretch. That wasn't on his agenda. Samson would kill me to keep me quiet. He wouldn't think twice about it.

61

SAMSON

The element of surprise had done its job. Roscoe and MacKenzie looked like they were going to shit themselves when I approached the car. They were well and truly cornered this time. There was nowhere to run to. I stared into Roscoe's soul as I pumped the side of his Jag with bullets. When his expression changed from fear to agony, my lips stretched into a smile. I'd enjoyed every second of his suffering. Getting even with that fucker had been long overdue.

One down, one to go. It was time to turn my attention to my wayward former employee. Was MacKenzie so naive that he thought I'd issue an empty threat? He should have known I'd never do that. I had zero tolerance for people not following through on an agreement, especially where money was concerned. The scrote's card was marked the minute he put his sticky mitts in my safe and cleared out the contents. I can still picture the lying little shit's Oscar-winning performance when he swore blind that Eden's had been robbed. Did he seriously expect me to believe the pile of horseshit he'd tried to feed me? I didn't come down in the last shower.

I wasn't exactly flush at the moment, so I couldn't afford to lose a pile of cash, and MacKenzie didn't appear to be in any hurry to return it. I wasn't prepared to wait a minute longer. He'd fucked me around enough, and my patience had worn thin. Nobody stole from me and got away with it. MacKenzie's days were numbered. He'd made his bed; now he had to lie in it.

If grudge-holding was an Olympic sport, I'd be a gold medal winner. Petty was my middle name. When somebody wronged me, no matter how slightly, they could expect serious repercussions. My fearsome reputation was built on that. MacKenzie was about to be taught a very valuable lesson. Loyalty counted for nothing. The shit was about to hit the fan.

MacKenzie had run back to his old boss with his tail between his legs rather than face up to what he'd done like a man. I took umbrage at being mugged off. He should have known Roscoe couldn't protect him from me. Nobody could. His punishment was going to be long and drawn out. It was only fair that the payback matched the enormity of his betrayal. I was a man of principle and never went back on my word.

Even if MacKenzie hadn't just seen me turn Roscoe into a human colander, he knew too much about how my operation ran to stay alive. There was no way I was going to spend years of my life behind bars like my old man did. Just thinking about being banged up made my blood pressure soar.

Gary had a firm grip on MacKenzie to stop him from doing a runner. I saw the scrawny fucker flinch as I closed the gap between us. When I headbutted him, he went down like a sack of spuds, so I took advantage of the fact that he was lying helpless on the ground and started booting him into the ribcage and stamping on his bandaged hand. He drew it towards his chest, then curled into a ball, moaning and yelping as he accepted what was coming. I was going to take my time with this, eek it out and make him suffer for as long as possible before I finished him off once and for all.

'Get him in the car,' I said once I'd beaten the living daylights out of him.

MacKenzie was the lucky recipient of a one-way ticket to my mansion in Sutton Lane. I had a fully equipped torture chamber in the cellar for just such occasions. And thanks to the hiding I'd just given him, he'd be in agony for the whole journey. The thought of that brought a smile to my face.

62

DAISY

Wednesday 7 January

I woke to find sunlight pouring in through a gap in the blackout curtains, so I pulled the pillow over my face. My head was throbbing. Bernice and I had sunk two bottles of wine and God knows how many Tequila shots celebrating Lily's freedom last night. I was feeling the worse for wear. Too much booze and a lack of sleep were taking their toll on me.

My tongue felt like it had doubled in size. I was in desperate need of water, caffeine and a greasy breakfast. A fry-up would either kill me or cure me. I threw back the quilt and dragged my sorry arse out of bed. Then picked up my mobile from the bedside cabinet and glanced at the time. It was half past eight. No wonder I felt like shit. We hadn't gone to bed until about three in the morning. I was tempted to dive back under the covers. But I was awake now and had a hangover that needed feeding.

'Hello, darling,' Bernice said when I walked into the kitchen. She must have read my mind. She was frying bacon and sausages in a pan. 'How did you sleep?'

'Like a log, but I feel like death warmed up after all the booze,' I replied. 'How about you?'

Bernice had drawn the short straw and had slept on the sofa bed in the open-plan living area. I'd offered to swap with her, but she wasn't having any of it.

'Not bad at all. It's surprisingly comfy. Do you want a coffee? I'm just about to make one,' Bernice smiled.

'I'm gasping, but let me do it. You've got your hands full.' I wasn't used to being spoiled like this.

Bernice cut two thick doorsteps from a white bloomer loaf. She covered every inch with butter before layering bacon and sausages over one of them. 'Would you like ketchup?'

'Yes, please.'

Bernice zig-zagged the buttie with Heinz, then cut it in half. 'Get your chops around that,' she said, putting the plate down in front of me.

My eyes were on stalks. 'Thank you, it looks lovely,' I said. The weight of the sandwich nearly snapped my wrist as I lifted it up to my mouth. Talk about a gutbuster. It was just what I needed.

Bernice and I sat opposite each other at the table. We weren't locked in conversation like we'd usually be. She just stared into space like she was in a world of her own with her hands wrapped around her mug of coffee.

'Aren't you going to have anything to eat?' I asked as I wiped sauce out of the corner of my mouth with my ring finger.

She shook her head. 'I'm not hungry.'

'I feel bad that you've gone to all this trouble on my account.'

'It's no trouble.' Bernice forced out a smile.

'You don't know what you're missing.' I grinned before taking another huge mouthful.

Something was definitely wrong. Bernice wasn't her usual self. She seemed troubled. Distant.

'Is everything OK?' I asked, reluctantly placing the remainder of my sandwich down on the plate so that I could give her my full attention.

'I don't know. Roscoe didn't reply to the text I sent him last night.'

I hadn't known Roscoe for that long, but he didn't strike me as the kind of man who'd get the hump over being asked to give MacKenzie his old room back at The Castle so that Bernice could stay with me in the apartment now that she'd convinced me to leave London. She'd decided not to mention anything about Lily. She wanted to break the good news in person.

'It's still pretty early. Maybe he ended up having a late night. You know what boys are like when they're left to their own devices. Roscoe and MacKenzie probably stayed up half the night getting pissed and putting the world to rights.'

That seemed like a perfectly reasonable explanation if you asked me. That was exactly what Bernice and I had done! Come to think of it, I hadn't heard from MacKenzie either, and he'd been messaging me constantly since my dad was attacked, checking to make sure I was doing OK, which was so sweet of him. Perhaps there was hope for the two of us after all. Were they just on the lash? Or should we be worried?

'I'm just going call Harvey to see if Roscoe or MacKenzie are around,' Bernice said, then she slid back the full-length glass door that led off the kitchen onto the balcony.

I couldn't hear what they were saying, but Bernice was pressing her right hand onto her forehead. She looked stressed out, so I didn't think Harvey had managed to put her mind at ease.

'What did he say?' I asked as soon as she walked back in.

'They're not at The Castle. He hasn't seen them since yesterday morning. I've just tried Roscoe's mobile again, and it's gone straight to answer. I'm getting really worried now.'

I could see Bernice trembling. Her calm facade had slipped, s●
I got up from the table, walked over to her and threw my arm●
around her. She'd been so good to me. She'd taken Lily and m●
under her wing, protecting us like a lioness would her newborr
cubs. So, I wanted to repay her kindness and help in any way
could.

Lily had been out for the count, catching up on some much
needed sleep, when the sound of knocking on the front doo●
roused her from her bed. Roscoe and MacKenzie had keys. Wh●
the fuck was out there? I was scared to look.

63

MACKENZIE

It had been a long night. I'd slipped in and out of fitful sleep. Being chained to a wall wasn't compatible with rest and relaxation. It had stopped me from drifting off fully. My eyes fluttered open. I sensed somebody was staring at me, so I turned my head in their direction. Samson was standing inches away from me with a maniacal grin painted on his face. I felt my guts rumble. My body was already aching from the beating he'd given me. The shackles pinning my arms overhead in an unnatural position made my shoulders scream while the burn on my hand throbbed in time with my heartbeat. I couldn't take any more punishment.

'So you made it through the night then?' Samson sneered.

When he prodded me with his foot, I instinctively drew my knees up to my chest. My body was in bits. Samson stared down at me, arrogant. Uncompromising. The power he had over me made my insides turn to jelly. I was trying to take what I had coming like a man. But I didn't know how long I'd be able to keep up the pretence.

Samson could have killed me in the Jag along with Roscoe,

two for the price of one, but he'd deliberately spared me. It was a miracle I hadn't been caught in the crossfire. It showed he was a skilled marksman, but by the time he was finished with me, I had a horrible feeling, I'd be wishing that miracle had never happened. I wouldn't be wallowing in survivor's guilt. I'd be praying for deliverance.

'You're tougher than you look. But it's hard to kill vermin, isn't it?' Samson laughed and then spat in my face.

I didn't dare lapse even a millimetre into any kind of involuntary, fear-conditioned reaction, or he'd attack me again. Samson preyed on the weak. He ate the vulnerable for breakfast. I was full of uncertainty. The only thing I was sure of was everything that was about to happen to me was out of my control. There was nothing I could do to stop it. There was no point in begging for forgiveness. Samson wouldn't listen. I knew from experience that he wasn't a man you wanted to be on the wrong side of, so I faced a terrifying prospect.

'I'd like to say this is nothing personal, but I'd be lying. You brought this on yourself. So, you deserve everything you're going to get.' Samson shoved his finger in my face, and I felt myself flinch.

'I'm sorry I let you down. I scraped together as much as possible at short notice, but you hardly gave me any time to come up with the money. I was good for it. I just needed a bit longer...' I knew what I'd said sounded lame.

I'd worked for Samson for ages, but he hadn't cut me any slack. He'd given me an impossible deadline. It was almost as though he didn't want me to be able to pay back the cash.

'This isn't just about the dosh. It's about the loyalty you didn't show me. Your desertion. Your betrayal.' Samson was boiling mad. His face had turned red with temper. He was ready to blow his top any minute. 'You think you're a master at duping people, but you've got a lot to learn. What pains me the most is that I let you into the fold. You're a scruffy bastard. I'd never have employed you in the first place if I hadn't been poaching you from Roscoe.'

The mention of my old boss's name tugged at my heartstrings. He'd been one in a million before Samson had snuffed out his life as though it meant nothing.

'You turned up to your first day of work wearing a faded T-shirt, ripped jeans and battered trainers.' Samson looked down his nose at me.

That was a long time ago. I couldn't remember what I'd been wearing. But his description matched nearly all my clothes, so I was sure he was right. I wasn't going to dispute it. Samson had an eye for detail and my wardrobe choice had clearly offended him. But instead of mentioning it to me on the day, he'd stored it up to throw back at me at a later stage. Another nail in my coffin, so to speak.

'I should have shown you the door, but I turned a blind eye so that I could get one over on my old rival,' Samson smiled. 'And look how you repaid me?' Samson's features darkened before he dropped down in front of me and wrapped his hands around my throat.

I desperately wanted to get him off me. Claw at his skin. Do something to overpower him, but my hands were out of action, restrained above my head. I thrashed about, trying to break his grip, but he kept squeezing and constricting my airway. I could feel the fight start to leave my body. I felt myself slipping away. As my head lolled forward and my eyes began to close, he released his grip. I gasped for air as my eyes sprung open.

'You didn't think I was going to let you off as easily as that, did you?' Samson laughed. 'The interrogation hasn't even started. Gary, get your arse in here.'

A moment later, Gary burst into the basement, unlocked the

padlocks on the chains securing me to the wall and bundled me into a chair equipped with leg and wrist straps. He knew what was required of him without Samson uttering a word. It made me wonder how many times he'd done the routine before.

'Now that you're sitting comfortably, I'll fill you in on some of the blanks. You were never going to come up with the money in time. That's why I didn't bother waiting for the deadline to expire before I hit you where it hurt the most. There'd be no greater punishment than killing your innocent girlfriend, would there?'

Thoughts of Daisy raced through my mind. I started to struggle. Samson looked so smug. I wanted to lash out at him and wipe the smile off his face. He was going to kill me anyway, so I didn't have anything to lose. But the straps on the chair were holding me too tightly. My efforts were in vain.

'You fucking bastard. What did Daisy ever do to you?' I shouted.

Samson threw his head back and laughed. 'Don't go jumping the gun. She was still alive and kicking last time I checked.'

'You just said you'd killed her.' I could feel my nostrils flaring.

'I'd intended to. I still do, in fact. I need to rectify my mistake...' Samson said.

Mistake? What mistake? I was still trying to make sense of what he was saying, piece things together, when he started talking again.

'I thought I'd had Daisy kidnapped in lieu of the debt. But when she turned up on my doorstep looking for Lily, I realised my guys had ballsed up. I should never have left Gary in charge. You always fuck everything up, don't you, Gary? You're about as much use as a one-legged man in an arse-kicking competition.' Samson's eyes flicked towards his second in command.

'Sorry, boss,' Gary said. He was wearing the guilty expression of a man caught knocking one out by his nan.

Samson turned his attention back to me. 'Now it's your time to talk. Did you really think you and Roscoe would get away with flogging my cocaine? How did a pair of clowns like you intercept the shipment? Who tipped you off?' His questions came in quick succession. One after the other. Like rapid fire.

'I don't know what you're talking about,' I replied.

'Don't talk shit, MacKenzie. I bet you're going to deny killing two of my men and taking my hostage as well!' Samson's jaw was twitching. 'Answer me! I know you and Roscoe were behind this,' he roared, not bothering to hide his impatience.

'I swear, we had nothing to do with any of it.'

'Wrong answer,' Samson said. 'This is your last chance. Roscoe's paid the price, so either you confess your involvement, or I'll go after Daisy...'

I couldn't tell him what he wanted to hear, so I stayed quiet.

'Take his jeans down,' Samson said.

I tried to swallow the huge lump in my throat, but it sat wedged in position like the giant iceberg waiting for the *Titanic*.

I tried to put up a fight but failed miserably. Once Gary had done the honours, Samson attached two metal crocodile clips to my gonads. Wires ran from the clips to a box with a switch, a button and a small lever. When Samson turned the lever, electric shocks hit me in agonising waves. I'd never felt anything like it. I gripped the armrests as my whole body rose up in the chair. White lights darted around my eyes like shooting stars. Samson grinned with delight. I lost count of how many times I passed out. He'd allow me to recover, then turn the lever again. The pain was so excruciating I lost control of my bladder and bowels.

Samson grabbed a handful of my hair and pulled my head up. It lolled around on my neck like a newborn baby's. 'You might as well release the straps; he's not going to give us any more hassle.

After you clean this mess up, make sure you dump his boc where nobody will find it.'

Samson's words floated around me as I felt myself slippir away.

64

DAISY

The moment I set eyes on the two uniformed officers, I knew something terrible had happened.

'Are you Roscoe Allen's wife?' the policeman asked.

'Yes,' Bernice replied as the colour drained from her face.

'Could we come inside for a moment, please?'

Bernice didn't reply but turned on her heel and started walking down the hall. The two officers followed. I closed the door after them, and was about to join the procession when Lily caught my eye.

'What's going on?' she mouthed.

I shrugged my shoulders and then rushed to catch up with them.

Bernice was already perched on the edge of the sofa when I walked into the open-plan space. I sat next to her and took hold of her hand. Time seemed to stand still while we waited for the police officers to speak.

'I'm sorry to have to tell you this, but your husband's dead,' one of the policemen said.

My mouth dropped open. I couldn't believe what the officer

had just said. I turned to look at Bernice. She was in shock. We both were.

'Noooooo! I *knew* something was wrong,' Bernice wailed as her body crumpled.

She was devastated. I wanted to start sobbing, too, but I had to be strong for her.

I supposed there was no easy way to break news like that, but the way he'd delivered it was very matter-of-fact. I got it. In his line of work, you probably had to emotionally distance yourself from situations like this, but I couldn't help feeling it wouldn't have killed him to show a little more empathy. Be a little kinder to the newly widowed woman sitting in front of him. As Bernice started to sob, I let go of her hand and threw my arms around her shoulders.

Bernice pulled away from me. 'What happened?' she asked in between heart-wrenching sobs.

'He was shot.' Another clinical response.

Bernice gasped. 'When? Where?'

'Yesterday evening. We don't think it was a random attack. It's much more likely your husband was targeted. His car's full of bullet holes,' the officer replied.

The contents of my stomach somersaulted.

'Oh my God. Poor Roscoe,' Bernice said, then covered her mouth with her hands.

'Whoever did this, set out to kill him. Can you think of anybody who might have wanted to harm your husband?' the other officer asked.

His question implied that the police had no idea who was involved. Roscoe's murderer was still on the loose.

Bernice shook her head as tears poured down her cheeks.

I doubted I was the only person in the room who suspected Samson Fox was responsible. I couldn't begin to imagine how

Bernice was feeling. I was completely heartbroken, and I'd only known Roscoe for a short while. Talk about history repeating itself. Bernice's previous partner had also been shot dead.

'We won't take up any more of your time, but if you think of anything that might be useful, please call me,' the officer said before they both walked out of the room.

MacKenzie seemed to have disappeared off the face of the earth. It was odd that he hadn't been in touch for a while. Agitation began swirling inside me. I suddenly felt anxious. Had something terrible happened to him, too? The police hadn't mentioned anything about him, so he mustn't have been at the scene when Roscoe was discovered. Surely, he wouldn't have abandoned his boss in his hour of need.

'This is all my fault.'

The sound of Bernice's anguished voice broke my train of thought. 'Of course it's not,' I replied, but Bernice wasn't having any of it.

'Samson must have thought Roscoe was behind Smithy and Tank's murders. So he took his life as payback,' Bernice sobbed, then covered her face with her hands.

I peeled her fingers away and looked into her tear-filled eyes. 'What happened to Roscoe was horrendous, but you didn't know how Samson would react, so don't you dare blame yourself,' I said.

'I should have realised something like this would happen. Samson thinks he's the top dog, but back in the day, Roscoe was the main player around Brixton. That was until Samson muscled in on his territory. They fought over it, but Roscoe lost. That evil bastard punched my poor hubby so hard in the face his left eye popped out of its socket.'

My gasp interrupted Bernice's flow. I knew there must be a story behind what happened to Roscoe's eye, but I hadn't liked to ask.

'The man's an animal. He beat the living daylights out of Roscoe. His wounds were going to take time to heal, so I convinced him to step aside and accept defeat gracefully. I'd already lost one partner over a turf war. I wasn't about to lose another. And now look what's happened,' Bernice's voice cracked with emotion before she broke down in tears.

Bernice had been incredibly unlucky. Nobody should have to experience something like this more than once. But you'd be hard-pushed to find a more resilient woman than her. I was confident that she'd get through the dark days ahead and come out the other side stronger than ever.

'Roscoe's dead because of me.' Bernice had drawn her own conclusion.

'Listen to me, it's not your fault.'

When I looked into Bernice's eyes, she shook her head. As far as she was concerned, she was guilty as charged. There was no convincing her otherwise.

'I have to shoulder some of the blame, too. You only killed Smithy and Tank because you were trying to free me,' Lily said.

I turned my head towards the sound of her voice. I'd completely forgotten she was there. She'd been hovering in the background like a spare part, not knowing what to do with herself, while Bernice poured her heart and soul out to me. There was no denying Lily had been through a traumatic time, but the last thing we needed was her offering herself up as a martyr.

Fat tears rolled down Bernice's cheeks. She looked distraught. I didn't know what to say to comfort her. There were no words.

'I can't believe Roscoe's not coming back. I keep expecting him to walk into the room any minute.' Bernice stopped talking and glanced at the empty doorway. 'Why didn't I handle things differently? I never got the chance to say goodbye. Tell him how much I loved him...'

The speed at which everything had changed was shocking. morrow wasn't guaranteed for any of us.

'What you've been through is heartbreaking. Don't be too hard yourself. Just focus on the basics. Eat, drink and sleep. It'll take ne to get over this,' I said, offering her a sympathetic smile.

'Nothing's going to bring Roscoe back, but I'm going to get en with the bastard who took his life. I won't rest until Samson x is six feet under,' Bernice replied, wiping her tears away on e back of her hand.

Revenge wasn't what I had in mind; me and my big mouth. I dn't doubt Bernice felt bitter. Betrayed. Resentful. Who could ame her? But she'd be stirring up a hornet's nest if she tried to ttle the score.

'I'm going to drive over to Samson's house and plant a bullet etween his eyes,' Bernice said.

My stomach lurched. I had to talk her out of that. It would be a uicidal move. 'Please don't do anything hasty. Sleep on it.'

I had to find a way to stop Bernice from doing something so ckless. Enough blood had been spilt.

65

DAISY

Thursday 8 January

Even though a couple of days had passed since we'd rescued Lily
hadn't plucked up the courage to tell her that Dad was fighting f
his life. There was no easy way to break the awful news, so
intended to avoid having that conversation for as long as possible

Bernice was sitting at the counter with her long finge
wrapped around a mug of coffee when I walked into the kitche
She didn't acknowledge me. She was in a world of her own.

'Good morning,' I said to get her attention.

'Morning, darling,' she replied, giving me a half smile.

Bernice was doing her best to put on a brave face, but she wa
pale and drawn. Dark circles nestled under her eyes. She looke
exhausted.

'How did you sleep?' I asked to make conversation, but
already knew the answer to my question.

'I didn't,' she replied.

No surprise there. I'd been tossing and turning all night, too
and it wasn't my husband who'd been murdered in cold blood.

'I know you asked me to give it some time, but I don't feel any differently about things this morning. Every fibre of my being is telling me I have to get justice for Roscoe.' I was about to voice my objection when Bernice held her hand up to stop me. 'Before you try and talk me out of it, I know it's going to be dangerous. But whatever happens, happens. If I lose my life getting even with Samson, then so be it.'

Bernice's blue eyes filled with tears, and my heart went out to her. I'd somehow convinced her not to storm into Samson's house with both barrels loaded yesterday. Reacting while her emotions were running high wouldn't have been smart. She hadn't been thinking straight. She was blinded by grief and rage, and that would have clouded any decisions she made. I wanted her to wait until the shock had worn off. Until she'd had time to digest what had happened. But she was hell-bent on seeking revenge. So I knew better than to try and talk her around a second time. I couldn't bear the thought of losing her, too. I felt my eyes mist over, so I turned away and walked over to the sink.

'Do you want a refill?' I asked, to break the heavy silence bearing down on us.

'No thanks,' she replied.

I lifted a mug from the cupboard and placed a tea bag inside. As I waited for the kettle to boil, I discreetly studied my mentor out of the corner of my eye. She looked broken. A shadow of herself, which was gutting. Bernice used to be a force to be reckoned with. She was strong and feisty. An inspiration for the female race. She'd taught me so much in the short time I'd known her.

Bernice was on the ball where most things were concerned, but I couldn't help feeling she was about to make the biggest mistake of her life. Going after Samson would be a disastrous move, whichever way I looked at it. Maybe in years to come when the dust had settled, but if she struck now, in the heat of the moment, the consequences could be deadly for the wrong person.

I'd thought about nothing else since Bernice shared her desire to wipe out the man who'd ruined her life. Lily and I also had good reason to want him dead. So did MacKenzie, for that matter. That was if Samson hadn't got to him first. My head was whirring. The day had barely started, and I was already stressed out.

My tea had brewed, so I couldn't put off going over to Bernice any longer. I had to drag myself across the floor. My feet were glued to the spot. I didn't want to have this conversation with her. How could I give her my blessing to do something so reckless? If all of this backfired, I'd have played a part in her destruction. I wanted to have her back, but I wasn't sure I was prepared to give her the green light.

'I'm not going to kill him quickly. I'm going to make him really suffer before I let him take his last breath. And I'm going to enjoy every torturous minute,' Bernice said with an evil glint in her eye.

I'd taken a swig of tea as I listened to Bernice plotting Samson's murder as though she was Lady Macbeth. Her words took me by surprise, so I spat the mouthful across the kitchen tiles and then started coughing and spluttering.

'Are you alright, darling?' Bernice asked, springing into action. She slapped me across the back so hard she almost loosened my teeth.

'I'm OK,' I said, gasping for air. 'It went down the wrong way.'

'It's horrible when that happens,' Bernice replied, instantly switching back to her caring self.

Bernice was going after Samson with or without me. I respected her decision, but she'd never be able to get inside his fortress without him realising. He had more security measures in place than Buckingham Palace. She'd have to outsmart him.

'I'm not going to let you go through this on your own, but we'll need to put our heads together and work out a plan. Come up with something that catches him off guard. He'll be expecting you to turn up on the doorstep demanding answers,' I said.

Silence spread out between us for what seemed like an agonising amount of time as we racked our brains. Then I suddenly had a light bulb moment.

'I've just had a brilliant idea. If we use me as bait, Samson won't be able to resist.' I smiled.

'I can't let you do that, darling. It's too dangerous,' Bernice replied.

But that wasn't her decision to make.

66

SAMSON

MacKenzie's piss and shit were splattered across my porcelain tiles. The spineless git never mentioned he needed to use the crapper before I got to work on him. It was almost as though he'd dropped his load all over my white floor as his parting gesture to spite me.

'It fucking stinks in here. What are you waiting for? Clean it up,' I roared.

Gary stared at me with a look of disbelief on his face, but somebody had to do it. I could hardly ask my housekeeper. She didn't even know my dungeon existed. The basement of my house was strictly off-limits to everyone apart from my trusted inner circle.

Gary knew when he was beaten, so he sloped off to the cupboard. He was just lifting the mop and bucket out when the buzzer went on the intercom.

'Hello,' he said when he answered it.

'I'm sorry to disturb you, but Mr Fox has a visitor.'

'Who is it?' I bellowed from the other end of the room. My

nvited guest couldn't have picked a more inconvenient time to
p by unannounced.

'She said her name is Daisy Kennedy.'

I felt the hairs on the back of my neck stand up. 'Well, well,
l,' I said.

'I'm sorry, sir. I didn't catch that. Do you want me to let the
ly in?'

'I wouldn't call her a lady but show her into the living room
d make sure you stay with her until I arrive. You'd better come
th me, Gary. Your domestic duties will have to wait until later.'

Gary's face broke into a big cheesy grin.

r fuck's sake,' I said under my breath when I opened the door
d saw Daisy standing next to her sidekick. I shouldn't really
ve been surprised, but my housekeeper hadn't mentioned
ything about her being with an old battle axe.

'Why did you do it?' Bernice shouted the minute she clapped
es on me.

'I would have thought that was obvious,' I replied. I wasn't
ing to deny murdering the gammy-eyed prick.

'Well, it's not, so maybe you'd care to elaborate.' Bernice
shed out at me with her poisonous tongue.

'The job I did on your old man was some of my finest work, and
n proud of that. You should be thanking me. Being a grieving
idow suits you.' I smiled, which didn't go down well with Mrs Allen.

She was ready to fly at me, but Daisy stopped her in her
acks, and a wordless exchange passed between them. It was
uite endearing to watch. The pair of brainless idiots must have
atched a plan to bring me down. As if that was going to happen!

'What have you done with MacKenzie?' Daisy asked.

I knew it wouldn't take long before she confronted me over whereabouts. I briefly considered letting her see for herself, the thought of going back to my torture chamber before bodily fluids were eradicated turned my stomach. Gary neede sort that out before it stank the house out, so I wasn't going waste time on this pointless conversation.

'He's dead. Boohoo,' I replied. Then I began rubbing my e with my fists to mock her.

I'd been busy watching her struggling to compose herself, hadn't noticed Bernice pull out a gun. I didn't have time to re before she pulled the trigger.

'Look out, boss,' Gary shouted, then he dived in front of me.

It felt like it happened in slow motion. Gary gallantly took bullet, but it wasn't a heroic act. The lengths some people wor go to just to avoid doing a job. But he wasn't going to get out cleaning up MacKenzie's crap that easily. I wasn't about to get hands dirty.

I was going to say as much when the sensation of bei punched in the gut by a cannonball winded me. It took me moment to realise the bullet must have passed through Gary a hit me as well. A second later, the two of us dropped like flies. T last thing I remembered before everything went black was Dai saying, 'We need to get out of here before the police arrive.'

67

DAISY

Everything inside the rustic farmhouse was old and creaky. It was a far cry from the plush, newly renovated apartment I'd been staying in. But that didn't matter. The most important thing was that it was in the middle of nowhere, set deep within the Kent countryside, surrounded by tall trees and high hedges.

Thoughts raced around my head as I sat in the kitchen at the large oak table opposite Bernice and Lily. So much had happened in such a short space of time. I was struggling to make sense of it. We all were. We were together but apart, locked in our private worlds. You could have heard a pin drop as silence stretched out between us. But that suited me fine. I didn't want to get bogged down in meaningless conversation. I was beside myself with worry. What the hell had happened to MacKenzie? He'd vanished into thin air. I kept checking my phone to see if he'd messaged, but I'd heard nothing. No news was good news, I kept telling myself.

I glanced over at Bernice. She was trying to put on a brave face, but it was plain to see she was devastated. Her life would never be the same again. It was going to take time to adjust to

Roscoe's loss. But she could rely on me to support her every step of the way and help her through the dark days.

I tore my eyes away from her and turned my attention to Lily. She was pale and drawn. She looked haunted. Traumatised. I felt a bit deceitful not telling her about Dad, but I was keeping her in the dark for her own good. She needed time to heal. He was somehow managing to cling to life by his fingertips. Knowing he was at death's door would be too much for her to handle. She was too fragile. Too emotional. What she didn't know wouldn't hurt her.

Warren Jenkins still posed a massive threat to us, so going to the hospital would be too dangerous. He was bound to be sniffing around waiting to see if my dad pulled through or not. Mum and I had witnessed what he'd done. I knew what he was capable of. I couldn't put Lily at risk.

Samson was gone. It was the end of an era. The end of all the bloodshed. I hoped. Although his housekeeper knew my name, I doubted very much the police would bother to look for his killer. They'd most likely see it as a case of one villain snuffing out another. It wouldn't be worth wasting precious resources getting to the bottom of their feud.

And anyway, she'd very obligingly told us that her memory was terrible when Bernice reluctantly held the gun to her head. She would never have followed through with the threat to blow her brains out if she blabbed, but we had to cover our backs. Nobody wanted to face the future looking over their shoulder. I'd seen enough drama to last me a lifetime.

I'd been trying to block out the last conversation I'd had with Samson, but it forced its way back inside my head again. He'd told me MacKenzie was dead. I didn't want to believe him, but had he been telling the truth for once? While the police hadn't found a body, I was clinging to hope. Was I in denial? Maybe. But I wouldn't give up on him. I couldn't bear the thought of him not being part of my life.

MacKenzie had disappeared before. He was probably just lying low, waiting for the dust to settle. He'd resurface when the time was right. I just had to keep a level head and not panic. Be patient. But that wasn't my strong suit. I was going out of my mind. I needed to do something to distract myself.

'Who wants a cuppa?' I asked, pushing my chair back and getting to my feet.

In times of crisis, there was nothing a good brew couldn't fix. It was a well-known fact that tea solved everything!

ACKNOWLEDGEME

Firstly, I'd like to thank my amazing editor, Emily Ruston for your help and support. It's been a pleasure working with you again.

I'd also like to thank Nia Beynon, Jenna Houston, Debra Newhouse, David Boxell, Colin Thomas, Ben Wilson, Gemma Lawrence and Chris Simmons.

Finally, thank you to the amazing readers, reviewers and bloggers. Without you, none of this would be possible. I hope you enjoy the book!

ABOUT THE AUTHOR

Stephanie Harte is the bestselling gang-lit author of seven crime novels set in London's East End. Previously published by Head of Zeus, she lives in North West London.

Sign up to Stephanie Harte's mailing list for news, competitions and updates on future books.

Visit Stephanie's website: www.stephanieharte.com

Follow Stephanie on social media here:

facebook.com/stephanieharteauthor

x.com/@StephanieHarte3

instagram.com/stephanieharteauthor

ALSO BY STEPHANIE HARTE

The Kennedy Twins

Double Trouble

Double Dealings

Double Cross

PEAKY READERS

GANG LOYALTIES. DARK SECRETS.
BLOODY REVENGE.

A READER COMMUNITY FOR
GANGLAND CRIME THRILLER FANS!

DISCOVER PAGE-TURNING NOVELS
FROM YOUR FAVOURITE AUTHORS
AND MEET NEW FRIENDS.

Boldwood

Boldwood Books is an award-winning fiction publishing company seeking out the best stories from around the world.

Find out more at www.boldwoodbooks.com

Join our reader community for brilliant books, competitions and offers!

Follow us
@BoldwoodBooks
@TheBoldBookClub

Sign up to our weekly deals newsletter

https://bit.ly/BoldwoodBNewsletter

Printed in Great Britain
by Amazon

51284292R00178